MADE
IN HEAVEN

MADE IN HEAVEN

a novel by
TRACY HOTCHNER

WILLIAM MORROW AND COMPANY, INC.
New York   *1981*

Library of Congress Cataloging in Publication Data

Hotchner, Tracy.
    Made in heaven.

    I. Title.
PS3558.0813M3   813'.54   81-4299
ISBN 0-688-00663-9   AACR2

Printed in the United States of America

First Edition

1 2 3 4 5 6 7 8 9 10

BOOK DESIGN BY MICHAEL MAUCERI

For my sister Holly, with love

Acknowledgments

They say that writing is a solitary endeavor . . . Well, it is something I could not have done alone. I had the support, advice and love of many people:

Rennie Airth, Sherry Arden, Daphne Astor, Andrew Boose, David Brown, Yvette Mimieux Donen, Roz Doyle, Blake Edwards, Sam and Beryl Epstein, Judith Freeman, Brendan Gill, Pat Golbitz, Jorie Graham, Nancy Hardin, Jessica Harper, A. E. Hotchner, Holly Hotchner, Sally Hotchner, Ursula Hotchner, Joan Hyler, Jill Jakes, Owen Laster, Robert and Susan Lescher, Louis Massa, Ileen Maisel, Ron Mardigian, Ron McDevitt, Patricia McGerr, Thom Mount, Thad Mumford, Nancy Neiman, Peggy and Arthur Penn, Carolyn Pfeiffer, Jean Picker, Joan Rivers and Edgar Rosenberg, Melissa Rosenberg, Sonny and Howard Sloan, Joanne and Alfred Stern, Jamie Wolf, Digby Wolfe, Frank Yablans and Helen Ziegler.

My love and gratitude to each of you.

Cortona, Italy
Summer, 1980

"The true paradises
are the paradises
we have lost."

—PROUST

One

My blood goes cold. If I see fire, I feel it flowing icy through my veins. I am terrified of fire, of that bonfire one autumn day when I was nine and it seemed as though the whole world were up in flames. It may be something more than the fire itself that causes the panic and grips me, because it was my mother who started that fire and could not stop it. My palms go sweaty if I even see a fire on the news. There was only one other thing my mother couldn't overcome, the cancer she fought years later. She wouldn't acknowledge either adversary, but they both won out.

The lies my mother taught me were that the world would love me as she did and that she could manage anything.

It was an October day, 1959, Long Island ablaze with trees turning red and golden, aromatic leaf fires and the sweetness of the last apple crop. A piercing sun, the grass no longer summer's lush green, the air thin and clear and very bright, stripped of all artifice. It was a good time to build wooden boats on the turpentine-stained floor of the toolhouse; Jim gave Cassie and me lessons in sawing and hammering beneath the shelves of jars and nails and screws lined up like preserves. It was the time of year when the lily pots came out of the lily pond and we could run around barefoot for just a little longer, the grass so cold we couldn't really feel our feet after the first steps across the lawn.

Bonfires. Fall was the time for bonfires, gathering piles of twigs and branches, sweeping up mounds of leaves from the acres of lawn. Even though there was a gardening crew that came in, Cassandra and I were expected to make a contribution. Our own small rakes hung beside the big ones on the toolhouse wall, but we were too small to be of any real help. We couldn't pull enough leaves with our rakes, so we'd switch to big wooden ones with a fan of bamboo curled over at the tip like Turkish slippers. But those were too long and heavy for our toothpick arms, so we didn't get stuck for long with the hateful raking. We much preferred driving an obstacle course around Jim, the gardeners and our parents, who loved to garden and would often pitch in with raking. Cassie and I took our replica Model T Ford out of the green garage Jim had built for it and asked Papa for help in starting its outboard motor. Then we drove merrily through the edges of the piles of brown leaves, the car's red body bright against the fading fall earth tones as we wended our way around the rakers. While I steered, Cassandra waved to the workers as though she were a princess in a carriage.

The leaf sweeper was the best thing in the world. Cassie and I squealed when we sat in it while Papa propelled it across the grass, a shower of musty, crinkly leaves thrown back at us by the powerful brush that rotated in front of our feet. Sometimes we'd take Pango and his daughter Pandora in with us, and there would be leaves everywhere; in our hair, down our clothes, even in our mouths when we opened them in shrieks of laughter. It smelled like the beginning of the world.

But my father was not around the day the fire started. He was off on one of his art dealing trips somewhere in the world. Even if he'd been there the disaster might have happened, but all the same, a man's presence gives the illusion of protection. I don't know at what point the fire leapt off the pile and trickled through the "safety zone" and into the field, but once it had made that break, the light wind carried it onto the dry wheat. Mother took a shovel and hit at bits of flame as they jumped off the main bonfire, but no sooner had she stopped one spark than there were three more. "Girls, get shovels from the shed and we'll tamp this out," she commanded. Jim, who was gone on an errand, had shut off the outdoor water supply with the first frost.

By the time Cassandra and I dragged over shovels, the fire was already moving down the field. The wind was dancing with the flames, spinning like Fred Astaire and Ginger Rogers, showing off.

"Mommy!" I yelled, trying to swallow my panic. "We'd better call the fire department." The fire was headed downfield, a determined platoon marching to war. I was immobile with fear, unable even to help hit at the flames near us. I could see that nothing we did to a few sparks was going to make any difference now, but Mother was completely concentrated on beating the ground around her, refusing to see the bigger picture.

"Don't be silly, Blake," she said with her Scotch Presbyterian nothing's-bigger-than-me spirit. "We can take care of it ourselves. Now go get a bucket of water," she ordered, a hint of nervousness poking through.

/   15

"Mama, *please!*" I begged her. "We *have* to call the fire department."

She brushed a wisp of strawberry blond hair out of her eyes and continued to attack the flames near her, oblivious to my entreaties or to the speed with which the fire was consuming the field.

It was a dreadful decision, the sort of dilemma the bible is full of: whether to follow my instincts or have faith in my mother's insistence that she could handle it. I ran to the telephone and gave our name and address to the operator.

"Where's your mommy?" the woman asked slowly, patronizingly.

In horror I realized she might not believe a little girl, that even she wouldn't help. "She's out there, she thinks she can stop the fire, but hurry . . . we're burning up."

I looked out the service-porch window at Mother in her faded green corduroy jacket with the plaid wool collar. Her blond hair, swirling in the wind, was the color of the wheat before the fire got to it. For a terrible minute her hair seemed to turn the color of the fire and I thought she was aflame. I ran out onto the steps and yelled at her to come away, but she was in the thick of it.

"It's all right dear. I'm getting it under control," she shouted back, sounding quite rational. "Just hurry up with that bucket."

More than half an acre was in flames when the firemen arrived. I held my breath as I heard the sirens getting close, afraid that Mama would be angry, wouldn't let them come on the property. The trucks came to a thunderous halt; there was a moment's silence more frightening than the scream of the sirens. Then I heard the firemen clambering out, shouting to each other. Mother didn't even look up. The fire seemed to dance higher in defiance of its enemy in the red trucks. The field was so far from the hydrants on the road that the firemen had to put on back-packs with chemicals to spray the flames. They emerged through the hedges like spacemen with astronaut headgear and hoses pointed like weapons at the base of the flames. Time seemed to have stopped.

The fire chief rushed over to my mother. "You can take it easy now, ma'am," he said. "We'll take care of things from here on out." She kept right on pounding at the flames with a shovel, as if to demonstrate his rudeness in underestimating her ability. He looked intently over at the fire fighters covering the field. He shouted at Mother over the rushing sound of the fire and the voices of his men, "Smothering the embers with wet cloths is better than fanning them with a shovel." He ran back into the flaming field.

Cass and I began a relay into the kitchen on our mother's orders to soak anything and run back to her with it. I was wearing a green sweater my grandmother had knit for me. It had plastic buttons of dogs peering out of their dog-houses. It was my favorite, but I ripped it off, hoping Grandma would understand, and dunked it in the butler's pantry sink. Cassie and I left a watery trail as we dashed back and forth between the kitchen and field with anything we could get our hands on, dripping wet. Maria seemed more interested in the mess we were making than the fire. She muttered to the saints and mopped up behind us. The whole world was in flames and all she cared about was the floor; it made me wonder whether Mama was right and this wasn't as bad as it seemed.

The squad of firemen left the ground black and smol-dering behind them as they went after the flames, their movements as jerky as robots in their asbestos suits and gas-mask helmets. The fire was racing towards the towering pine trees at the far end of the field; I knew how willingly pine burned. I was bracing myself for the crackling, pinesap-pungent flames that would soon shoot up to the heavens. I was numb, my mind and blood drained by the terror, so that it didn't really feel as though I was there.

As suddenly as it started, the fire was out. Small stumps of wheat continued to smolder, but the flames were gone; the wind had only the smoke to push around now. The entire field was flattened black. A few wiry bushes had survived the fast-moving flames and stood self-consciously, suddenly naked without the wheat around them.

Field mice ran crazily across the smoking ground, driven from their nesting places. It must have been terrifyingly hot on their tiny feet, this decimated landscape. A few years before, I had touched lava in the volcano at Pompeii, hot, bubbling sand inside the caldron. For the animals this was like Pompeii, where people were caught in the middle of an ordinary day. Without warning, death came spilling out of nowhere.

The fire chief came over to my mother and asked questions about how the fire had started. Her replies were matter-of-fact, punctuated by her sooty hand as she wiped ashes from her face. She spoke in the supercilious tone I heard Papa use when he ushered trespassers off our property. "Another few minutes and that house beyond those big pines would've gone up," the fire chief said. "It's a good thing you called us when you did," he added soberly. I glanced over at Mama but got no response. She thanked him for the job they'd done—the way a tennis player congratulates her winning opponent.

Mother's face was puffed up and continued to swell as they talked. "You should see a doctor right away," the fireman said. "That's a bad burn."

Mama pooh-poohed his suggestion. She considered it an affront to her hardiness, even the following day when her face was bright red and so swollen her eyes could open no more than a slit. It must have been painful, but she'd entertain no discussion of it.

Cassandra and I played in the blackened field, investigating animals' tunnels, pretending we were explorers on a new planet. When green shoots began to sprout up in the field, Mother said that farmers often burned fields on purpose so they'd grow back better.

TWO

The wedding was a hot, green day. It was almost too beautiful, Blake thought, months later, an insult to the gods who frown on such dreamlike perfection in the lives of mere mortals. She wondered if that was why the wine turned to vinegar so fast; a punishment from on high?

She had fantasized about her wedding for years—not about being married; that had always made her queasy. Marriage seemed to Blake the kind of thing other girls desired, not a worthy goal for her. Looking forward to being "Mrs. Something or Other" seemed a repudiation of the independent life she had been raised to lead. But the wedding itself she had envisioned a hundred times, walking white across the green, green lawn of her childhood. That hot June day surpassed anything she had imagined; it was as sweet and delicate as the spun-sugar pastry decorations on the *Ile de France* that had delighted her as a child, when teatime on transatlantic crossings was the most magical hour of the day.

Blake's wedding was perfect. The loveliest single day of her life, the payoff for her fantasies, a marriage made in heaven. It was a day she paid for through the nose every day thereafter.

They were so certain the gods would smile on them that they didn't even set up a tent. The sun blazed fiery across the velvet-green front lawn, a carpet unfurled in front of the stately white-stone house. During all those years of travel, the East Hampton house remained the only constant, the closest thing that Blake felt to roots. It had been on that lawn that the massive Easter-egg hunt took place every year the Marshams were not in Europe, the first rite of spring. Eloise and Baa-Baa, the pet sheep, wandered loose with yellow ribbons around their necks; the fat white ducks—which the Easter before had been only a handful of yellow fluff—waddled officiously, taunting the dogs who didn't dare get too close to their snapping yellow beaks. Fortune Cookie begrudgingly pulled a hand-painted Italian cart with flowers woven through the leather harness on his back; his ears lay flat, protesting the imposition of pulling cheering children instead of being able to watch the festivities from a dignified distance in his grazing field. Isabel oversaw the games—sack races, raw-egg-in-a-spoon relay races—and for each child there were chocolate eggs and marshmallow bunnies in a straw basket they would use for the egg hunt. Blake and Cassie decorated dozens of eggs the day before, the halls of the house filled with the smell of warm vinegar, their fingers dyed a rainbow of colors. Early Easter morning Marsh snuck out and planted the eggs around the property, first choosing easy hiding places for the littlest hunters, who were allowed a ten-minute head start; then finding sneaky repositories for the eggs so that the older kids would have to scurry and scramble before they could shriek triumphantly when they outsmarted the Easter Bunny.

Blake had always wanted to get married on the lawn she rode across with Lancashire Lad, who once took off and jumped clear over the lily pond with her like a steeplechaser, the lily pond beside which she would stand under a flowered gazebo and pledge herself for ever and ever. The lawn across which Lannie had pulled a long, boatlike fiberglass sled on deep winter snow, Isabel an Indian princess sitting cross-legged in a ceremonial canoe as Blake ran beside Lannie's head. The lawn where she and Cassandra had searched tirelessly for a four-leaf clover the day before the gardeners cut the grass. Dreams die hard.

The day before the wedding Blake and Cassandra went into New York and through the red door at Elizabeth Arden. They spent a day pampered from head to foot: hair treatments and facials, massages and leg waxings. Blake remembered the first time she had gone through the red door, her hand firmly in Isabel's grasp. Her mother had admonished her never to shave her legs, but when she was thirteen Blake had succumbed to peer pressure. Although she wouldn't directly defy Isabel and try a razor, she did sneak to the drugstore and get a jar of Nair. She nearly fainted from the putrid sulphur smell when she spread the gunk on her legs; just before asphyxiation, when the ten minutes were up and she was about to wash the depilatory off along with the blond peach fuzz on her calves, Isabel knocked once and came into the bathroom. "Why didn't you tell me, Blakie?"

"I was afraid you'd be mad, wouldn't let me."

"My pussycat, afraid of a few golden hairs. OK, get that crap off your legs, and we'll have our legs waxed together next week."

It had been one of their most fun days together, an hour of being encased in hot yellow wax side by side at Elizabeth

Arden and then lunch at the Palm Court to recuperate from the shock of having hairs ripped out by the roots. Cassie and Blake got used to the pain after years of practice, Isabel insisting that if they ever shaved their legs, it would come back black and bristly. The girls trepidatiously tried a razor once, not quite believing Isabel's warning. They waited with bated breath during the days following, dreading the dark stubble. When all that grew back was the same pale downy hair, they were relieved—glad to have had the courage to try it but glad of the inconsequential results. They never shaved again, keeping their appointments at Arden.

Cassie stayed with Blake in her childhood bedroom the night before the wedding; they took hot, buttery popcorn to bed with them and giggled as though it were a teenage slumber party. Michael went to a stag party at the Harvard Club and was going to stagger up to East Hampton the morning of the wedding.

"How bad a hangover you have is your decision," Blake had teased. "But it's going to make me very short-tempered if you get the clap from whatever entertainment is procured by those perverse old cronies of yours."

The morning of the wedding Cassie gave Blake an antique mother-of-pearl rosary. "From the part of us that is Isabel," the note said. No one but the two of them could have understood that while their upbringing had been steadfastly atheistic, churches and religion had been a deeply important part of their travels and cultural exposure. Blake wound the rosary inside the bouquet of spring flowers that matched the band of flowers that held back her hair. The photographer—who did *Vogue* fashion layouts and had never shot a wedding before—took dreamy pictures of the bride and her sister in the boudoir, primping for the main event, photos like Gainsborough paintings. Blake's favorite was the one of Cassandra fixing flowers around Quickly's neck, pale blue and white blossoms to match Cassie's chiffon dress and bouquet.

Blake looked out her childhood window, peeking through the silk swag curtains. The lawn was a page from a hazy, romantic nineteenth-century novel: starched children cavorting past women in flowered pastel dresses and wide-brimmed garden hats, past the complacent nods of watch-fobbed fathers in cream-colored summer suits. The lily pond was full of blooms, and the bronze stork fountain that Isabel had given Marsh one birthday spouted a high, thin arc of water.

In the center of a group of people Blake saw Lily, her surrogate mother, the woman who had healed her heartbreaks over men, tucked her into the guest room in their country house in Bucks County, gone clothes shopping with her and traded juicy gossip the way boys trade baseball cards. Lily had a son and daughter but always introduced Blake as her older daughter, which sent a warm thrill through Blake like hot cocoa after ice-skating. Although younger than Isabel, Lily had been very close and amazingly like Blake's mother. Both raised as Scotch Presbyterians, they had married non-religious Jewish men who became renowned in the literary art world. Both women had raised their children as atheists but found Judaism admirable. They both were delighted with what they took to be expansive Jewish blood in their offspring. Blake had never quite understood their eagerness about Jewishness, the hunger for Jewish emotionality, warmth and intellectual drive, compared to their severe Calvinist origins.

Lily had referred to Blake as her older daughter even before Isabel died. Blake wondered if it had been to acclimate her slowly, the way you buy a puppy in anticipation of the family dog dying. The Marshams had done that with their adored dog Pango when he got on in years; bred him so that his daughter Pandora would overlap his death and outlive him. The plan had backfired: Marsh had been alone in the house when the highway patrolman drove up and asked if he owned a white dog. When Marsh nodded, the cop took her limp body off the back-seat floor of his car and handed the lifeless ball of fluff to Marsh, leaving him with the nine-month-old corpse.

The wedding was achingly beautiful, Cassandra leading the way from the arched front door to the edge of the soft lawn where a quartet played baroque music under the leafy curtains of the old willow. Cassie and Blake's five-year-old half-brother, wearing pale blue French shorts and a lace-trimmed top, carried the rings on a heart-shaped lace cushion. Michael's niece was the flower girl and walked beside the ring bearer with a basket of petals that she scattered now and again, whenever she could stop staring long enough at the huge crowd to remember her duties. Quickly, fluffy white as a lamb and festooned with flowers, trotted alongside, the children's guardian. Behind them came a bevy of beautiful women: Blake's friends and Michael's sister, parading two by two, holding a rope of flowers that joined them together.

Blake could see Michael at the flowered gazebo where he waited, dazed by the floral opulence and Monet beauty of the procession. Blake's little half-brother, joyfully solemn-faced with the importance of his ring-bearing mission, held the white cushion as though it were an offering to the gods. Blake floated towards Michael, a short train of Victorian lace trailing behind her on the emerald grass. Her wedding dress had been designed in an antique style, using old lace. There was a deep "v" of transparent lace from the high collar right down between her breasts, which gave a demure bawdiness to the elegance, the pink swell of her cleavage amidst all that white. Blake shone with happiness as she moved towards Michael under the flowered arch. She kept her hand on her father's arm.

She had to chuckle at how Marsh had tried to argue his way out of escorting her.

"It's foolishly old-fashioned," he'd said. "You should walk with Michael; there's no point in carrying out the absurd hypocrisy of the father giving away the virgin bride."

"You mean I should wear a scarlet letter around my neck because I'm not?"

"And I still don't see why you wouldn't rather have the money for you and Michael than put up with a mob scene."

"Ah, Papa, what a sentimental description of a wedding." Blake kidded him, but it made her feel lousy. She wondered if beneath his protest was his dislike of giving her away.

They exchanged rings, repeated words in a dreamlike state, characters in their own imaginings. Michael folded Blake into his arms for the kiss, and it was everything she thought the first kiss should be—assertive without being blatantly sexual, a long, ardent kiss that made the onlookers squirm just a little. When Michael let her go, Blake looked past him at the house, smiled at the long window to her room. She used to sit with her legs dangling through the wood-slatted floor of the balcony, blowing bubbles, floating orbs that descended in rainbows onto the lawn.

All of Isabel's friends pressed in on Blake after the ceremony, moving in slow motion across the fragrant, jade lawn. This was the wedding she'd always wanted, in the house her mother had filled with such pleasures for everyone. Isabel's friends were gathered to give her blessing, Blake thought, since she could not be there herself. As she kissed and hugged the multitude under the hot sun, Blake glanced over their shoulders, looking, just in case Isabel had made it, after all.

Three

I t was hard to grow up inside a fairy tale, a constantly caressing life. Sometimes Cass and I dressed up as poor people, like *The Five Little Peppers and How They Grew*, one of our favorite books, a tale of a happily hungry family that bordered on saintliness. Cassie and I put on tattered layers from our carved wooden chest of dress-up clothes and went into the back guest room, the chilliest room in the house. We got friends to play with us; I was the mother who buoyed the spirits of her hungry brood as they huddled together for warmth.

One day as I leaned over the chest, I felt queasy. It might have been the camphor smell; maybe I was sick with myself for pretending about something so serious. Cassandra couldn't understand when I refused to play the game anymore; just hours before, we'd been playing another game, the one where we tried to calculate how many plane trips we'd taken and how many countries we'd been to, counting the stamps in our passports. I just couldn't play both kinds of games anymore.

Although I couldn't quite believe them, I loved hearing the stories Mama told about "the chicken coops" we'd lived in before the big house. They were three little wooden buildings which she called "the chicken coops," creating a bizarre image of the four Marshams bent double, ludicrously squeezed into stubby, slant-roofed chicken houses. She was pregnant but still working for *Look* magazine, writing and doing publicity, when they took the little cabins in the country while they were looking for a proper house.

I loved hearing the tales of comic hardship, of how they couldn't heat the buildings and would find my thumb frozen in the morning, iced over after it had gotten wet from being sucked. I could not discern fact from fancy, yet I loved the notion of us as struggling pioneers—despite the fact that I knew Isabel would stop at nothing, least of all the facts, to embellish a story. She also talked about Dora, the big, fat maid who drove my parents crazy because there was never any cream for their coffee. Dora would drink the entire bottle when the milkman left it and hide the empty container at the bottom of the garbage. It seemed too absurd to me that we had a maid while living in chicken coops, that my thumb actually froze over, but in a box of old photographs I did find one of a plump black lady in a white uniform with our dog Pango at her side, still a frisky puppy. So Mama hadn't made the whole thing up. The three little cabins must have existed, because they were moved onto the new land when we bought the house in East Hampton. One of them became a playhouse for Cassandra and me. It was disturbing, this strange, rags-to-riches story. Mama and Papa had slept in one chicken coop, Cassie and I in another and the third had been a study for my father to write in, was how the story went. And then, supposedly, my house became my playhouse overnight.

One day after we'd lived in the big stone mansion for several years, I was driving up to the country with my father. He didn't take the usual exit from the expressway. When I asked why, he smiled secretively and said, "You'll see . . ." It was a September afternoon, the treetops a patchwork quilt of red, orange and yellow, the air pungent with bonfires and the first-day-of-school smell of newly sharpened pencils. My father made turns onto old back roads, their age evident from the thick-branched trees that plunged them into churchlike shadows despite the piercing, late-afternoon sun.

We drove up a steep hill and around a bend; Papa pulled off onto a dirt road, tire tracks with a high tuft of grass straight down the middle like the ridge of hair on a Mohawk's head. He drove the car a short distance and cut the engine. He looked out contemplatively over the apple-tree-studded hillside, then turned to me.

"Do you know where you are?" I shook my head, looking right at him, waiting to be told. "Come on," he said, and I followed him out of the car, snagging my socks on some brambles. I had to run to catch up with him, and he looked almost surprised to see me appear at his side, he was so caught up in his thoughts.

Papa gazed across the gently sloping hill and pasture, where birds pecked at fallen apples, like a man appreciatively inspecting his territory, at peace with the world. Finally he said, "This is where the chicken coops were," in a quiet voice that made it sound like the good old days, the start of something so sweet in his life that it made him smile even now, though that early promise had never been borne out.

It must have been different between Mama and my father once, in the beginning, when he was starting his career and she believed in him, believed he could go all the way to the top, believed life could be dreams made real. Papa didn't see life that way, coming from a meager family that had its back broken by the Depression; Papa and his sisters were raised by a taciturn father when his mother went into a sanitarium for TB. They fled from unpaid rent and went hungry a lot. Mama told stories of Papa's childhood with incredulous amazement, as though she were telling an Aesop's fable about a man of the world, the apple of her eye, this prince of a man who had actually once been without clothes, had nearly starved, had lived without love. He grew up without ever hearing the words, "I love you." No wonder he thirsted after an oasis like Isabel, a fount of feelings. He was drawn to her ebullience, to the devotion that filled him up to overflowing. She believed in him like a religion, but implicit in that faith was the expectation of godlike achievements; it was a dreadful burden. Deep down at the bottom of himself, he couldn't believe all the adoring things she said about him. She was like a mirage; as he got closer, it was too much, overwhelming. He was a man in the desert so parched that when he found water he couldn't believe it was real.

Had they ever loved each other madly? What was it he saw in her that he later became blind to? After she died, he wouldn't talk about her at all, would cringe perceptibly as though a dirty subject had been raised. He claimed ignorance if I asked him direct questions. "How did Mama feel about *her* mother dying?" I asked, eager to know something of the dramas that had preceded my own in the family.

"I don't know, dear," he replied impatiently, as though her death erased the past. But I didn't want to dangle in a void—I wanted to know her history, place myself in it. "I was really little then," I explained to my father, "and

I'd like to know. Was she close to Grandma Nellie? Was Mama there when Grandma died?"

"I don't remember," Papa said dismissively. "You should ask one of your mother's friends." He said it as though I'd asked what size nightgown Mama had worn. They didn't have a good marriage, but that's no explanation. Their early days together were filled with adventure, discoveries of shaping a life together. When she was eight months pregnant with me and they went down to Barbados to visit a famous painter my father represented, Mama swam off on long, aquatic explorations from the side of the deep-sea fishing boat. They laughed later about everyone's daily dread that she would give birth to me right there, under water. He must have loved her spirit, her strength. She was reminiscent of Katharine Hepburn: a bit arrogant when she set her jaw defiantly and a bit irresistible when she let her hair down. Mama even walked like Hepburn, long, purposeful strides in faded khaki gardening pants, refusing to look or behave like other women. Was that what made Papa love her?

We stood looking out at the chicken-coop hillside, and he said, "Don't you remember?" in a tone that made me want to say yes. I could feel how much he wanted to reminisce, for the other person to say, "Remember the time that . . ." so that he could say, "Yes! And what about the time that . . ." My mother, in other words. She was long gone, as were those tender, early times.

My father pointed to a clearing at the end of the overgrown road, a forest glade that showed no sign of human trespass. "That's where Pango had the three-hour standoff with the woodchuck," he said, referring to the often recounted story of our dog's bravado. "And over there were the chicken coops," he added.

I remembered the home movie of me pulling Cassie in a red wagon in this place. The movie made us howl with laughter, because Cass was crying, inspiring me to cry while continuing to pull the wagon, urged on by my father, the film director. It was a wonderfully funny silent duet of two crying angels in seersucker romper suits; but I couldn't remember the chicken coops. Damn, to have forgotten those intense joys, fierce frustrations, intrepid explorations of every hour of childhood—lost somewhere in the brain. Those moments of being hugged suffocatingly by arms as long as your own body; of running bare-assed under a sprinkler; of seeing your father look at your mother the way he looked at you, full of love, and give her a big, fat kiss. All buried, while certain trivia inexplicably remains: the words to a nursery rhyme; the castles of transparent peach and yellow shells that Maria glued together after a day at the beach; the way that tuna fish tasted at other kids' houses on white bread, which we never used. But the memories that matter, dammit, the ones that could stick to your ribs, are gone forever.

I glanced discreetly over at my father, not wanting to disturb his privacy but watching intently as he stared out over the woods. I wondered if by concentrating hard I could get inside his head, recapture for myself those cider-sweet memories; whether I could share his reveries back to happy times. When he and Mama spoke of the chicken-coop days, their faces lit up with that early energy and passion. It was a wealth they'd had together and later lost—or squandered, I don't know which. I was too young to see.

She was too much for him. Isabel wanted so much from life, from every moment, every person, *right now*. Malcolm was a man who reserved for his work what passion there was in his nature, rather than spill it on the thirsty brick of daily life. They were a bad match that worsened as time went on. The fights between them were not loud but charged with a terrible tension. She criticized, made demands; he withdrew into silences which incited her to further rebukes.

One time she pushed just that little too much. They were arguing in the butler's pantry and didn't know I was right outside on the service porch, brushing the dog. "I refuse to take any more of this," he said. He threw his gin and tonic in her face and stormed out of the house. There was utter stillness. Through the screen door I could see the mint sprig from his drink stuck in her hair; I could almost smell the bitter sweetness of the quinine evaporating. He had never done anything like that before, and I knew then it was pretty bad between them. There was the spinning crunch of tires on the gravel, and he was gone.

Years later, driving into the city in the same red sports car he'd had back then, I asked Papa where he'd gone that night. His laugh was a bark of surprise.

"Nowhere! I realized I didn't have anywhere to go. . . . I just drove around for a while and came back."

It was always very special that our father had a sports car, a red Alfa Romeo with a convertible top that leaked here and there in the rain. We tolerated gladly the discomforts of a luxury, like buying a thirteenth-century villa in Venice with windows that don't close properly. Cassandra and I didn't know other fathers who had sports cars. Families had station wagons for the procession of food, critters and guests that trekked up to the country on weekends. But a sports car, a fast, flashy two-seater? It seemed anti-familial, un-American, intriguingly forbidden. No one else was ever permitted to drive it: it was Papa's private territory, like his third-floor office, or his pied-à-terre in New York where he sometimes worked.

The best fun was when my sister and I rode with him, our voluminous red tresses flying madly in the wind,

Cassie's darker curly hair tangling with my straight, blond-streaked hair so that we became a two-headed mythological creature woven together. If we stopped for cones at the ice-cream parlor, it was always a race between our tongues and the wind, which dissolved the ice cream faster than we could consume it. As Papa accelerated, our flying hair dipped into the flying ice-cream drips and we yelled at him to slow down, laughing like capuchin monkeys, trying to eat the cones while they melted. Papa drove fast up the driveway, breaking his own rule and spraying gravel off to the sides as he screeched to a stop by the hose. We staggered from the seat where we'd been squeezed together; before we could get away, he sprayed us soaking wet, washing off the sticky goo. Three musketeers, we always had a laughing good time with him. Oddly enough, the best times with Mama were also when we were just three intrepid travelers to new lands. Three and three. The best times did not seem to be as a foursome. In some peculiar sense, we became a family of six, three and three, a mathematical expansion to compensate for how hard it was for them to be together.

Cassandra and I are probably what kept their marriage together. They didn't do it *for* us, but our presence made their union possible. And the travel, being constantly on the move, also took the heat off. They both had a strong drive to try new places, but the difference was that underlying Papa's compulsion was a sense of escape; Mama's need to travel seemed a running-towards, a search for something missing. In both cases, Cassie and I helped to justify their craving for change; they pledged themselves to making a delicious life for us. They treated us as equals, including us in dinner conversations or decisions about our collective life. They didn't have to face their problems head-on because they could direct their energies to us, away from the half-life they had as a couple.

Isabel refused to acknowledge the slow disintegration of their marriage. By the second time we moved to Rome, Cassie and I were just becoming teenagers, and Papa had already been spending a good deal of time at his own apartment in New York. My sister and I had each quietly accepted the fact that our parents were not happy together. Isabel would not give up her illusions. She was the only one who had any solid hopes that Papa would really come live with us in Rome the way he had when we were little girls. Once the bare truth had stared at her long enough, when we'd been in Rome for two months and the lawsuit with a painter that had kept him in New York was long settled, it hit Mama like a hardball in the shin. She focused on the immediate pain, unable to see that she didn't get any more chances up at bat, that the game was over. "Your father has left us," became her incantation; her tone was by turns astonished, mournful and angry.

Unlike the divorced parents of kids we knew, who bent over backwards to assure their children that the split had nothing to do with them, our mother insisted upon including us. "He's left us," she'd say, and Cass and I didn't need to say anything; we just gave each other a there-she-goes-again look. We knew Papa had left her, that it was unbearable for him with Mama; we also knew that she refused to face it. Christmas vacation was approaching, and she made elaborate plans to go to Sicily, allowing for the possibility that he might show up, after all, but also inviting a woman archaeologist who was interested in archaic religious celebrations. But I wanted to see my father, not Catholic rituals. Knowing better than to ask Mama's advice or permission, I called New York and said how much Cassie and I missed him. He invited us to join him for the end of a national tour for a collection of abstract expressionists he was promoting. I steeled myself for breaking the news to my mother. I felt badly that we might disturb her carefully planned trip and hurt her feelings, but my loyalty did not run so deep as to rob me of seeing my father. As it stood, her inability to see or change what had gone wrong between them had cheated me of his presence.

"What do you mean, I'm not invited!" Mother exclaimed.

"I guess Daddy's not ready to see you yet," I said apologetically. "I guess that's why he hasn't come to live here," I added in the patient tone one would use with a slightly dim child.

"That's ridiculous! How could he not invite *me*, for God's sake!"

I could not fathom where her indignation sprang from, what streak of stubbornness kept her from seeing that this man had been leaving her, bit by bit, for years. All that was missing now was his physical presence—the less tangible elements had been gone for some time. Yet Mother was sincerely stunned and stung by the rejection. A dynamic had built up between them in which he would try to take control by withdrawing, and she would wrest it back from him by pursuing, imploring him to return and give it another chance. They were trapped in a hopeless deadlock.

Cassandra and I had such a wonderful time over Christmas that we forgot about the problems between them. We slept together on the sofa bed in Papa's pied-à-terre and went to a stream of cocktail and dinner parties with him.

"You two get more attention than Willem de Kooning," Papa said after a few days. "These two breeze into town and steal center ring from the big shots," he quipped. "The only answer is for me to become a fifteen-year-old girl."

"Forget it, Dad, you'd hate it," I said. "Adolescence stinks."

"They're only interested in us because we live in Europe and speak languages," Cassandra said, eternally the precocious diplomat.

The tour was our first peek at America, a foreign place to us. The only trip we'd taken in the United States was to Hollywood when we were younger and Papa had to go on business. We adored the Beverly Hills Hotel, the tile-roofed bungalow cottage, an utterly pink world with mazes of gardens and lunch al fresco in a pink-arched patio.

The hotel suites arranged could hardly compete with the grand old European hostelries we'd visited, but we had a heavenly time. One morning in Chicago I couldn't decide what to order for breakfast. Papa said to have one of everything. I gave him a look that told him I was going to take him up on it; he smiled broadly.

"All this for only three people?" the room-service operator queried. "Are you certain, dear?"

The room-service carts arrived in a caravan procession, their small wheels barely able to roll forward with the heavy load. I had ordered every single thing on the menu. Cassie and I descended like starved madwomen on the tables of food they had prepared—fruits with cream, waffles and syrup, omelettes and muffins, sausages, ham and kippers. As we lay spread-eagled on our beds afterwards, Papa laughed and suggested, "Maybe we should think along the lines of a light lunch today?"

When we left Toronto, Papa had us smuggle Cuban cigars in our suitcases, as we'd been doing from childhood. It made me a nervous wreck, more so as the years of crime accrued. My palms went cold and sweaty; I picked a fight with Cassandra to divert the customs man's attention. I'd been smuggling for Papa for years, but I still didn't believe his assurance that if they did find the wooden box, nestled deep in a pile of sweaters, they wouldn't send me to jail. Yet, trembling, I kept on doing it. I would have risked anything for that man.

"You are the most important thing in your father's life," Mama once said solemnly. "He loves you more than anyone."

As things went bad between them, she found comfort in Papa's delight in me; I was so much like her it must have felt as though he loved her that way, a vicarious validation. I was a buffer, a bait. By the time I was old enough for an Electra complex, it wasn't a question of competing with my mother. She had more or less given him to me for safekeeping; if *she* couldn't have him, at least she could keep him in the family.

Four

I t was Blake and Michael's first trip away together, to a dinner party in East Hampton. She
loved it out there, the way the wide, flat fields
fell away on either side of the road at the beginning of the Hamptons. The houses and barns were
acres away from the road, set almost at the horizon. The
soil was dark and loamy, as fertile as the banks of the
Nile, Blake thought. Such a nice sense of decency, proportion, that the land was used for its oldest purpose, that
agriculture could thrive despite the chic, rich people from
New York who tried to make it another playground.
Blake liked the way that potatoes grew down the road
from Old Eastern Money wearing lime-green trousers—
from people who called pants "trousers," for that matter.
Corn grew next door to the urban writers and painters
who wore conspicuously weather-beaten khakis and Top-
siders, to give the impression of being Old Money. And
although there were opulent mansions set on dunes above

the ocean, it was the corn fields and stern houses of weathered gray wood that made it balanced, palatable.

They had been invited to dinner by a film director Michael knew, and as they drove past the well-manicured lawns of Lily Pond Lane, Blake recalled the various sprawling houses her parents' friends had rented during the summers and what fun it had been to investigate the seemingly endless guest bedrooms that looked out on sloping, green lawns. They pulled into the driveway of Lester Kaplan's house, and Blake thought what a charming, rambling place it was, not at all the oppressive sort of spread that an equivalent millionaire director would have in Hollywood. Kaplan came bounding out of the house to greet them, with the exuberance of a springer-spaniel puppy, ears flopping as he jumped in welcome. Lester's wrinkles put him near fifty, but he was no taller than a twelve-year-old and seemed to have retained a boyish energy to match his height. When Michael introduced Blake, Lester perked up and asked if she were Marsh's daughter.

"That's what he claims," she replied, annoyed by her own smart-ass discomfort at being perceived as a branch rather than a tree.

"Those were the grand old days," Kaplan said delightedly. "The greatest painters worked out here and your father made them all rich and famous."

Lester put his arm around Michael—a difficult task because of the full foot of difference in height—and headed towards the front of the house. "Come see the place," he said, putting his other arm around Blake's waist. "This is just the greatest place in the world to live. The best," he bubbled.

Blake put her arm around Lester, touching Michael's arm in back, a moment which struck her as comical, this bouncy little man between them as if he were their child. They reached the rushes on the bank of an inlet that flowed past Lester's property. The tributary was lined with spiky reeds and widened out into the ocean beyond. Blake had a sense that this was how the Hamptons had looked before men had encroached; the tall, harsh rushes seemed to be waiting, marking time, and would be there long after mankind had passed on.

"Now, what do you make of this?" Lester queried. He was standing beside a mound of turds which he studied intently. "What kind of animal is this? A deer, a fox?"

"Deer droppings are pellets, like rabbits'," Blake said.

"So what could this be?" Lester continued excitedly. "A bear?"

"I hate to disappoint you, buddy," Michael said, "but this is dog shit. Some neighbor's dog prefers your lawn, Les."

Kaplan looked crestfallen. The three of them stared at the pile of turds a moment longer. It reminded Blake of those wonderfully paradoxical scenes in Buñuel movies, the elegant characters hovering over a heap of shit on a gorgeous lawn.

Lester took them to a dinner party at Marguerite Damson's, the recent widow of a Pulitzer-prize novelist. He had been the central figure in the East Hampton hard-drinking literary group. Many years before, the Damsons had formed the nucleus of a similar circle in Paris, made up of expatriate intellectuals, wanderers and movie people, who congregated at their huge apartment on the Île St. Louis. Those were the days when many Hollywood films were shot in Paris, so there was a constant flow from America with fat expense accounts, movie people who would hook up with the ex-pats living abroad—painters, poets, writers. Beckett used to hang out at the bar beneath the Damsons' apartment, and American visitors were thrilled that they could just go down and talk to him. And the Parisians were fascinated by the Hollywood types—fledgling filmmaker Truffaut practically fell to his knees when idolized figures from classic American movies turned up at the Damsons'. It was a rich, innocently sophisticated time.

Lester walked into the Damson kitchen ahead of Michael and Blake. A voluptuous woman in a caftan greeted him, her hair pleasingly askew and her hands full of thick white plates. She welcomed the young couple with such enveloping warmth that all at once Blake remembered Marguerite from her childhood. Blake and Cassandra had gone to the Damson kids' birthday parties, but there had been a celebratory air there even without a birthday: the air was alive at their house, a ribald energy from Marguerite that hit people as soon as they walked through the door. Her husband had been a brooding, taciturn man—as befitted a renowned literary figure—contrasted with Marguerite's wild spirit and ringing laugh.

"Lester! You adorable man!" Marguerite called out. "Just in time, everyone's coming in to eat." She turned to Michael and Blake and added, "Hello, welcome!"

Lester introduced them, and Marguerite handed the stack of dinner plates to Blake, looking her up and down. "And is this little freckled Blake Marsham, all grown up?" Blake nodded, smiling; Marguerite placed her strong hands on Blake's shoulders, inspecting her for another moment, then pulled her in for a big, bosomy hug. "My, oh my," Marguerite said, turning back to the stove as the other guests drifted into the kitchen.

Blake was reminded of the Sunday night spaghetti dinners at the Damsons' in Paris, when loads of people showed up and ate and drank and smoked grass all night long. Early in the evening the guests crowded around Damson, but as he got drunk he lost them, one by one. He wasn't a sloppy drunk, more like a mummified one, asleep open-eyed on his feet; the people gravitated towards Marguerite, enchantingly ebullient. People came to see her as much as the great man of letters. Blake and Cassandra played with the Damson kids on the upper floor of the apartment and fell asleep to the music of chatter and laughter below.

People drifted now into the big, warm, beachy kitchen, and introductions crossed back and forth. Blake heard the names of two well-known writers, a painter and his sculptor wife, a Broadway composer, a literary critic and a TV commentator as she set out the plates Marguerite had given her. It was a long, battered, wooden table, reminiscent of the dark, carved, Italian dining furniture in their Paris apartment, straightbacked monkish chairs at a long refectory table. They had been just the right size for children, but the adults were always grumbling about how much smaller people were in the eleventh century.

Blake wound up at one end of the table and had to strain to hear the man at the other end, who was telling a story from the Île St. Louis days.

"So Faulkner was supposed to come to Paris for rewrites on *Land of the Pharaohs,* which was a tits-and-sand flick that had started out with loftier aspiratons." The table got quiet as everyone listened, and Blake could hear more easily. "First, Faulkner was found wandering on the Left Bank, a bottle of brandy in each hand. One of the expatriates found him, rescued him, learned that the crazy bastard was supposed to be in Egypt and got him on a plane to Cairo. Only hitch was, Faulkner wasn't letting go of those bottles. He stepped off that plane into the desert, still hanging onto the damn brandy, and immediately holed up at Shepherd's Hotel. Everybody is out in the desert waiting for this rewrite: herds of camels, tribes of Bedouins, et cetera. One day passes, then two, with thousands of dollars down the drain, waiting for this rewrite so the cameras can roll again. Finally, on the third day, Faulkner emerges from the hotel. He's holding a bottle of brandy, nothing else. He looks out at the assembled crew, shakes his head and says, 'I just can't seem to whup this cold'—and he goes back into his room and won't come out!"

Blake joined the other guests' laughter, and the spaghetti passed from hand to hand.

After fruit and cheese, the assemblage moved back to the living room, gravitating towards the semicircular stand-up bar that dominated the room. Marguerite stood behind it, bottles in various stages of depletion around her, looking like a kid whose lemonade stand wasn't doing too well. There was something just in the way she offered guests a drink, Blake noted, that revealed her desperation. It made Blake want to hug her. Marguerite's blowsy gaiety was only a thin veneer over the awesome grief she was still suffering from the loss of her lifetime husband.

Robert Damson had been a formidable drinker, and the crowd that orbited around him had shared his fondness for alcohol. When Lester was driving Michael and Blake to the party, he had said, "It's really such a terrific love story: Marge was never much of a drinker, but over the years she began to drink to keep him company."

Lester had paused, waiting for Blake or Michael to say something, but they had remained silent, faced with Lester's demented sentimental praise for alcoholism as an expression of love.

"How they loved each other!" Lester had continued.

"And what a knockout of a body she had, once upon a time . . . gone fat from drink now, but those were the days."

Blake remembered how her teetotaling mother used to comment about the amount of drink at the Île St. Louis apartment—Isabel used to say that Marguerite did not seem drunk but gave the impression of being in a perpetual fog. So many people came and went at the Damsons' that Blake wondered whether Marguerite remembered much of it.

"Love your father," Marguerite said, leaning over the bar just a bit too close to Blake. "How is he?" She gave Blake only time enough to nod, then said, "He visited us in sixty-eight."

"Were you still in that great apartment?"

"Ah, yes . . . such good times . . . great times . . ." Her voice trailed off, and her dark, disheveled hair bobbed as she emphasized with nods, her eyes far away. Just the mention of it had taken her back there. "And your father is wonderful . . . what wonderful times those were." She luxuriated in her reverie.

Blake recalled the Damson girl, Lucy; a proud little face, square-cut, ringed in blond curls, as if she were a formal portrait of herself. "I remember going to the Jardin D'Acclimatation with your kids," Blake said to Marguerite.

There had been a zoo with moats instead of bars, little trains and planes to ride on, and a sandy playground with pools and sailboats and a huge slide with three bumps that took the mothers' breath away. Blake had a flash of the mothers standing at the bottom of that slide, their hands at their throats or covering their mouths like heroines in Victorian novels, holding their breath until the jeopardy passed and each of their little angels had made it safely back to earth with a thump in the sand. On the way home, Blake and Cassandra used to get a thin, piping-hot waffle dusted with powdered sugar that burned their fingers through the square of tissue paper and left them with white whiskers.

"Yes, le Jardin," Marguerite mused. "I drove down that street to the Bois not long ago—how it had changed. The street is lined with car hookers now." She added an ironic, "Huh!" then saw that Blake was puzzled. "You know, darlin', the *putains* who pull their sweaters up over a tit as a car goes by." Marguerite's face went dreamy again, and she drifted away. "Ah, but those were the days, weren't they?"

A burly hulk of a man grabbed Michael's arm. He was the stinking-drunk author of half a dozen commercially successful novels. The cognoscenti knew to call him before eleven A.M. because he'd be too drunk to make any sense after that. After his sorry excuse for a marriage had finally given up the ghost, he was attended by a succession of willowy socialites, English majors from exclusive colleges who found their degrees quite useless once out in the world. Blake couldn't imagine what any of them saw in him: it was a mean, broken-blood-vesseled face without so much as a friendly wrinkle on it.

"They just ruined my book in a fuck-all mini-series," he growled.

"That's too bad," Blake said, instinctively trying to rescue Michael from his grip, get the man's attention on her, like the assistant bullfighters do when a matador is in danger.

"Which book was it?" Marguerite asked, solicitously refilling his wine glass as if that would make it all better. Maybe she was right.

" 'The Moneylenders,' " he snarled. "Jesus—I've been

on this fuckin' diet for a *week*," he added, glaring at the glass she had just filled for him. "No booze, just this grape piss, and another friggin' week to go." His reddened face was woeful with self-pity.

"But you must feel better in the mornings when you wake up?" Blake prompted cheerfully.

"No, I feel like shit. And why don't you tone it down?"

"But she's adorable," Marguerite countered, a rescue dog, too.

Several people were making tipsy good-byes, and Michael pantomimed leaving to Blake, who nodded. Marguerite and the Broadway composer had begun to dance in the front room, swaying to a scratchy record. He and his lady writing partner had written some of the most enduring Broadway musicals; he seemed compelled to act out his reputation, working hard at being very Fred Astaire. He wore a sailor cap that gave him a jaunty air, but his belly hung over his belt a bit too much for him to pass as a debonair hoofer. Marge was working hard at being a bon vivant, the gay-hostess-overcome-by-the-beckon-of-the-music. She succeeded only in underscoring her terrible loneliness. She missed Damson so much that Blake could almost feel her dead husband in the room.

There had been one Sunday at the Paris apartment when everyone was talking about how Camus had just died, what a tragedy it was to die in a car crash, and only forty-six! No, he wasn't drinking, just some crazy French driver, yes, instantly, no pain . . . and then the doorbell rang. Everybody at the Damsons' had known Camus and his girl friend slightly. It was she at the door. They had all felt important, connected to his important death, even though they hadn't really known him in life. No one said a word when his girl showed up at the door— she wasn't a regular visitor. They were all chagrined to have been talking about Camus as though it had anything to do with them.

She stood on the doorstep, plain in her pain. "I'm lonely," she said. "I need company."

Marguerite had enfolded her in an embrace, welcoming her as she did anyone who came to her door. Now the people in East Hampton had come to keep her company. Those years in Paris had been stylishly decadent, Fitzgeraldian, holding court for international artists. Now it seemed sad to Blake.

Five

Isabel Blake Marsham was an anachronism, an exuberant creature who had managed to flourish in an environment of tough, dour prairie people. Raised as an ingenuous aristocrat with the severe doctrines of a Scotch Presbyterian mother, my mother grew up in Calgary, Canada, with pioneer spirit and puritan ethics. Mama managed to accommodate her warm Mediterranean soul to her harsh surroundings—by the time my sister and I got to know her, Isabel preached sensible tweeds while practicing silk and cashmere. She didn't see the contradiction in comparing the prices of cans in the supermarket, yet never buying a piece of clothing in a store. Mr. Gwinn's flowing signature adorned the lining of everything she wore, yet Mother managed to feel frugal because, unlike her friends, she didn't have a famous designer like Adolfo or Galanos. Her proud stories of her brutal Canadian upbringing, walking five miles to school through tunnels of snow, didn't keep her from hailing a cab to go ten blocks. She didn't have a limousine, did she?

Cassandra and I evolved with a rosily warped view of the distribution of wealth in the world. If we were "just middle-class," with a castle for country weekends, trips to hot places during cold vacations and nothing we couldn't have—be it chocolate soufflés for dessert or horse shows all summer long—then what did rich mean? Mama told us we weren't rich, but it was hard to understand when Cassie and I lay stomach-down on the prow of our boat, with Papa at the helm and weekend visitors stretched out in white canvas chairs, the gleaming chrome railings sweeping back on either side of us as the sharp nose of the boat cut through Long Island Sound and Reggie popped open bottles of frosty beer for the guests.

"That's where the rich people live," Mama would explain as we passed waterfront mansions.

Isabel's friends may have thought she was being facetious, but Cassandra and I accepted her lifelong insistence that we were just middle-class, that The Rich were someone else, not us. It seemed an unappetizing thing to be, judging from the huge houses on deserted private beaches, boats tied to the weatherbeaten docks, but no people, nobody having any fun. It made Cassie and me glad we weren't rich, living in listless tranquillity in some gloomy old place where people didn't even come outdoors to play.

Every time the boat slid past a certain ultra-modern glass house on the bay, Mama would say to her guests, "Poor Henry Berger, he's so unhappy about being rich. All he has to do is wake up in the morning to rake in millions. I think being born into it depressed him a little—also, it wasn't terribly glamorous, all that money, because his family's company makes the bags for every supermarket in America. Poor Henry. Now, everybody has to promise not to ask for double bags at the A&P, or the money will pour in *twice* as fast and he'll feel even worse!"

The guests would laugh and sip their beers, and Cassie and I would smile at each other as the salty spray came up at us, so glad we were sisters, that Isabel was our mother, that we could skim the ocean with Papa at the wheel and nothing could harm us.

The contradictions were woven all through our life: Mama's lavishness on the one hand and penny-pinching on the other; her ambivalence about the horn of plenty. Every time we ate dinner in the country I would study the ceiling, the candlelight playing against the burnished gold. When they had bought the house, the entire dining room was gold-leafed: the swinging door to the butler's pantry, the walls, the ceiling.

"It was just a touch too Louis the Sixteenth," Mama said with an edge of bitchiness when she took people around the house. "The Rockefellers did one hell of a job commissioning this dear old place, but, really, who do you know who feels royal enough to eat in a golden box? I didn't see how our meals could ever live up to it, so we kept just the ceiling."

She had the walls and door painted ivory; sometimes I would investigate them close up, thinking about that layer of real gold that Mama had covered up under there.

There was always something that Isabel was proclaiming we couldn't afford, but it didn't matter if it was a new septic tank that Jim said we needed, if it was a winter blanket for the ponies or tickets to a new musical. We would wind up getting whatever it was eventually, but she needed to feel the pinch, to prevent any of us from getting complacent. But it was confusing. She would tell us that we couldn't afford new tires for the station wagon, that in Papa's business one never knew where the next dollar was coming from, we had to be careful; but when we knocked on her bedroom door and she said, "Come in, dear," we found her stretched out on a portable, red-vinyl massage table with Helga, a broad-shouldered Swede, kneading Mama's thighs. She had massages twice a week—she explained that it was good for muscle tone, and I never questioned her indulgence.

"Ven will ve start vit you, little von?" Helga would say when I came in to talk to Mama. I didn't understand how we could be poor and afford a masseuse, but I figured it was something all grown-up women did, and one day I would, too.

One of the major ways for Isabel to be a spendthrift was that Cassandra and I rarely shopped for clothes. We wore the pass-me-downs of Mama's rich friends, whose children grew out of their clothes almost before they had time to wear them twice. It was a mini-Christmas on the day one of those gift boxes arrived: we dumped it upside down and the tissue-wrapped clothing spilled out, many things with their price tags still attached, never worn. Cassie and I bargained for the nicest things and made giddy fun of the rejects, like picking a baseball team at school: we each got our first choice, and then subsequent choices were in a descending order of desirability.

By the time we reached the bottom of the pile, there were clothes strewn all over Mama's bedroom, and we were punchy, bursting into hysterics when Cassie put a particularly dowdy plaid skirt on her head and danced around the room. Mama would admonish us to be grateful, suppressing her own laughter as she lay on the gray-and-black-striped silk of the chaise longue, the light through the tall elms dappling through the window. She would try to be serious: "If it weren't for my extravagant, generous friends, you'd never have that English coat with the lamb's-wool collar and matching muff," she'd say. Then Cassie would collapse in laughter when I got down on my hands and knees and bowed to the coat in question. It was hard to take Mama's frugality too seriously, because as soon as we were off home turf we got custom-made clothes the way Mama did. Riding clothes in London; copies of Chanel suits in Rome, where the dressmaker lined the jacket with the same silk we'd chosen for the blouse; dresses of Egyptian cotton and nightgowns of heavy striped flannel in Cairo. In Athens we went to Mrs. Kokos' workroom and stood behind the weavers, choosing the pattern we wanted for long mohair skirts to wear when company came to dinner in the country.

Although we accepted our mother's definition of us as middle-class, my sister and I knew that our life wasn't ordinary, that we weren't anything like the normal American people we sometimes longed to be. We were fascinated by the family that lived over the stone wall up in the country, whose daughter Jenny sometimes played with us. Cassie and I had been all over the world but never encountered anything so startlingly foreign to us as the Walds. They had speckled linoleum in a basement room called "the family room"; they had a father with a crew cut and a lawn mower, and a mother perpetually in curlers covered by a triangular kerchief with the ends tied underneath in back. Climbing over the wall to dinner at the Walds was a mysterious adventure. Cassandra and I were baffled that a small glass of tomato juice was served as a first course, and the vegetable was always an odd frozen mélange called succotash.

We had only ever seen succotash in the little tin hollows of TV dinners, an exotically American treat that Cassie and I could have only on nights our parents went out to dinner. Even then, there was a sense of the forbidden. Cass and I were allowed to pick out five-course

TV dinners at the market, which we huddled over in front of "Lassie" like fugitives from our real life. Maria once ruined the whole experience by transferring the dollops of food from their metal compartments onto plates, where they looked quite grim and skimpy. We ate things called "fish sticks" and "Salisbury steak," which bore no resemblance to real food and didn't exist anywhere we'd ever traveled—except the succotash over the wall at Mrs. Wald's, where she served it up proudly as though it were a natural vegetable. Our parents came into the upstairs den to say goodnight on their way out to dinner and invariably shook their heads in mock dismay.

"Could these be *our* children?" Mama teased.

"The same two girls who order a dozen escargots when we go out?" Papa continued. "And beg for more?"

Mama left a heavy cloud of Guerlain perfume in the air, and they went out looking achingly elegant; it felt deliciously sinful to stay behind and be so all-American, just like people on television.

My being both my mother's and my father's favorite made life brutally confusing for Cassandra. She had all the external pleasures I did but couldn't satisfy her parents. It was a no-win situation: she'd been born to people whose hunger was sated, who already had what they considered a perfect child. Anything she did was measured against the past triumphs of her eighteen-month-older sister; regardless of all the privileges of our life, Cassie had no way of capturing our parents as I had, evoking a shower of love. She was often chastised for not keeping up. It was an enchanted existence that could whirl around at any time, a sleeping snake, and strike at her.

Her natural personality was different from Mama's and mine, from our high-key, bursting-at-the-seams energy and enthusiasm. Isabel was impatient with her second daughter's differentness, as though it were a deliberate slap in the face that Cassandra wasn't more like her. I had been naturally receptive, willing to become whatever my mother wanted . . . which was to become her. She had such a malleable piece of clay in me that one would think her need for a replica, immortality, would have been pacified. Yet she was forever criticizing Cassandra, asking her rhetorically why she couldn't do things the way Blake did. I wondered why our mother dressed us as twins in matching outfits: lace-pinafored party dresses with wide, yellow satin sashes; Easter dresses with a design of apples around the hems and on the matching parasols; silk kimonos and wooden sandals that Papa brought back from the Orient. Did it make her feel better to dress us alike, to mask how differently she treated us?

Despite the way she fanned the flames of sibling rivalry, stabbing at Cassandra and hurting me by making me the sword, we were still both proud to be her daughters. Her way of being a mother eliminated the rigid rules and humiliations usually imposed on children. We were treated as independent, free-thinking people, encouraged to decide for ourselves what time to go to bed, what to have for breakfast and what school we preferred. She even let us choose our own middle names.

"I picked unusual names for both of you," she explained, "so I didn't give you middle names; in case you didn't like what I'd chosen, you could rename yourselves."

We spent weeks toying with everything from Elizabeth to Nicole before deciding we preferred what Mama had chosen: her maiden name for me and the ancient prophet for my sister.

As Isabel's daughter, it was impossible to feel that anything in life could take the upper hand. She was like a westward-bound pioneer in gold-rush days: she viewed life as a vast land to conquer and be enriched by. My sister was not as wholehearted as I was in accepting Mama's philosophy that there was no such thing as an insurmountable obstacle, that the world was a playground to make of what you dared. I still don't know, after all, whether Mother was dead wrong or dead on. Cassandra says I viewed life like the line from the children's song, "Merrily, merrily, merrily, merrily, life is but a dream . . ."; that trusting Mama left me ill equipped for the world outside our enchanted castle. Ah, but those were the days: a field full of pet animals, adoration from parents, a life that never said no. Days had a clear, clean shape: take a perfect jump; execute a symmetrical figure eight. There, you are master of your world, sleep, dream, in peace. My horse, Lancashire Lad, carried his tail like a flag, the glint of majesty in his dark eyes—I kissed his soft nose so much I felt sure he'd turn back into a prince someday. Imagine, my horse had a barn with French windows. The universe was ours.

Nothing daunted my mother. She was chronically late for everything, so that airplanes were often already taxiing down the runway by the time we breathlessly reached the gate. I can't board an airplane to this day without seeing the cold stares of all the passengers we had delayed back then. Those were days with less air traffic: Isabel concocted fantastic tales about our future health or happiness in order to have the plane turned around on the runway; we scrambled up the hastily assembled metal stairs, then had to walk bravely down the aisle past angry people who wondered who we were to merit such VIP treatment. We knew it was just Isabel Marsham, mountain mover.

It was the underlying message that nothing was bigger than we were . . . germs, for instance. "We don't believe in germs," Cassie and I would say to other kids when they told us not to eat candy that fell on the ground or pat strange dogs. We thought germs were something—like God—that more timid people believed in but that we,

Isabel's daughters, didn't have to worry about. Or banks, for another example: Isabel's financial habits made me think that balancing a checkbook was the waste of time she pronounced it to be. I thought one just wrote checks, the bank put up the money and later on you settled things. Noblesse oblige. Every time I went into the Westport Bank & Trust with my mother, the president, Mr. Block, would greet us warmly and then chastise Mama gently for overdrawing her account. He did his finger wagging without much conviction, knowing that she would charm him to death. Isabel's presence was overwhelming to men, and she thrived on the way she could wrap them around her finger. She wasn't a femme fatale, she wasn't beauty-parlor beautiful, but she had a great figure and a way of making a man feel ten feet tall. Whether it was a policeman, a car mechanic or a hotel manager of a completely booked hotel, Mama always emerged with a suite with a view.

Life with my mother meant it was OK even when it wasn't, that everything would come out happily ever after. When we were living in Rome, I lost the navy-blue kid gloves lined in gray rabbit that she had bought as a no-occasion present. I took them to the ballet, my first date with a tall fellow of Dutch extraction who was a class ahead of me at St. Stephen's. In those days Mama said that a lady must always wear a slip and carry gloves. When he dropped me off in a cab he kissed me, and I floated out of the cab. At sixteen, it was my first kiss on the lips.

I got inside our apartment, only to realize I'd dropped one of my new gloves. I searched outside but couldn't find it. I was horrified, losing one of those luxurious gloves before I'd even had it on my hand. I cried and cried, begging my mother's forgiveness even though she said it didn't matter, that things were just things and never deserved that much attention. Nonetheless, I berated myself all the following day, kicking myself for the stupidity of my carelessness. I came home to find a slim package on my bed from the glove store at the Piazza di Spagna. Along with the replacement pair of gloves was a note from Mama, saying how little the little things mattered since I was perfect in the big things. I was amazed. Once again, Mama confirmed that I could not lose in life, no matter what. It was an awesome feeling, slipping my hand into that soft, gray bunny fur and knowing that life was fur-lined, too.

Mama made everything around her luminous, stretched even the simplest things to heroic proportions. There was one summer evening when Cassie and I went out to collect fireflies; the night air felt as if a storm were gathering and the south field was glittering with neon flickering. We ran through the grass with jars from the toolshed, opening the lid just enough to capture a flying dot of light without releasing the ones already trapped in the jar. Maria called our names, and Cassandra opened her jar as we usually did and released the fireflies on our way back to the house. But I wanted to keep mine this once, keep them with me as a night-light.

Cassie and I lay in the dark, watching the jar on the bedside table as the little bodies turned on and off. Mama came in to say goodnight, walking across the moon-dappled rug. I wasn't sure if she'd be mad that I'd brought them inside, that I hadn't let the poor things go, but she didn't say a word, just sat down on my bed and watched the jar with us. As dark as it was I could feel her smile at me, could see a faint glint off her front teeth as she radiated love at me like moonlight. Everything I did pleased her, it seemed.

"Wouldn't it be swell if we could have fireflies all over our room, twinkling like stars?" I said.

"Twinkle, twinkle, little star," Cass mumbled sleepily.

Mama reached over and uncapped the jar, turning it sideways. For a moment the room remained dark and still; suddenly a firefly lit up above the end of my bed, then another one across the room. None of us said a word, peering out into the dark, looking for the unpredictable flickers. After a while Mama leaned over and kissed me on both cheeks, then on the forehead. She got up and did the same to Cassandra. She walked quietly out of the room. I looked at a few more flickers after she left, then fell into a sound sleep that was as deep and calm as the womb.

The sound of thunder woke me up. As I slowly came awake I remembered the fireflies and opened my eyes, expecting to see them still twinkling, but there was no sign of them. They had died or found a way to freedom. A loud crack of thunder and a ribbon of lightning lit up the window beside me. I slipped out of bed and looked outside at the night lit up with storm. A wide band of lightning brightened the sky, and suddenly I saw my parents down there, a dreamlike apparition, skinny-dipping in the lily pond. Moonlight gleamed on their bodies as they splashed, two baby seals.

I dashed downstairs and outside, my nightgown instantly soaked by the heavy rain. I pulled it off over my head as I ran. The lily pond had been recently recemented so the goldfish had been taken out, and the water lilies were perched around the edge in wooden pots. My parents looked up with delighted surprise as I appeared, my little body streaming with rainwater and lit up by slashes of lightning. Papa put out his hand, and I stepped into the warm, shallow water; we three embraced in a hug filled with the soft, thundering storm.

"What about the lightning, with us in the water?" Papa said, suddenly cautious because I was there.

In her wonderfully insouciant way Mama replied, "Don't be silly—there are lightning rods on the house."

We laughed and splashed until the rain made the water too cold to stand it anymore, and we went inside for cocoa and cognac. Papa and I had stopped worrying when swords of lightning had cracked open the moonlit sky; our faith in Isabel was so complete we knew no storm would dare to harm us.

Six

I sabel ignored the first warning about a lump in her breast. She simply did not have the time for an interruption in her life. She was in the middle of getting a doctorate in comparative religions from Columbia, and she had also planned a triumphant return visit to Easter Island. One of her finest hours had been her coup in arranging to bring an Aku-Aku head to New York. She had been bowled over by her visit to the primitive island and was dismayed when she learned that funds had run out for further archaeological explorations. First, she charmed the local Easter Island officials into allowing one of the enormous heads to make a goodwill journey; then she sweet-talked an air force colonel into donating a military transport plane to bring the two-ton head to New York; finally, she convinced the people at the Seagram building in New York that displaying the head in their plaza would be worth a fortune in publicity. Once she'd gotten the mayor to officiate at the unveiling and had saved the archaeological future of the massive heads, the foundation that had been sponsoring Easter Island invited her back. And she was damned if a bunch of over-eager doctors would stop her. After being examined by half a dozen of them, who all agreed emphatically that she needed immediate surgery, she finally found some barely intelligible Indian doctor, who said it could wait. She was delighted; her tenacity had been rewarded.

Eventually, Isabel could not avoid the mastectomy any longer, but she didn't allow her chin-high outlook on life to be undermined. She viewed it as one of life's nasty little ironies and poked fun at the grisly affair. It wasn't just false bravado for our sakes; it was simply out of character for such a vibrant, never-sick-a-day-in-her-life woman to be struck by a deadly disease. She told humorous anecdotes about the little old ladies in the special department at Bergdorf's, who fitted mastectomy victims with "fake bazooms." Mama mimicked their enthusiastic sales pitch about the wide variety of texture and bounciness available to those who found themselves suddenly breastless. We all laughed as if there really was a joke.

She not only had to get a false breast, but the operation left a shrunken cavity where the muscles and glands under her armpit had been cut away. All her clothes had to be recut to camouflage it. "It will be an inspiring challenge to Mr. Gwinn," she declared sardonically, "to mask the deformity." Her clothes were designed with no eye to current fashion, only to what she liked on herself: a close-fitting bodice, tight waist and wide, billowing skirt. She often brought back pieces of Peruvian weaving or Egyptian cotton for Mr. Gwinn to incorporate into his designs. Just before Cassandra and I became full-fledged teenagers, we were self-conscious about our mother at school because she never looked like the other prim and proper mothers. Isabel stood out because she didn't look like anybody else:

she wasn't sedate; she walked with a purposeful, eager stride as though she were in a hurry to get somewhere. It made you want to run and catch up and go there with her.

Mr. Gwinn worked on Mama's suits until he devised a capelike attachment that covered her carved-out armpit. She swam in Long Island Sound even after the season was over and it was cold as hell. With her inimitable vigor, her arms lashed out at the water as if *it* were the enemy that had cut away at her. She didn't go down easy. She managed to cajole Cassie and me to go to the beach with her, despite our protests that there was already enough of a nip in the October air for us to be wearing plaid kilts to school. Sometimes we'd brave the chilly water with her; other times we'd walk along the shore, paralleling Mama hundreds of yards out at sea, watching her churn through the water with the determination of a marathon swimmer attacking the English Channel. It reminded us of one winter's trip to Israel. We arrived at the Dead Sea and Mama insisted we all go in, that the experience could not be passed up despite the frigid temperature. Cassandra and I were splotched blue with cold just putting on our pink suits with a seahorse design stitched into them. The driver, who'd brought us out to see the caves where the Dead Sea scrolls had been found, looked at us pityingly, his face suggesting that our mother was mean or crazy. Cassandra and I boldly plunged in, floating like toy boats in the heavily salted water. When Mama dried off her two blue-lipped, shivering little girls, we thanked her for making sure we didn't miss the thrill of floating in water that held you up like the hands of a friendly giant.

We all assumed that Isabel's insouciance, her sheer life force, had defeated the cancer. But it can be a devilish disease. There were five years between the first lump and the time it surfaced in her other breast. We were living in Rome the second time, and she refused to go back to the

United States until after a snake-worship festival near Perugia.

"These are very special pagan rites," she said impatiently, as if it should be obvious to anyone. "The divine sort of thing you don't find anymore—and I'm not going to miss it for this goddamned cancer."

They put Mother right into the hospital when she returned. We had buried our lifelong canine companion Pango in Rome, and Papa had promised we could get a new dog, maybe even a pair, as soon as we got back to the States. My father wasn't living with us any longer by then —the farce was exposed as far as my sister and I were concerned—but Isabel clung to her diehard belief that he was the only man for her and there might still be a way. We had lost Papa gradually over the years—forfeiting him was preparation: now it looked as though we were going to lose Mama, too. Getting a new dog seemed the most important thing in the world.

We made telephone calls to Bedlington terrier breeders from my mother's hospital room and settled on a female puppy from Boston; Reggie picked her up at LaGuardia. She was already turning from the bluish black of puppyhood to blue-gray; she was chubby and cheerful and was to be Cassandra's. We drove to New Jersey to pick out the male puppy, a skinny, runtish fellow who stood up on his hind legs and put his paws around my neck when I bent down to pat him. Falstaff became my dog, and we named Cassie's Mistress Quickly. We would arrive at the hospital with progress reports on the puppies' devilish antics, which delighted Mama no end. It gave us all the courage of new beginnings, renewed life, to counteract the harsh whites of the hospital, the sinister, shiny radiation machines and Mama's bandages.

"The puppy has distemper," the vet told me, shaking

his head discouragingly. "He's very bad off—I can't honestly give you any hope of his making it, Blake."

I was not angry and I was not frightened, I was simply determined to prove him wrong: I would not let this dog die. The doctor prescribed medicine to give Falstaff every four hours but warned me that distemper was nearly always fatal, because the puppy eventually couldn't breathe from the congestion and suffocated to death. I held the puppy's warm, limp body in my arms as we went to the car; I saw him smile back at me from behind his clouded eyes.

At home I kept him swaddled in blankets, took his temperature and forced pills down his throat. I took him in the bathroom with the shower running so hot the room was thick with steam. For a few hours afterwards he could breathe without gasping. In a couple of weeks the wallpaper had peeled away—the clowns and horses that had danced across the wall since my childhood were waterstreaked and wrinkled. But Falstaff lived: sheer will and determination were all it took. I had triumphed over death.

I cooked chicken soup up in the big country kitchen and brought it into the city in a gray and pink thermos. Mama hated the food in the hospital but also wasn't very hungry, so I tried to think of ways to please her palate. Flushed with my success as nurse to Falstaff, I applied the same optimistic energy to my mother. Chicken soup to cure cancer. I suppose it was as good a remedy as any. For a short time it wasn't even too gloomy in the hospital: there was still Mama's undiluted life-loving spirit, her plans for trips we'd take in the future and her general refusal to toll any somber bells.

But once the doctor's knives had ravaged the other side of her chest, the cancer didn't let up at all, eating its way out of her with a vicious hunger. She had watched her own mother die a terrible death from it.

Mama joked with me, saying, "I don't want to kick the bucket the way poor Grandma Nellie did—promise that you'll hit me over the head, Blakie, if it gets too bad?"

Her talking like that seemed Isabel's usual flippant nose thumbing at the world. Even at the end, when she got skinnier and weaker by the day, Mama never gave in. She had the raw persistence of a bird that sings in the middle of the night, oblivious to the darkness. How could I believe that this unquenchable mother of mine would really die?

The doctors tried to keep pace with the disease, racing it neck and neck, yet always a step behind as it coursed through her body. They put her back in the hospital for a hysterectomy, hoping that would slow the cancer. She made light of it, saying it was a good opportunity to replenish our linen closet. For two years Cass and I had been pointing out that it wasn't very cheery to wake up at home with "University Hospital" stamped all over our beds. Mother dismissed our complaints and said we should think of them as designer sheets, no different from having Vera's signature on them. Isabel sent home all the sheets and thermal blankets she could get her hands on. She ordered several sheepskin bed pads, sending word that they would make excellent saddle pads for Lancashire Lad. I guess she figured they owed her.

The bombardment of radiation and chemotherapy pills made her feel sick and her hair thinned out, but what bothered her most was that the male hormone treatments lowered her voice. I wasn't aware of it, the way a parent doesn't notice an adolescent son's voice gradually dropping, but it disturbed Mama when strangers on the phone referred to her as "sir." It was harder for her than the pain. *That* she bore gallantly, with the high head of a political prisoner who will not break down under torture.

Mother vowed she'd never let them cut her again after the last operation. "They can teach students on me once I'm a cadaver," she quipped. "But I'm not going under their knives anymore so some snot-nosed students can learn how to take out a uterus without mashing the kidneys."

When her stomach began hurting they put her back in the hospital and treated her for an ulcer, sending food devoid of any taste or texture. She had no appetite anyway, but when her tray of plastic containers arrived I would take charge of it: I'd sprinkle on herbs or butter or mix together two of the ingredients to make it tastier. But the food was awful, and her stomach hurt too much anyway. Visitors brought paté and caviar, but Mama couldn't manage them, so they wound up eating the gifts they'd brought.

It was always a lively cocktail party in her room, Mother made sure of that. There were mobiles hanging in front of the river-view windows, prints we'd brought in and hung on the walls and a small Giacometti sculpture on the window ledge. As a child I had been fascinated by the horse; now I was struck by the man riding it, his exaggerated tall skinniness that so much resembled Mama. Despite the illness she was an exemplary hostess, mixing drinks and guests, walking around in the lavish peignoirs friends had given her. The nurse's station became resigned to supplying extra ice, and when our hors d'oeuvre supply ran low, Mother had a friend in the restaurant business who sent food the minute she called.

I hovered constantly, protecting Mama from her own determination. I made her lie down when I saw that the pain had gnawed through her medication; I'd go out to the nurses and cajole them into more painkillers. Even then Mama would not allow the guests to leave; she didn't want to worry them by appearing weak, nor would she give the disease the upper hand by letting it take control. So it fell to me to keep the three-ring circus going: introducing new arrivals, making sure drinks were filled and people were amused, all the while keeping an eye on Mama so she'd get some rest in spite of herself. In flash moments I could hear myself imitating Isabel's social style so exactly—the big laugh, the coy flirtation, the saucy comment—that I felt as though she had already left and they'd accepted me as her replacement.

My mother didn't have any ulcer. The cancer had spread to her stomach, but no one would say that aloud. Her mother's cancer had been there. I would get migraines so fierce I would have to lie down on her hospital bed. Mama caressed my forehead with her cool hands, which had gotten even silkier from their months of rest; she stroked my brow as she had through all the earaches and heartaches of my life, taking away the pain, soothing the fever. How could I do that for her? She would stroke my head, gazing down at me until some nurse came in and insisted that the beds were only for patients. I got up but wanted to spit at the stupid woman who spent her days caring for the dying and had not yet figured out that those around them died a little each day, too.

They let her go home, but the cancer had gotten to her bones. Mama's legs would hurt after just a short walk. Sometimes at school I had to sit down in the hall because my legs would ache, too,

It was Christmastime. Mother was getting rapidly worse, but she insisted that Cassandra and I do all the traditional Christmas things without her, go to *The Nutcracker* and the holiday parties. Isabel adored any occasion for celebration and always made a grand production. We never had just one birthday, always three: one at school, one in the city and one in Connecticut. But Christmas was her favorite, a chance to decorate the New York duplex and have a modest tree, then go hog-wild up in the country, decorating the house stem to stern with holiday trappings and two big trees: a tall stately fir in the formal living room and a rotund Scotch pine for the tweedy downstairs sitting room. It took Cassie and me five straight hours to open all our presents, a mountain under the tree. All our lives it had been Mama's abiding desire for us to have a good time, and she'd always seen to it that we did.

I didn't totally believe in Santa Claus—that he went to every kid's house in the world—but I did believe that he came to ours. On Christmas Eve Cassie and I left all sorts of things for him on the mantelpiece: a jar of cold cream for his windburned cheeks, cookies from the French bakery in New York with a glass of milk and a fat red apple that Maria shined until it looked too good to be real. Below it we hung our stockings—and ones for the dogs and ponies—and then sealed our list of requests. Cass and I decided what gifts to ask for during the weeks before Christmas, adding things, crossing others off, asking our parents' advice. We took the task seriously. It never occurred to my sister and me to ask for something outrageous, because we knew that Santa was really going to read that list and we would get whatever was on it.

Cassandra and I had a torturous wait before we were finally allowed into the living room on Christmas morning. Papa had to have his coffee and set up his movie camera and lights; Maria had to braid our hair and dress us in the dressing-gown sets that Mama had designated for Christmas morning. Reggie would open the double French doors that led from the dining room to the living room—which were impossible to peek through because of the closely pleated beige silk stretched taut from top to bottom—and Papa's bright lights shone in our eyes. His camera caught our amazement at the presents that were three feet deep under the tree and spilled almost all the way to the door. There was a child-size grocery store, with two shopping carts and shelves filled with miniature boxes and cans of household supplies and food. There was a Good Humor truck run by pedals that opened on the side and was filled with plastic replicas of toasted-almond and chocolate-fudge-cake bars. There was a complete doll-bathing set: a collapsible bassinet that held water, with shelves underneath stocked with diapers and powder and bottles. We had to open our stockings first, which were topped off with the customary Italian gift, black coal, a traditional joke about what naughty children would receive. Except that it was candy coal, spun-sugar-flavored licorice. Even the coal in our Christmas was sweet.

During endless hours of unwrapping, Maria saved the ribbons and unwrinkled paper, while Reggie kept us fortified with glass dishes of the thinnest crunchy ribbon candy and homemade cookies. Afterwards we'd get dressed and go out and play in the snow, plopping down on the sparkling field of white on the front lawn and making snow angels, flapping our arms and legs like marionettes, until the cold flakes seeped through the back of our knitted caps and tingled our heads. Reggie heated up maple syrup for us, and we'd pour it on a mound of fresh snow, gobbling it up as soon as the steamy syrup hit the feather-light ball. Best of all was playing snow tag with Mama: first we tramped down a wide circle, stomping our feet until it made a path; then we made two paths cutting straight across the center of the circle like spokes of a wheel. Mama would start out being It and stood in the center of the circle. She could come after us down any spoke of the wheel, but no one was allowed to put a foot outside the confines of paths. There was a great deal of shrieking and slipping and shouts of, "She cheated!"

When we were very little we spent one Christmas skiing in Switzerland, snuggled up in an inn at St. Moritz, with a sleigh and fat horses to pull us into town. Cassandra and I whizzed down the mountain just like the Swiss children in our Tyrolean coats with wooden buttons closing the teal-blue wool. But we were the only ones with a father who took each of us up in the chair lift, leaving his poles at the bottom, and skiied down the mountain with one of us between his legs. It was a life where you were carried up mountains and flew down on angel wings, held between your daddy's legs, his thick mittens strong under your arms.

Cassandra and I didn't want to go to the holiday festivities and leave Mama at home in bed, but we followed her wishes, giving her at least an impression that life was continuing. The cancer continued to chew her up despite the operations and drugs, reducing what had been a robust woman to a skeleton. She was so repulsed by her own body that she wouldn't let us help her in the bathroom, but I got a glimpse of her getting into the tub after I'd drawn a bath for her. Her chest was all bone and ribs slashed with wide, bold scars, the emaciated body without any curves, carved away to its bedrock. It was like the shock of seeing a premature baby: the raw ugliness, the frailty, the vulnerability. All Cassie and I could do was please Mama, so we dressed up in our winter velvets and black patent shoes and went to the parties without her, trying hard to be jolly but betraying ourselves in the way we clung to each other's arms.

On Christmas Eve Mama rallied for us and invited a few people over. She came slowly, painfully, downstairs, but the minute she made eye contact, she smiled, covering. There were decorations all over the apartment, and Mama made conversation about the heavy snow outside, how nice it must be up in the country and that we'd go up soon, just as soon as she felt a little stronger. There was a stuffed crown roast of pork for dinner. Cassandra got everyone laughing with the story of our Christmas in Jamaica when the cook at our house in Round Hill asked if we'd like a suckling pig for Christmas dinner. That afternoon a young black boy walked up the driveway with a small pink pig on a length of rope, trotting merrily along beside him. "Wilbur!" Cassie and I exclaimed simultaneously. None of us could face the poor little fellow when he came to the table with an apple stuck in his mouth; Christmas dinner that year had been mostly fried plaintain chips and okra.

Mama took a piece of roast pork, but it was hard not to notice that she pushed it around her plate discreetly. She hadn't been able to eat solid food for some time; she drank ginger ale and juices from a machine that pulverized fruits and vegetables into a liquid. We all tried unbearably hard to be festive.

It must have been a cold, burning hole for her, knowing that life was being taken away. She loved it so dearly, endowed it so fully. Cassandra and I carried on As If—which meant Mama could have illusions, too—As If she weren't dying, As If she hadn't failed with Papa.

The last really great trip we'd had as a family was to a swanky dude ranch in Arizona. It was wonderfully all-American, families all done up in their spanking-fresh cowboy hats and boots, the men in string ties with silver closures, although striped silk ties were all they'd ever had around their necks before. We got to watch cattle roping and branding by sun-bleached cowboys in chaps worn smooth from years in the saddle. One day we all went out on a hike high into the mountains, our family and two others, led by a wrangler who squirted long jets of brown tobacco juice onto the parched ground. When we reached the highest point overlooking a crater lake, we spread out our picnic lunches. The sky got dark and the high mountain air turned chill; suddenly it began to snow. Everyone started to panic, to throw things together to beat a hasty retreat.

"Everybody hold on!" Mama called out in her charmingly authoritative voice. "We had these sudden storms in Canada, and they pass quickly. The children should just cover their heads so they don't catch cold."

The wrangler looked worried; it was nice to have someone take over, but who was this dame? The other people were fussing around, trying to figure out a way to cover their children's heads. It had been so hot when we'd left the ranch that everyone was wearing shorts with tank tops or short-sleeved shirts.

"Take off your underpants, kids," Mama commanded with a smile, "and we'll all bunch together over by that rock and tell stories until the cloud passes over." The group moved hesitantly to the designated boulder, wanting to trust my mother but unsure whether they should. "Come on, girls," Mama urged Cassie and me. We ducked behind the rock and got our underpants off, proud to have a mother who knew so much but mortified by her instructions.

In a few minutes we were all huddled together, the wet snow falling all around us, the children sitting cross-legged in a circle with Carter Spanky Pants draped on top of their heads, giggling at the sight of each other. My father began a story, and, like the bedtime stories he made up for Cassie and me, it was a fanciful saga that included our snowbound predicament. As Mama had predicted, the snow stopped before long. We were all having such a good time, entranced by Papa's story, that it was with great reluctance we put our underpants back on and headed down to the ranch.

One of Mother's flakier friends learned of a fly-by-night cancer cure developed from animal serum by a doctor in upper New York State. Her friend bundled Mama into a car and drove her up the Hudson. Mother returned with a handful of vials filled with frightfully expensive yellow liquid and some disposable hypodermics. They had given Mama a quick lesson on how to use the needle; she practiced at home on an orange before injecting herself. "My horse-piss shots," was what she called them with a bitter laugh. She was a bit embarrassed to have stooped to such quackery, but at that point she was game to try anything.

It was no more futile than the renowned cancer specialist she'd been waiting four months to see. When the day of her appointment arrived, she was so weak and doubled over in pain that it took Cassandra and me an hour just to dress her. Getting her in and out of a cab took so long there was a honking line of cars impatiently blasting us for holding them up. If I'd had a hand grenade, I would not have hesitated to pull the pin and throw the bomb right in the middle of them, blowing them to smithereens. With one of us on either side of her, Mama made her way slowly into the doctor's office, which was on the ground floor of a high-rise apartment building. People are living here, I thought, as Mother forced her body to walk, there are people doing their laundry in the basement and burning English muffins above us. Mother was a woman who had never complained a day in her life, but her pain was so excruciating that she had to lie down on the couch in the waiting room. Cassie and I hovered over her, two nervous hummingbirds above a feeder. The doctor kept her waiting an hour, spent five minutes with her and sent her home without any hope.

She got the Hong Kong flu, and it sapped what little strength she had left. Not one doctor in the city of New York—even with the intervention of influential friends—would make a house call. Cassandra and I could not understand why no one would help, how they could let this woman suffer, turning their backs as if she were a leper. "Now we know what life is like for poor people," Mama said, turning it into a lesson in ethics.

In the middle of this, her cancer surgeon called to say they wanted to put her back in the hospital and remove her pituitary gland. They had cut out everything else they could think of by then. As she talked into the phone, Isabel began to cry; I could see her conviction drain out with the tears, her will to live running down her sunken cheeks. She had vowed never again to submit to the indignity of the hospital. She had little strength and nothing really to fight for anymore.

That afternoon Mama went to sleep, and we couldn't waken her for her medicine. Her lips had gotten all dry and cracked. Cassandra brought a slice of orange upstairs and held it against Mama's mouth, but she wouldn't wake up, wouldn't suck on it. We debated and decided to call Papa at his apartment where he'd lived for several years, although the divorce had been final only a few months. It had been one more blow to Mama, the divorce becoming final right in the middle of her dying, two big black birds with one stone, right between her eyes. We had tried to cope by ourselves but this time it felt different, too serious for two girls to handle alone. Our father called the doctor, who ordered an ambulance.

Cassie and I each held one of Mama's limp hands; they felt as extraordinarily soft and cool as the Pope's hand had felt that time we'd kissed it, as though mercury—something more exalted than blood—flowed in the veins. I felt as though we were on stage, a spotlight pointed at us. It was hard to feel real; it just didn't sink in that this was our life, that this was happening. We sat there for an hour before calling the ambulance company. They said the car was on its way.

"Good thing it's just a slow death from cancer and not a heart attack," I whispered to Cassandra angrily.

"That sounds like one of Mama's wisecracks," she whispered back.

We didn't say another thing, keeping our vigil nearly another hour until the doorbell rang.

The ambulance attendants came upstairs, and Quickly, who was normally placid, growled so ferociously at them that we had to lock her in the bathroom. The two men jerked my semi-comatose mother out of bed, her neck and legs wobbly at the joints like a rag doll's. Her nightgown slid up as they moved her. I reached hastily across them and pulled the lace edge down, protecting her privacy. They put her onto a chair, tilted it back and carried her to the first floor of the apartment. They lifted her onto the stretcher they'd left by the front door, but it wouldn't fit in the small, European-style elevator. They raised her above their heads and started down the stairs to the street. Cassandra and I followed, watching fearfully as Mother's body slid precariously on the narrow stretcher. The man who owned the town house and lived in the bottom duplex came to his door in a plaid bathrobe, awakened by the bumping and banging in the middle of the night. I shook my head as if to say, "It's OK, it's only us, everything's under control," but I could see that he took my headshake to mean, "It's all over." I wondered whether his first thought was about the apartment, whether he'd have to find new tenants. I wondered where we would live now.

It was bitter cold out on the sidewalk. The little wheels on the stretcher clacked on the cement like chattering teeth. Cass and I got into the back of the ambulance, and I held Mother's hand tightly, bent over her protectively. She squeezed back hard, with more strength than I thought she had, as if my hand were a lifeline. She had half-awakened and was frightened by how fast the car was going. Perhaps she thought we were rushing her to her death. She winced when the long ambulance swung around corners. "Slow, slow . . ." she moaned.

Each time I called out, "Slow down!" to the driver, but he spoke Spanish and either didn't understand or didn't want to. He hadn't hurried coming to pick us up, but maybe he was speeding now because it was what he'd seen ambulances do in movies.

"Why aren't you using the siren?" Cassie asked.

He said private ambulances weren't allowed to. It made me feel they didn't think my mother rated a siren.

Looking down, it was hard to comprehend that this had once been our tower of a mother. She had always been there: omnipotent, all-caring, even magical. Like the time we were in Greece visiting the outdoor theater at Delphi. We had already been to the spot where the Delphic oracle used to sit, and now the guide was reading aloud from Euripides in Greek to demonstrate the acoustics of the amphitheater. Mother was riveted on the guide; she loved anything that brought her closer to a foreign land, an ancient civilization. But it was broiling hot, and Cassie and I were bored, so we took refuge beneath Mama's full skirt. There was a tourist photographer who delivered a photograph that evening to our room at the Grand Bretagne in Athens. It showed a tall, blond woman looking regally off into the distance, her attention transfixed, apparently oblivious that underneath the hem of one of Mr. Gwinn's most flattering dresses were four skinny, freckled legs poking out into the sun.

Suddenly our guide had stopped reading aloud. Cass and I peered out when we heard her gasp. Tiny pellets of hail were falling from the sky, right there in the middle of a dusty, Greek August. The guide was fluttering with excitement, and several tourists nearby crossed themselves furtively.

"I wonder whether we've pleased the gods or annoyed them," Mama mused.

The hailstorm lasted only a minute, and calm descended again. Cass and I went back under her skirt; we were with our mother, so nothing seemed too extraordinary.

We pulled into the emergency entrance to the hospital and got another faceful of biting, cold air as the back doors of the ambulance swung open. I kept hold of Mama's hand as they wheeled her down the long, white corridors, bending low over the stretcher so that my hand wouldn't pull her arm up. I did not want her to think I had abandoned her. She had been so adamant about never wanting to return to the hospital. I was too young and too scared to protest the doctor's orders and protect her wishes. We had yanked her from the warmth of her own bed and denied her the quiet sleep she had tried to slip into forever. The least I could do was hold her hand.

I looked over at my sister scurrying along on the other side of the stretcher as the attendants pulled it. Her sweet little face was clenched as tight as a drawstring purse; we smiled at each other over our mother's body, connecting in the darkness. I looked down at Mama's anguished face, her eyelids squeezed shut. It was the same look our old dog Pango had worn when we'd had him put to sleep in Rome. He'd been eaten alive by a tapeworm undiagnosed by the Italian vet; the cancer devouring my mother had been treated by the best of American know-how.

The dog had been old and sick. He seemed resigned to the death he sensed was imminent, but there was also a look of accusation in his eyes that had burned into me. I saw that same wounded, angry, vacant stare in my mother's eyes when they fluttered open, the deep pain of feeling betrayed. I wondered if she were thinking of Pango, too, remembering how they'd given him the injection to put him peacefully to sleep; it hadn't worked, and he had jumped off the table with a yelp.

They wheeled my mother into a room and pulled a curtain between her and the sleeping figure in the other bed.

"Gently, gently," I urged the two brusque orderlies as they lifted Mama onto the hospital bed and raised the metal side rails.

She curled up into a childlike ball. A nurse gave her an injection. Mother's face was twisted in such pain I thought the shot had killed her. But they wheeled her into a private room and waited hours to declare her officially dead. After seeing her death mask, there was no suspense in the waiting.

Our father met us at the hospital; the three of us sat silently in the plastic waiting room, waiting. There wasn't a whole lot to say. We hadn't been close to him for some time, a year or two since there had been trust and spontaneity. It hadn't been possible to live with the paradox of maintaining a closeness to him while we watched Mama die her slow death, helping her through it while he led his separate life at a safe distance from it all, leaving us to cope, to do his job. We resented him for making her so unhappy, but also for sticking us with the burden of the woman who had been his wife.

Papa said that Cassie and I had to try and sleep, so we lay down on the acqua vinyl sofas, eyes open. Our sleeplessness was interrupted by a solemn-faced young doctor who came out to ask what religion she was.

"None," my father said, but I added, "Atheist." I didn't want him thinking we were wishy-washy fence-sitting agnostics.

I didn't understand why we weren't with Mama, why I couldn't have her head cradled in my lap like the Virgin holding Christ in the pietà, why Cassie couldn't hold her hand like Mary Magdalene and put a cool cloth on her brow. Where was the sense in isolating us from her at the end, in denying her the comfort of our flesh pressed against hers so that the last thing she felt would be her babies, the skin she had powdered and tickled, or our kisses softly on her cheek, the scent of our breath reminding her of the life she had started and cherished as jubilantly as her own? I lay there unable to move, unable to make my plea, but I knew it was wrong ever to have let go of her hand, to have allowed them to break the bond that could have allowed her to slide away still holding me, me holding her, and I knew I would regret it as long as I lived.

The next time the doctor came out, he was wearing his death face and said she had passed away—that was how he put it. He asked if we wanted to go in and see the body. My father said no for all of us. The doctor left us: Cassandra crying out loud, my father at a loss what to do, while I fought back tears. I had to struggle for breath as though an East Hampton wave had broken on top of me, churning me in the sand so I didn't know which way was up for air.

"It's okay to cry, Blakie," my father said gently.

"I *am* crying," I snapped back at him. He had no way of knowing that the few tears that had escaped were the only ones I could risk. I was the replica of someone who no longer existed: I had to keep control, stay whole.

My sister and I went into the neon-lit bathroom. I permitted myself a slow stream of tears. Through her heaving sobs Cass said, "At least she *loved* you." I looked at her sweet face twisted in pain equal to what I had seen on my mother's, and I let myself really cry. I cried for the blind way my mother had held me up to Cassie as an example of the perfection she'd never attain, for the rivalry Mother had created between us. I fit Isabel's mold, but Cassandra had suffered a constant rebuke for not conforming. I cried because my mother had died when she had made me believe she would not, for all the things I hadn't said and now never could, but most of all I cried because that hardheaded woman had left behind a girl who felt unloved.

It had been more of Cassandra's lousy luck that she had lived alone with Isabel in the last year, the hardest one, in the town house off Fifth Avenue. I was away at college, and Cass was trapped with a woman dying in front of her eyes. She wanted to do things for Mother; Cassie did her damndest to break through a lifetime of being deemed incompetent, but Isabel wouldn't let her off the hook. Even when she was bedridden, Mother continued to dismiss my sister's clumsy attempts at helping with the familiar, impatient threat, "Never mind . . . Blake will be home on the weekend."

From the moment our mother died, there was the possibility for the first time that Cassie and I could be friends. Our tears for our mother, for ourselves, extinguished the fires of sibling rivalry that she had fanned between us for so long. We had shared a very special growing up, a charmed childhood that no one else on earth could truly understand. We had a shorthand of words and looks we'd never learn with anyone else unless we were married for twenty years. And we were two parts of Isabel: only by staying close, reflecting off each other, could we make even a dim outline of the woman in whose shadow we had lived.

It was three or four in the morning when we left the hospital with Mama's dead body in it. Father took Cassandra and me back to our apartment in a cab. He stood awkwardly at the front door while I fumbled with the key.

"I'll stay with you girls, if you'd like," he offered. His discomfort was almost visible, like steam on a bathroom mirror.

"The couch isn't too bad," Cassie said.

None of us quite knew how to behave, now that Papa had become our sole parent overnight, our protector again.

We went upstairs, past the conglomeration of Christmas decorations: the brass angels that revolved around a candle, the little painted-wood tree that held miniature candy canes, the live branches of holly woven through the banister. We heard a whimpering sound and realized that in the confusion of departure we'd forgotten poor Quickly in the bathroom, where we'd locked her for growling at death's messengers. As we went past Mama's bedroom I shut the door, unable even to look in there. The empty place where the sheets had been pulled back was a gaping wound. Cassie and I sat down on the floor of the bathroom, the scent of Mama's Guerlain perfume clinging in the air, and we stroked the dog. Our fingers brushed as we ran our hands along Quickly's soft fur from opposite sides. Christmas was over, sad at the best of times.

We lay down in Cassie's room to sleep, the dog on the floor between our beds. There was a stillness, like after a heavy rainstorm.

"Sing to me, Cass," I said, and she began to croon a little song.

When we were kids she'd sing me to sleep sometimes, such a peaceful way to drift into dreams. I had missed it when I'd moved into my own room. Cassandra had felt betrayed, rejected, that I wanted privacy as I got older. The night our mother died was the first time I'd shared Cassandra's bedroom in years, and it tied us to our past.

I slept for a few hours, awoke unsure of where I was and saw that Cassandra's bed was empty. Downstairs, I found her doing the tedious chore of putting decorations away in their boxes. The tree was a shabby skeleton with only a few wisps of tinsel clinging to it. Cass had removed the tinsel without tangling it, laying it flat in the box as Mama had taught us so it could be reused in years to come.

Seven

Blake blacked out when a new gynecologist said there was a growth on her ovary. He slapped her face, made her lie back down on the examining table and drink a paper cupful of water that a nurse rushed off to fetch. During her checkup the previous year, Blake's doctor had found an ovarian cyst and said she had to be operated on; she'd gone to a second doctor, whose opinion was the same. When she found a third doctor who said there was nothing there, that it was just a tipped uterus, she was delighted, vindicated. She shopped around for medical advice in the same way that her mother had, never questioning why her uterus would suddenly tip at age twenty-six.

When she told the most recent doctor that he wasn't the first to find the growth, she could see the veil come down over his eyes, the shielding curtain she'd seen on the doctors around Isabel.

"It's best not to leave growths in the body too long," he said, "because the nature of the cells can change."

Cancer, you mean, Blake said to herself. She knew it would catch up with her eventually—her grandmother, her mother, now her. She figured it was part of the balancing system in life: you get a mother that special, a childhood that sweet, you're due for some bad to even things out.

"You mean it becomes cancerous," she said to the doctor, making it a statement. She was not going to have any pussyfooting around *her*.

When she was a teenager, Blake used to talk about how much she looked forward to being a spry, wry old woman, mischief in every wrinkle. "What's your hurry?" people would say, or, "Who wants to get old, for Crissake?" But Blake protested jubilantly, "I can't wait to be a cool old broad; I'm looking forward to it." Blake had never questioned her desire, but as she lay naked on the slick, crinkly paper at the gynecologist's, it suddenly came to her. She had dreamed about becoming an old lady because her mother never was. She wanted to become the *grande dame* that Isabel had not had a chance to be.

It was impossible to know anything was wrong with Blake until the doctor reached way up inside her, poking with his rubber gloves. It would hurt, he'd apologize; then he'd call his colleague who would stick *his* rubber-gloved hand up there. Then they'd huddle together, taking refuge behind their doctors' expressions of willful calm. It had grown larger, they agreed. It had to come out. Blake couldn't help but wonder how something the size of a grapefruit had taken up residence inside her when she didn't feel a thing. It was easy to imagine that it existed only when she was in the doctor's office. The only reason she believed it was there was because she'd expected it someday.

Blake decided she couldn't talk to Michael about her fears, about the worst that could happen. He was so afraid of losing her as it was, continuing to say that their problems weren't serious, they just needed time to iron things out. He was shattered by the possibility that he might now lose her before that happened.

"It's okay, Pookie," he said as he held her the day she came back from the doctor. "Everything's going to be all right."

He needs convincing comfort more than I do, she thought. Suddenly that idle phrase " 'til death do us part" meant something. Blake realized that despite how wrong things were between them, she had harbored visions of them growing old together, becoming Garson Kanin and Ruth Gordon across the breakfast table at the Algonquin.

She and Michael talked about other things in the weeks before the operation; they said little and kept busy. They suffered alone, together. A barely perceptible distance slithered between them, a poisonous snake neither of them dared arouse.

There was only one person who could have held her tight enough, to whom she could have admitted how frightened she was, who could have made it all better. "Mama, Mama," she whispered when she was alone, soothing herself with the rhythm of that powerful word, the first sounds she had ever made. Blake crooned the word, rocking herself back and forth, a benediction over her own head. To the outside world she stayed calm and cheerful, knowing it would have pleased her mother, angry that no one saw through it.

Once the date was set for the operation, Blake walked around numb, plodding through the routines of daily life in a fog, each trivial activity magnified by the enormous effort it took. Unloading the dishwasher took forever; Blake held each dish a long time, thinking about the past it represented, saying good-bye. It wasn't the pain she feared; she'd had migraines for years and was masterful at living with pain, concealing it. She was afraid of how well she'd handle herself when they told her she had cancer, when she woke up and they told her they'd done a hysterectomy, when they came back with lab tests that said she didn't have much longer. . . . It was imperative that she keep her cool, be "Grace Kelly under pressure," as her mother used to call it. Blake could not let anyone know about her fears, not when Isabel had been so nonchalantly brave. Isabel had shown Blake how to die, how to avoid sniveling self-pity, how to protect the fears of people around you. If there is a true test of mettle, of class, Blake thought, it is in living your dying with such stylish aplomb.

It wasn't easy for her to talk to Cassandra about the lump in her body. She didn't want to stir up memories or create fears for her sister. They shared a suspicion that they carried their mother's disease dormant inside them, a sleeping dragon. Blake wondered if Cassie had come to the same conclusion—that the odds were that Cassandra would be spared now that her older sister had gotten it. It seemed ironic justice: Blake's early years had been pure pleasure, while Isabel had bludgeoned Cassandra, using Blake as the weapon of comparison.

Blake talked to Cassie on the phone every day. They didn't speak of the past, although it hung in the air. They exchanged the only comfort there was: they were friends; they had grown to love and trust each other; they were the only thing that helped when they felt lonely for Isabel.

"Shit, what would Mama have said?"

"Shit."

"She didn't swear, did she?"

"No, I guess not."

"She would've turned it into an event—I would've racked up thousands of presents."

"Then I would've had to 'catch up,' though."

The girls laughed at Cassandra's self-mocking; all those childhood years of jealousy, bartering, making sure both girls got their fair share, Cassie always feeling she came up short, had to "catch up."

"It's just as well; we had her for the right amount of time."

"Yeah, the first quarter—spend the next three recovering," Blake said.

"Remember when that woman at the Otis' dinner party asked which of us benefited more from her death?"

"Yeah, and we tripped over each other to say, 'Me'!"

"Weird." Blake recalled the way they had turned and stared at each other in surprise, startled to hear the other claim to be the beneficiary, like a puppy catching sight of itself in a mirror. "Oh, well, guess I'd better go wash the windows or write an article or fix a tequila gimlet."

"I love you, Blake."

"Hey, thanks, Cassie." Blake was surprised at her sister's forwardness. Blake was usually the one who said things like that.

"It's hard to say to you, Blakie. Taken me twenty-five years to figure out how to love you." Cassie still felt oppressed by the way Blake overwhelmed a person, doing and giving and saying so much that there was never a chance to reciprocate, to catch up. Just trying was intimidating, as it had been with Isabel.

"You're doing a tip-top job, kiddo."

"I'm working on it—just give me some time."

My time's run out, Blake thought, but she controlled herself. Cassie could have handled hearing it, would have expected Blake to fall into Isabel's style of morbid death jokes, her routine of "hit me over the head if it gets too bad, ha-ha-ha." It was a good feeling to have a sister who knew it all, to whom you didn't have to explain.

Blake's father didn't call her during the wait before the operation. He learned particulars from Cassie, expressed concern through her, but did not go directly to his first-born child. Blake hated him for his weakness, understanding at the same time that he simply could not deal with it; he had been through it all before. After countless years of yielding to Isabel's pleas—yo-yoing back to that impossible marriage only to be driven from it again—Marsh had finally kept on going, hadn't looked back over his shoulder. All the family friends had turned against him when Isabel was going-going-gone and he didn't rally to her side in some final display . . . of who knows what false sentiment, Blake wondered. She thought her mother was out to lunch on the subject of Marsh: insisting that they could make it work, insisting that something wrong was what she wanted, that no other man would do, that she could love only Marshie.

It was because of that neurotic insistence that she had left him everything in her will. It made Blake angry, because Isabel had been such a foolish romantic, sacrificing the last years of her life to an impossible dream when there were several good men courting her, wanting her, even with both breasts gone and time running out, men she could have had something with. And then to leave everything to Marsh in one last grand gesture, proclaiming her love even into the grave, holding him on that hook. But what had she imagined would become of her two girls, protecting them with one ambiguous phrase in her will, suggesting that he "provide for our daughters as I would"?

It was only years later that the girls talked to each other about the way their father had pulled away from them, pushed them out of the nest after Isabel died. She had been dead five years when Blake brought it up one night. They were at a Brazilian restaurant with their father, dishes of black beans and slices of orange crowding the flowered tablecloth.

"How come when Mama died you didn't make a home for us, so we could live together like a family?"

"But you were grown up," Marsh replied, stunned.

"I was a *teenager* and my mother'd just died! All I wanted was to feel loved, that I had a home," Blake exclaimed.

"But you did have: you had better than that; you had your own pad and I was right downstairs."

"Hooked up to that intercom, a gray plastic box with wires climbing up the outside of the building from your window to mine. 'Just buzz if you need anything' was hardly a cozy family chat around a fireplace."

"Good Christ, all this now? I thought how swell it was for you, how jealous your pals at school must have been that you had that freedom, no parents to breathe down your neck."

"*I* was the jealous one: of kids who had a mom, a dad and a dog. English muffins and bacon at a breakfast table together. I wanted someone to come home to. Cookies and milk after school, dinner at eight."

Marsh looked over at Cassie. Did she think this was madness, too?

Cassie put a fingerful of toasted coconut in her mouth.

"I don't know what to say; you were two young ladies with boyfriends, lives of your own. I didn't think you wanted some grizzled old father plunking you down at a dinner table every night. You didn't need me anymore."

"Just because we acted grown-up doesn't mean we felt it."

"We needed you more than ever," Blake said, tears rolling down her cheeks as she thought of herself and

/ 89

Cassie, two little orphans left alone to face a treacherous world.

"Oh, girls, girls . . . I felt you guys left *me*: Blake off in the Ivy Leagues, Cassie going away every weekend with, uh, what's-his-name—whatever that winner's name was!"

The three of them laughed, remembering the insufferable photographer with a pubic-hair beard, whom Cassie had gone out with for a long time after Isabel's death, much longer than she would have otherwise.

"Thanks a lot, Dad. You don't hear me knocking any of those bimbos you dated before you got married."

"Bimbos!" he repeated in feigned indignation. "My daughter the feminist calling a *Vogue* editor and a financial analyst 'bimbos'?"

"I see," Blake teased. "Are we just going to sweep under the carpet that jet-set frog who showed up with a different fur coat every time? 'Oh, *bébé*, ve must be at Le Cirque in von hef hour; la Baronesse vants to meet you, *bébé*.' "

"Look who's throwing stones now!" Marsh exclaimed between gusts of laughter that Cassie and Blake shared with him. "Are we forgetting the short Russian who owned most of a movie studio, with the two-block long limousine and four A.M. discotheques every night? Who just happened to be old enough to be *my* father?"

"Truce!" Blake hiccuped. "Let's just say we've all been around the track."

They wiped their eyes from the tears of laughter and took sips of beer. Marsh considered for a moment, then spoke.

"You know, maybe that's one of the reasons I married so fast—to a woman with two children. I had lost you two." It was the most Marsh had ever revealed to them about himself. They both knew what a risk it was for him to open up, to dare to be vulnerable. It was a display of his love and trust that moved them both.

"Never, Poppy. You'll never lose us."

"No such luck," Blake added warmly, astounded that he had felt as they had but that none of them had said a word until now. When Isabel died they had carried on as the Three Musketeers, admitting nothing of their fears and loneliness and helplessness, tigers who had lost their tamer and crept off, snarling, into dark corners of the jungle.

And now, so many years later, Marsh didn't know how to reach out to Blake. She wasn't any better. She sat and waited for him to call, waited to pick up the phone and hear the slightly charged air of Long Island reaching out to New York. Blake was damned if she was going to break down and dial. *She* was the one facing the knife; she was the child. She still held it against him that he had pulled away from his two most adoring fans, who would have done anything, everything for him. Because he had spurned them, they turned away, had developed the very cold-shouldered independence that Marsh had feared. Unrequited love creates barnacles of bitterness, and they clung to Blake.

"Oh, Papa, I loved you so much," Blake said to him in her head. "This much and more," she remembered telling him as a kid, spreading her arms in a circle around her body until her hands touched in back, encompassing the whole globe, a universe of love. "Oh, Papa, how could you have let me learn to hate you?"

Three days before her operation, Blake developed a craving for chocolate-chip cookies. She went into a supermarket but couldn't make a decision; there were a dozen choices. She stood staring at the wall of cookies for a long time, paralyzed by indecision; people pushed past her, carts clanging. When Blake realized they were staring at her, she hurried out of the store, leaving the frozen orange juice to melt in her cart. She walked home and went into two neighborhood grocery stores looking for cookies, thinking it would be easier with a small selection. But they had the same packages, and she stood staring at them with the same idiotic paralysis. Tears threatened. She went home empty-handed. While she and Michael were dressing for dinner, she told him how she'd tried to buy chocolate-chip cookies and couldn't make up her mind.

"But you don't even like cookies," he said quizzically as he pulled on a pair of slacks.

"I know; but suddenly I wanted some real badly, but I didn't know what brand to get. They all looked kind of crummy."

"Why didn't you just go into Greenberg's and get some good ones?"

"God, they cost a fortune."

Michael gave her a you're-nuts-but-I-love-you-anyway look—he kept watching her face, giving her a chance to say something more.

"I mean, I probably wasn't going to eat them anyway; it was just this compulsion." Blake shrugged, fought back the tears that pressed into her eyes; she leaned over to do up the ankle straps on her shoes. "So that would've *really* been a waste."

"Whereas trekking into three different stores was not a waste?"

When Blake didn't look up at him, Michael went over and bent down beside her; he put his hand on the back of her neck, on top of her hair, silky and warm against her skin. "You OK, Pookie?"

She nodded, painted a smile on her face as she turned it towards him. "But can we stop later and get some?"

Michael nodded, straightened up and reached for his shirt. "Sure, honey." He buttoned the shirt, then undid his pants to tuck it in.

Blake thought it was the dumbest thing men did, to do up their pants and then undo them when they put their shirts on. Why not just put the shirt on first? Were they so afraid of being bare-assed? She laughed aloud, an unexpected burst of laughter that made Michael stop in the middle of buttoning his shirt cuffs.

"What?"

"Nothing. I'm just silly," she said.

Later that night Michael told the cab driver to pull up outside a corner deli near their apartment.

"Want me to come in?"

"Nope, I'm fine," Blake said lightly as she got out on the curb side. "Only be a minute."

But as soon as she got in front of the cookie display she felt the same horrible inability to do anything. Why the hell do I want chocolate-chip cookies? she thought. A picture formed in her mind: she was a little girl with red pigtails in a Norman Rockwell painting, leaning on the kitchen table and watching her mother pull a batch of cookies out of the stove. Isabel had never baked things, but that was beside the point. Blake hurried out of the store and burst into tears as she slammed the cab door shut behind her. She leaned her face against Michael's shoulder as the cab pulled forward.

"Couldn't find what you wanted?"

Blake shook her head, meaning yes, that's right. Michael didn't say anything else, just held her, a friend. Both of them understood only vaguely, but it didn't matter. Blake was glad to be married.

Once she was actually in the hospital, her fears dissolved, lifted away when they took off her watch and replaced it with a plastic manacle clipped onto her wrist. She made a big issue about her wedding ring; they put adhesive tape around it rather than taking it off. It created a sentiment about marriage that she hadn't felt since her wedding day.

She experienced a strange exhilaration, standing outside herself and watching the drama unfold. She had always known she would wind up in the hospital and found a certain smug pleasure in having been right. It was out of her hands now; the hospital personnel were in charge of her destiny, and it made her feel lighthearted. She made friends with the nurses, explored the closets, gave a blood sample and admired the flowers that had already begun arriving in cartloads. Like a precocious child, she asked the reason for each procedure, then submitted to it cheerfully.

"Wish they were all like you, honey," one nurse said.

It gave Blake great satisfaction to be a model patient.

When the anesthetist came in the night before, Blake chatted with her gaily. Michael sat in the corner, watching in horror as Blake pulled up her shirt in back and asked the doctor where the anesthesia would be administered. The anesthetist put her fingers low on Blake's spine, and it gave Michael a chill. Blake knew the doctor's fingers must be warm, but they felt like cold steel. She was eager for it, eager for them to get in there with their knives and tell her the truth at last. She looked over at Michael and made a gruesome joke, trying to lighten his agonized expression. She felt sorry that he couldn't share her excitement, her eagerness for the operation to begin.

That night Blake had a dream as sweet as honey, so plain and simple that it had to be real. . . . She is out riding with her daughter: Blake's tall, dapple-gray horse beside the little girl's fat, dependable pony. The big horse's ears are pricked forward, alert to danger. He walks like a regal old duke, setting the example for the cheerful pony, who is ready for mischief. Blake looks down at the top of her child's head, her hair shiny in the sun, her long, dark eyelashes extending in a sweep beyond the plane of her smooth forehead, and Blake is filled with admiration that such a small person can give what-for to such a big beast. "No funny business!" the little girl commands, giving a sharp tug on the reins as the pony tosses his head. Then she gathers up the reins and gives a good kick into his solid sides, and Blake knows the next words will be, "Race you, Mommy?" and the little girl is off like a shot. Blake knows they'll have a good laugh later about her ill-gotten gains, when she tucks her into bed with a merry scolding. The fat pony digs in its hooves and gallops off, Blake's horse on his tail, held back like a steam engine stoked for full speed but opened up only a little. Blake lets him pass the pony for a second, to make the race more exciting, then pulls him back into a canter so controlled he is almost running in place. "I won!" the child calls out triumphantly, standing in her stirrups from the effort of stopping her pony with deep-voiced "Whoas" at the edge of the field.

The cool of the forest enfolds them as they enter, walking alongside each other again, their horses still eager for the chase, the soft, hot sound of their nostrils blowing out in flutters, mingling with the bird-calls in the trees above. The back of the child's neck is damp from exertion, and a cluster of hairs has curled against her pale skin; her eyes shine with victory. She takes her feet out of the stirrups and swings her legs as though she were dangling them in a pond. Blake loves her so much at that instant it is too strong for words. "You've done it again, pussycat," is all she can say, and then they're back at the barn, feeding carrots and apples and talking about a family of field rabbits they passed on the way back. Blake's love blows around the child like a gauzy curtain in a breeze; the way the little girl looks over her shoulder and smiles when Blake says, "Ready to go, pumpkin?" tells Blake that yes, the child does know how happy she makes her, that she wants to eat her up with a spoon, that she's that scrumptious. . . .

Blake woke up feeling peaceful and happy. Michael arrived at six o'clock with the hair dryer she had called and asked him to bring. "Maybe you shouldn't be running around washing your hair?" he had cautioned on the phone. She was delighted by his concern; his show of affection over the past few days made her feel as loved as she had before they were married.

"Don't be silly, honey, I wash my hair every day," Blake said. She stopped herself from making an Isabel wisecrack about wanting clean hair for her funeral. He'd know soon enough.

Blake was sure she was going to die, but she didn't fight the feeling. She didn't act at all like a person condemned, however. She was so full of pep they had to give her a second knockout shot, and even then she wanted to climb onto the gurney by herself. She chatted with the puzzled orderly and nurse, who had never seen a tranquilizer act this way. They had to hold her down. Blake crooked one arm casually behind her head as though she were at the beach when they wheeled her down the corridor. Michael walked alongside; he tried to smile at her, but the anxious circles under his eyes betrayed him. He had to stay outside when they reached the automatic doors to the operating area. He kissed her cheek. Blake sat up and waved and blew him a kiss just as the doors swung shut. She was so pleased by the impression she left him with. She felt peaceful and carefree; the only thing she resisted was the drug racing through her, trying to put her under. Blake wanted to stay awake, stay alive, until her very last moment. She had made a will leaving everything to Cassandra and left it in her desk in an envelope marked: For Lily. She hoped Michael would understand: even if he *weren't* rich, even if things *had* been wonderful between them, Cassandra still would have gotten whatever there was. She was all that was left of Blake now, what was left of Isabel.

The friendly anesthetist leaned over the raised bars of Blake's gurney and took her hand.

"It's going to be fine," she said.

"I know," Blake smiled back. "Only I'm so thirsty I could die." She smiled when she said that, thinking what a grim little joke she'd just made, but the doctor missed it. Cassandra wouldn't have, Blake thought. She felt like a little girl, like Alice about to go down the rabbit hole, except she would not be coming back up. Peaceful.

They wheeled her into an operating room. Cold as a morgue, she thought to herself, shivering. A masked nurse put a blanket over her, and Blake asked what her job would be during the operation, how she liked this new wing of the hospital. They'd given her a third shot by now and she felt drowsy, other-worldly, but she refused to go under, a stubborn kitten who fights its head back above water when someone tries to drown it. Blake talked to the nurses and wondered what they must think of her, this girl who was about to die, gabbing away as if they were in a coffee shop.

Nobody told her she had cancer and was going to die, but Blake knew they wouldn't level with her. Nobody had ever told her and Cassandra, straight out, that their mother was going to die. One weekend Isabel's surgeon was visiting mutual friends near the Marshams' country house and said he would meet with Blake and Cassie. They had waited two days for his call, dreading it, yet glad that someone was going to tell them what was going on. Finally, Sunday night the doctor called and said he wasn't going to be able to see them: it confirmed Blake's belief that her mother wasn't going to die; that, regardless of what Isabel looked like, she would not die. When— a short time later—her mother did die, Blake realized that the doctor hadn't had any more courage to face it than she had had.

When Blake's doctor came into the operating room, she tried to sit up and nearly upset the whole spinal anesthesia. "Hi, Marty!" she said, all smiles; they had to hold her and make her lie back down.

"Well, you're full of beans," he said, nonplussed that she wasn't out cold by then.

Afterwards, Blake didn't remember the part about sitting up, but she figured she had wanted to ask him—to get the truth from somebody. The last thing she remembered was the burning sting of the needle going into the back of her hand. She wondered whether the final injection they'd given Isabel—on *her* white hospital gurney with the metal side bars raised—whether it had burned, too. Whether life has a last bright sting like a comet.

Blake's first stirrings of consciousness were tinged with disappointment—the anticlimax of waking from a suicide attempt. She was amazed to be alive. Michael was beaming down at her, his hand clammy—or was it *her* skin that was cold and damp?

"You're fine, it's all OK."

Blake could tell he meant it, that his smile wasn't just an encouragement for her but was of genuine relief for himself.

"Was it . . ." she began weakly.

Michael cut her off. "Benign."

Magic word. A terrible weight lifted off her, her shoulders lighter than they'd felt in ages, as though a hunch had been taken off her back. She wondered if that was what they'd removed in the operation. She felt like the nursery rhyme: with a flapping of wings the blackbirds flew out of the pie.

It was painful and boring in the hospital and she was hungry, but it didn't matter. Michael was there twice a day. If she called him at the paper, he took the call right away and didn't cut her short. Blake regained her faith:

he loved her, he cared, everything was going to be all right after all. When Michael visited, he bounded into the room, bringing with him the vitality of the outside world where people were well, where life went on. But Blake was glad to be in the hospital, so very glad to be lying there pale and pained, tubes and needles and stitches. Michael came in and made sure everything was fine, got instant action from the staff if she needed anything. She was passive and vulnerable, and Michael could take care of her; this was the way things were supposed to be.

"That man certainly does love you, sugar," Blake's day nurse said to her.

Blake felt like weeping for joy, to get such encouraging news from this nice lady with wise eyes.

Cassandra came to visit when Blake got home from the hospital. One afternoon the sisters were cooking together, talking as they puttered in the kitchen as a team—chopping, steaming, stirring, asking each other's counsel about seasonings—all the while discussing Blake's miserable marriage. For a short while Blake had been able to fool herself, but Cassandra's visit put into bas-relief the handwriting that was already on the wall. Cassie was a reminder of what life had been like, what they had been raised to be, to expect from life.

"I'm so unhappy, Cass, and I don't even know how to be it. Mama never taught me how to be unhappy gracefully."

Blake wiped the onion from her hands and took hold of the charm Cassie wore around her neck with several others. It was a dog charm, a likeness of Pango that Blake suddenly remembered she had once had, too. "Hey, where's mine?" Blake said, echoing that litany from their childhood.

Cassandra pulled back, remembering what used to happen next when her older sister wanted something. "Oh, no, you don't! You can*not* have mine!"

Blake smiled at her and marveled at the perfect golden likeness of a Bedlington terrier that their father had gotten them from the jewelry shop on Fifth Avenue next to F. A. O. Schwarz. It specialized in dog charms, and when Blake lost hers—Falstaff put his paw through the chain when they were swimming together in a lake—her father had taken her back to get a replacement. She remembered thinking how nice it was that there was a store with every breed of dog, where everybody could get a charm of their favorite kind. As Blake held Cassandra's charm, the onion oil scenting her fingers, she realized that Michael's criticism was well taken: she *had* grown up in an ivory tower. Her horse had a barn with French windows. She thought all people had purebred dogs that they'd be grateful to find carved in gold. She put her arms around Cassie and began to cry. She liked it in the ivory tower; she wanted to go there again, not live in the ugly dungeon of her sad marriage. Cassandra held her tightly, and Blake was surprised at how thin and supple her sister's body was, like hugging the life-size, dancing-partner dolls they'd had as children that attached to their feet, dancing with them like a whirling dervish. Blake thought of the time that she and Cassie had danced together on the tennis court under a full moon, stoned and silly, twirling like leprechauns on opposite sides of the net, trying to follow each other from twenty yards away. Hugging Cassie felt like that, as though she were hugging her own self.

Cass stroked her sister's hair and said soothingly, "Ohhhh, Blakie."

Blake ran home movies through her head: two chubby little girls together, playing with the red-nosed clown at their birthday parties; or running naked on sausage-fat little legs towards Papa behind the camera.

"It feels like being punished all the time," Blake said, easing out of the embrace. "I don't think I deserve it, but I wonder . . . there must be a reason."

"Nothing should hurt that much."

Blake had lived a totally unpunishing life until her marriage. As a child she had been spanked only once, two sharp slaps across the bottom from her mother because she'd awakened Maria early one Sunday with a trivial question. Blake had cried long and bitterly—joined by Cassandra in sibling sympathy, then joined by Maria who cried when she learned why her darling little girl had been swatted. Isabel had apologized profusely, explaining that she'd overreacted because she was upset about something else—and they'd gone to the ice-cream parlor and had a whole banana split each. Blake was not used to feeling punished, and the marriage kept smacking her with her own illusions, hitting her with the impossible expectations she refused to give up, battering her until she was punch-drunk. Yet she and Michael held on like shipwrecked rats clinging to a rotting log; anyone could see there was no hope of being saved, yet they would not let go.

"But we love each other, Pookie."

"That's no excuse for how horribly we treat each other," Blake replied.

They were locked together in fear and disillusion; they seemed to need to stay together. Unwilling to admit failure, afraid of aloneness, they kept calling it love.

Eight

C assandra and I didn't want a funeral, but family friends convinced us it was a good thing for everybody. Not a grim religious ceremony, just a few friends talking about Isabel. Our main concern was whether we'd hold up through it, since we couldn't even manage to answer the telephone. It rang constantly for days; people would start crying, and then we'd start up again after finally drying out. Thank God for Mama's dear friend Lily, who took over from that first morning. Maria didn't live with us anymore—we were too old for a nanny, and her grown daughter had moved to New York and shared an apartment with her. But during the rough days she was there to strip Mama's bed and make lunch and pat us on the head as she walked by, snuffing her sobs into a handkerchief. Lily took the phone calls, threw away the medical paraphernalia and helped open telegrams. It was overwhelming, an onslaught of feelings and duties, like opening the door of a jam-packed closet and having it all fall out on you.

Father went with us to make arrangements at the funeral chapel. The office at Frank E. Campbell was just like the inside of their deluxe coffins: gray and pink with satiny swag curtains and velvet chairs. The three of us sat rigidly while the gray-suited official practiced his well-rehearsed expression of gravity mixed with discreet compassion. Cass and I had to keep from looking at each other because we were on the verge of hysterical giggles. Papa could see that we were on the brink—over the years he'd seen us get punchy-silly from exhaustion or boredom or overstimulation—and rather than frowning at us, making it harder, he carried the conversation and distracted the funeral man's attention.

Even though Papa explained that we were going to have an informal funeral, the man said firmly that the chapel policy was that the body had to be in the room during the service. He scowled politely when Cass and I protested, explaining that we weren't at all religious and our mother had never been one for funereal funerals, anyway. But the Spokesman for the Dead had his way. Cass and I were squeamish about the idea of having to stare at the coffin, so Lily had her florist deliver a row of slender spruce trees to shield it from view. Isabel would have been aghast at the extravagance and would probably have devised a way to transport those trees to Long Island afterwards.

The three of us followed the funeral chapel man downstairs, where there was room after room of coffins to choose from, a veritable supermarket. We wandered through rows of satin-lined boxes, struggling to maintain our composure.

The man stopped beside one coffin and rested his hand lovingly on its tufted interior. "If I might suggest, I think she would be most comfortable here," he said piously.

I whispered to Cass, "If she was *alive*, she'd think it was dandy." We both nearly went into a fit of giggles; we bent way over another coffin, as if in deep study of its quality, to keep from laughing out loud.

One had to reach under the satin pillows for the price tag, a system we later decided was to discourage people who were afraid of appearing cheap. Cassandra and I went from room to room, checking all of them and poking each other when we found a particularly garish or expensive one. It had the same ludicrously macabre aura as the Roman catacombs we'd gone to with Mama: hundreds of mummified skeletons, some half-clothed, piled on the ground, perched in wall niches, hanging from hooks, leering at you around every dimly lit corner. It had made death visible, obscene, acceptable. I asked the funeral man if there wasn't something simpler; he gave me a look, as though he'd heard that line before from people trying to cut corners on their loved ones. What did I care what he thought? It was going to be burnt up anyway.

"Death is no different for you, me, a king or a mouse," Mama had said.

When we'd lived in Italy the second time, she had heard about the Florentine Cremation Society. She was so intrigued by the stories that on a weekend trip to Florence we went up to their offices inside a rococo building. We were greeted by two men straight out of a Dickens tale: one was short and jolly and wore a gaudy jacket; his partner was tall, lean and sallow.

"Anywhere in the world, all you have to do is call us," the short one proclaimed. "Just contact us when you're ready, and we take care of all the details," his stern-faced associate added.

When she found out how cheap it was, Isabel couldn't resist joining. She never missed an opportunity to show people the ghoulish membership card with a black border and a drawing of black flames surrounding an urn. She loved to watch them dissolve into laughter when she told the story.

The funeral went by like something you see through murky glass; I was so terrified of breaking down that I turned myself to blind steel. The guests gathered beforehand in a sitting room adjoining the room with the coffin, but they didn't know how to approach Cassie and me. We stood together self-consciously, smoking cigarettes to keep from crying, looking like the awkward teenagers we were. Just the sight of Isabel's two little lambs standing there was enough to make some people break down. Others wouldn't cry until they came over to comfort us and wound up sobbing on our bony shoulders. I chewed the inside of my cheek to keep from crying and patted their backs as if they were agitated babies in need of soothing.

Everyone filed into the other room. Cassie and I sat alone in the first row of chairs, and Papa stood up in front of the rostrum. It had to take guts to face a roomful of friends who had drawn the line: loyalty to Isabel meant hatred of him. They collectively pursed their lips when he said, "This is what Isabel would have wanted—something simple, all of you she loved coming together." He thanked them for what they'd done for Isabel, for all they'd given her, even though he could see bitterness and resentment in their eyes.

Now, *that* is grace under pressure, I thought, real class; at that moment I loved my father as fiercely as in my childhood fantasies of protecting him from an enemy army. Was this the army, these friends who had turned on him? It made me want to jump up and shout, "You don't know what she was like to live with, what it's like to live with a legend, a Paul Bunyan of a woman!" That was my bond with Papa, that Isabel called us both "perfect" and expected us to be The Best . . . because she said we were. We had both been crippled by that fierce love of hers; it was not humanly possible to live up to her fervent expectations . . . impossible . . . yet at the same time she could make you think you were capable of reaching that high. But I stayed frozen to my seat and fought back the tears as one friend after another got up to speak about Isabel, to contribute to the legend, to embroider upon it. To restate what we all knew: that we were lucky to have known her.

Lily had arranged for everyone to go around the corner to the Stanhope Hotel afterwards. Cassie and I walked down the block holding hands the way we had during ice-skating lessons in Central Park as children. At the hotel we milled around the room, holding a drink and chatting with people, going through the motions of real life; only when we caught each other's eye across the room did I feel the yawning despair.

Papa came to the gathering late. I went over to him as he handed his coat to a waiter. His cheeks were rosy from the frosty air outside, and there was a sparkle in his eye. "I went back for a last look—I tried to find you and Cassandra, but you'd already left. I asked them to open the coffin." My face wrinkled up in disgust and I was about to interrupt, but Papa stopped me. "Oh, no, Blakie, it was lovely, really." He paused, then added in a mystified voice, "You can't imagine how beautiful she looked." His voice was full of wonder, and I knew then how much he must have loved her.

Papa decided that Mama's ashes should be sent to Canada so that her father could have a funeral for his only daughter if he wanted or just bury the urn there. We had never been close to Grandpa, a self-centered character who always forgot my mother's birthday but managed to write her shortly before his own and remind her what kind of chocolates he liked. Not a mean man—he had raised Mama with buckets of affection between his bouts of alcoholism —just a selfish one. But we were unprepared for the shock of Mama's ashes coming back to us in the mail, marked REFUSED: RETURN TO SENDER across the discreet, gray-edged label from Frank E. Campbell. In a letter to Lily he later explained that he was miffed that we had only sent him a telegram when she died, that we hadn't telephoned.

Cassie and I were away when the urn returned. Papa mentioned it to us casually some weeks later.

"So then what?" Cassie asked, horrified at the insult.

"I buried the urn in the field," Papa said. He must have seen a look of dismay on our faces because he added, "You know how much your mother loved it up here in the country, and that's the field where your ponies lived."

"Where exactly did you bury it?" I asked, put off by the strained tone; it sounded as though he had made up the reason for burying it there.

"It doesn't really matter; we aren't going to put a tombstone up," my father replied, avoiding my piercing eyes.

"But what if we wanted to go to the place sometime?" Cassie persisted.

He walked with us out to the field and pointed to a general area. We could see his annoyance at being pressed for information so we dropped it, but we couldn't shake the feeling that perhaps he hadn't buried the urn at all.

It was the same field where we'd buried countless pet hamsters, goldfish, canaries and wild birds that fell out of their nests. Even Pango's puppy Pandora was buried there. Cassie and I prepared elaborate funerals, placing the body in a cotton-lined box with flower petals sprinkled inside. We each wrapped ourselves in white sheets, two small priestesses, and held candles as we made up liturgy. One inhabitant of the far-flung graveyard was a tree frog Cass had accidentally beheaded with an axe while we were playing. The saddest funeral for me was Chester's.

One Easter Papa got us a pair of chestnut-colored pedigreed rabbits. Jim added a hutch for them next to the one that already held a family of fat white bunnies. Chester became a gentle household pet and would even hop along beside me on a harness and leash. One morning when I ran outside to feed the brood of animals, I felt something odd in the air, something wrong. I slowed down as I reached the white picket gate of the animal pen. The chickens and ducks were strangely quiet. The two sheep ambled over with their heads low. On the ground in front of me was a clump of auburn fur, the same color as my hair. I picked up what had been Chester's tail. I had to swallow hard, to get my stomach back down out of my throat, as I went across the grass to his hutch. The heavy chicken wire on the front had been brutally forced open. Chester's mate was frozen in a wild-eyed stare; I picked up her body, but there wasn't a mark on it. She had been scared to death. There was no sign of Chester. The marauder had evidently taken his whole body, dropping his tail on the way.

I went screaming back into the warm, bacony kitchen and threw myself in Papa's lap, so violently that he didn't have time to get the newspaper out of the way. I handed him the fuzzy bunny tail and sobbed in his arms.

Later that day Cassie and I staged a royal funeral, with Chester's tail somewhat surrealistically nestled inside a velvet jeweler's box. We threw flowers into the shallow hole before covering it with dirt, and I cursed the vicious boy or raccoon or fox that had taken my pet away. I couldn't help envisioning the brute force of the cage being ripped open, my rabbit being devoured whole or carried away dying, leaving only his tail as a mocking symbol of how evil the world can be, how fragile life is, how ludicrous it is to imagine there is a safe harbor, that anyone can escape that brutality.

Nine

B|lake began having a recurring bad dream in which her wedding dress turned black. Then she had a nightmare so vividly real that it haunted her for weeks. The setting was the lawn of the East Hampton house. There was a grave beside the lily pond: the coverstone was askew, and inside there were brown, dried-up flowers and gift cards. There were also two naked dead people. The dead woman was short and blond; the man was tall and black. "But they don't belong together," Blake said in her dream. She looked at them again and saw there were many feet and legs in the coffin— she realized it was a mass grave. A beautiful naked woman took Blake by the hand—she had long blond hair and looked exactly like Botticelli's Primavera—and tried to talk Blake into joining the bodies in the tomb. She spoke soothingly, hypnotically, enticing Blake the way sirens did sailors in Greek myths, telling her how lovely and peaceful it was to be dead. Blake was beginning to believe her when she awakened, trembling, at the edge of her grave. Michael slept peacefully beside her, not even noticing when she got out of bed for a glass of milk to soothe her stomach.

Things were blissfully happy in the beginning, but Blake could not let go of her apprehension that something was going to go wrong, that they couldn't have gotten this lucky. Even though she believed she had it coming to her, that didn't mean she trusted the fairy tale. She couldn't quite believe that she had found her prince, that it had come true. It worried her. When things were wonderful, it worried her even more: did she really deserve it; would it last; was it for real? She couldn't leave it alone.

Michael's mother recommended a doctor when Blake's stomach pains got worse. She wasn't allowed to eat the night before, and when she got there she had to drink a thick, pink, chalky liquid. She gagged twice, letting go of the medical gown that was open in the back, cool air sweeping across her naked bottom. She was famished, and it disgusted her to have to break the fast with paper cups of vile, semi-liquid paste. She wondered why it was colored pink—to entice children to swallow it down? Did children get ulcers? Jesus, the agony that human beings inflict on themselves, against others.

She was sandwiched between two massive slabs of metal, her insides lit up for a white-coated man. His face was so close to hers that she could see where he had clipped the hair from inside his ears: up close the knob looked diseased, speckled black from the stubs of hair. He watched the chalky, pink stuff twist inside her body, quite at home with the revealed mysteries of man's innards, exposed. Blake thought about Michael's father, about the bleeding ulcer that had brought him to this doctor years before. How stiff that pain must have been, almost as bad as the pain of holding inside feelings so that they eat into you until you bleed. Blake watched the technician making photographs of her innermost depths, like flicking a switch to get photos of Jupiter or to split an atom. She figured there was only one mystery left for modern man, one invisible, undissectable mystery: the thing that happens between a man and a woman. Nothing casts enough light to reveal *that* secret, to understand what goes on there. Only poets can make sense of that.

Blake and Michael did lovely things together in the beginning. They drove to the Cloisters with a picnic on a Sunday to listen to baroque music played by a string quintet. Blake had spent most of Saturday preparing the food, an elaborate spread of poached chicken breasts in a walnut and basil sauce, china peas and water chestnuts in sesame oil, a cold rice salad crammed with diced cucumber and red pepper and artichoke hearts, and then multiple desserts. It was the sort of picnic Isabel would have given four stars to, a wonderfully absurd abundance, a recapitulation of the grand style of Marsham picnics in France when Blake was a girl, when they let down the back door of the VW bus and laid out enough goodies from the charcuterie and bakery to feed four families of four.

When Blake spread out a blue and white checked cloth from the deluxe picnic basket they'd gotten as a wedding present, Michael said in amazement, "Blakie, you've gone mad!"

She pinned him with a glare. "That's all you can say?" she demanded. She had worn herself out creating this picnic, and now he was going to ruin it all, miss the whole point of the opulence and be a spoilsport pragmatist about it.

"It's terrific, honey," he said, seeing how fragile she was. "It's just so *much*." He tried to make it sound like a compliment, but he could see she took it as a criticism, the injured anger in her eyes.

"You don't have to eat all of it, Michael," she said coldly, not looking at him, continuing to unwrap the food but wanting to fling it at him, or cry, she didn't know which.

Michael put his hand under her chin and said, "Hey?" in such a soothing, loving way she looked up, self-conscious tears at the rims of her eyes. "You'll see, I'll eat every last bite," he said, smiling away her unhappiness. "You are spectacular, have I told you that lately?"

Blake smiled sheepishly, knowing what a petulant baby she'd been. The problem was that no response could have come close to the reaction her mother would have had. Things were great, but Blake had an ominous feeling— that it wasn't as good as it seemed, or that it would change at any minute.

One day she and Michael went sailing, went up to Amagansett and took a boat out on the bay. The day was crystal blue, sky and water a perfect match, and they took swigs from a cooler of champagne and fresh orange juice and sang songs together, old Beatle tunes to which Michael sang the harmony and Blake made up new verses when she couldn't remember the words. Michael guided the boat and watched the sunlight glint golden off Blake's long hair in the wind.

She said to herself, "That gorgeous creature is mine and the circulation on the paper is up ten thousand and I got an assignment from *Esquire* for the first time and Michael is so beautiful and the world is ours." She thought the mimosa probably helped, but this must be what "rapture of the depths" felt like, the euphoria that scuba divers experience when they go too deep.

"I'm happy as a clam," Blake announced, lying back on the narrow deck as the boat sliced through the water. But she was aware of the padded orange life jacket, lumpy against her back, and it made her think that that was how marriage felt to her, just like this day. Everything seemed so hunky-dory, but you had to wear a life jacket, never certain when a squall would blow in suddenly and capsize the boat. Things had happened so quickly with Michael; he had dropped out of the heavens, taken her unawares. She wasn't in control; she didn't trust it. She couldn't help but wonder if this was how her parents were in the beginning; was it cozy and fun like this, and then suddenly the wine turned to vinegar?

Blake knew she was being foolish and tried to put a halt to her neurotic apprehensions by looking at the thing rationally. Michael was still tall and blond and said he loved her, and sometimes they made love at night and again in the morning. Twice he had come home during the day to surprise her. Once she hadn't been there, and Michael had left her a note scrawled on a piece of paper towel, "I LOVE YOU, 2:45 P.M., Sept. 11." Blake tacked it up on the bookshelf facing her desk in her study, even though it embarrassed Michael that guests would see it. She would not take it down until the soft paper curled up and sagged: she needed it there as proof, a reminder. "He loves me," she would say to herself, doubting it. He hadn't called her from the office in days—the way he used to before they were married, just to tell her. When she could not stand it any longer, she called him, but he sounded rushed and distracted, and she felt even worse when she hung up.

The other time he came home during the day, they made love in a pool of sunlight. "Right there," Michael said, pointing to a circle of sunny sheen on the cotton chintz sofa. As he lay on top of her, Blake felt disoriented: the sensations were pleasurable but seemed to be happening in a vacuum. She felt she should be happy—this was supposed to be every woman's dream, that her husband wanted her so much that he rushed home during the day and made passionate love to her. Blake didn't know what was the matter with her, why she felt as though she had awakened from an ominous dream that had hung over her all day, infusing her with a feeling of dread. Her fears were eating away at her, gnawing into her stomach.

Blake kept her eyes open while Michael made love to her: she looked at the living room and noted how adding just enough of her belongings had made his apartment feel like theirs; she looked at the pile of Michael's clothes on the beige carpet, his elegantly cut suit discarded with the blue tie she'd bought him at Battaglia one afternoon, and she felt as though she were an actress in a play. She couldn't relate to the business suit on the floor, to the harsh brightness of daylight as this man moved on top of her, to the interruption of the short story she'd been working on when he had poked his head into her study door and made her jump in surprise. Who was this stranger? A connection was missing; she was going through the motions of being happily married, but she didn't feel the intense depth of attachment to Michael that she had expected, that their whirlwind courtship had foretold.

When Michael left, straightening his tie and kissing her neck with little nibbles, she was amazed by how radiantly cheerful he was, a totally satisfied man. Blake hadn't been able to go back to work. She sat stonily at the typewriter for half an hour, immobile, feeling numb and lobotomized. Then she went into the bathroom, wiped the smudges of mascara from under her eyes and went to the health club. She walked right past the one nearest their apartment and continued uptown, walking dozens of blocks and then staying in the sauna until she felt nauseous.

Heartburn, they call it. That was precisely where the pain was: a sharp, stinging burn that spread fiery fingers around Blake's heart. The pain surprised her every time with its dagger. When she swallowed anything she held her breath, waiting for the burning stab when it reached the wound inside her, near her heart, then continued on its winding journey through her body. A knife in the heart. Sometimes when she passed a homey-looking coffee shop, Blake went in and ordered her security food, a coffee milkshake. Sitting at the counter she felt better; sucking down the cold, creamy drink gave her the satisfaction of sucking a bottle.

Michael knew something was wrong between them, but it made no sense; he couldn't understand where Blake's malaise came from. It was an underground spring that spurted up unexpectedly. They were on the floor, a fire crackling, playing Parcheesi, munching thick pretzels and drinking beer from silver mugs. Blake's attention wandered—she drew doodles in the frost on the side of her mug, thinking what a lovely wedding present they were, how perfect her wedding day had been. Her eyes misted over as she thought how much she wanted to feel like that again, a princess wrapped in white lace and flowers.

"What's the matter, Blake?"

"Things aren't the way I thought they were going to be."

"What things?"

"You, for instance. You're different."

"Different from what?" Michael asked with a sense of alarm. He had no idea what she was talking about, but she looked so miserable.

"From before we got married."

"People always act differently when they're courting," he replied, relieved that it wasn't really anything, just Blake coming a little unglued again. It seemed to be happening with greater frequency, though.

"But you don't have time for me—for us—the way you did then."

"What do you call this?"

"But this is the weekend. You used to make time during the week."

"I've got a paper to run, Ms. Marsham; this is the real world, not Shangri-la." He would have felt angrier, defensive, if she didn't look so pathetic. He put his arms around her and held her close, felt the beginning of tears in the way she was breathing. It was frustrating when she was childish like this, with a child's tunnel vision where all she could see was "I want," nothing else. "You know I love you, you impossible broad."

"Then why can't you make time now?" Blake asked, with a smile that suggested she knew better but wasn't going to give up.

"Christ!" Michael threw up his hands in mock desperation; he kept a jocular tone, but he really did feel desperate. "I see you every night, it's not as though I'm running all over town with the boys, and we play tennis and . . ."

Blake put her arms around Michael's shoulders from behind, covering his mouth to stop him from talking. His shoulder blades pressed into her breastbone, and a warm pleasure ran through her as she smelled the faint sweetness of lilac vegetal at the back of his neck. It made her think this was how he had smelled as a baby. "I'm a greedy bitch and I know I should be spanked, but you're too delicious, Michael Lowell; I want more of you, no matter how much I have." Blake rested her forehead on the back of his shoulder and tightened her face to keep from weeping; she could feel that the more she grabbed for, the further away it slipped, and yet she couldn't stop herself.

They looked out the picture window at the river, soaking in the sensation of her bosoms full and warm against the tight muscles of his back. Blake told herself to memorize the sight of a beat-up tugboat rocking and rolling in the backwash of a flatbed boat that had passed it. She knew this was what they had dreamed of, this moment of peace, of togetherness, and yet something was wrong, it was not going to last. She could feel herself saying things, demanding things, that she knew were out of line—yet if Michael could just pull the emergency brake, the train could be safely stopped, wouldn't hurtle recklessly into that cavernous tunnel. But he was new to all this. He'd had his share of affairs but they had all been rookies, so he thought he was a pro. Blake knew she was different: she had sharpened her blades on some very slick ice and could skate circles around Michael. All he'd have to do was make a couple of impressive blocks, a fancy shot at the goal, and she'd drop back. But he didn't know how.

Michael was as disoriented as a traveler who reaches a country he's always wanted to visit but once there can't speak the language, is lost. He had once told her that he'd never felt a full, one-on-one connection with another person until he'd been with Blake. He had grown up with doubts about whether his mother genuinely loved him. He'd felt the only way to win her affection was through accomplishments—he couldn't get approval for what he was, just for what he achieved. And then there had been his father's death. Those days with the body, insects in the heat, bitter-cold nights, thinking he was going to die, too— that it should have been he who drowned, not his father. Then coming back to civilization and having to walk around with that pain inside, the terrible hollowness of feeling unworthy of being alive. He told her that she had reached his soul, shown him a whole new world. Blake wondered whether she had done him more harm than good, opening those doors, because when things went wrong and they shut, he had no way of getting back inside. She sensed that Michael had never really experienced loneliness until their marriage, until he had fallen in love with her.

Michael reached his hands behind him and pulled Blake closer against him, holding her so intently that she could feel in his way of breathing that he was hurting, hoping. But she would not let herself feel responsible, guilty. Michael had wanted this, after all, maybe even more than she had. Before they'd met, the only thing Michael had wanted was to run his grandfather's empire, to take control of the newspaper in his father's name. Blake knew he could do it, that Michael was good enough that his mother would eventually step aside and yield to him. Then he had wanted something else—Blake—and had gone about getting her with the same arrogant self-assurance. He had pulled out the stops and swept her off her feet, propelled both of them headlong into it. But now that he had her he didn't know what to do with her, how to handle a relationship, how to negotiate with a complex female.

Michael turned around and held Blake tight against him, pressing her cheek against his. "But you didn't think it was always going to be like in the beginning, right?" Michael said, a rhetorical question.

Blake just stared at him. She heard herself saying, "Why not?" just like a kid asking an impossible-to-answer kid question that makes grown-ups want to shout, "Because I said so!" She didn't know how to control herself, to put aside the fairy princess who wanted to live up in the ivory tower forever. She had a doomed feeling she was recreating her parents' marriage, driving Michael away, when all she wanted was to feel that ethereal closeness again, the feeling during their courtship that life was golden, flowers and love notes, that nothing could touch them inside their gossamer castle.

"What is it you want, Blake?"

"To be closer, feel more intimate."

"Be patient, it'll grow."

"But how can it grow if we don't feed it?"

"Force-feeding will kill it, Blake."

Blake and Michael dovetailed perfectly: with each other they could recreate all the unhappiness they had seen growing up. Isabel had tried to change Marsh, transform him into a man who could meet her needs precisely as she wanted. In the process she destroyed what good there had been between them. Blake embraced her mother's tradition, trying to control a situation, to persevere, and Michael responded because it was so familiar. His mother had reacted to him not as a unique individual but as an extension of her, the beautiful blond son who excelled at sports and was on the honor roll and edited the school paper.

It drove Blake crazy when Michael came home and turned on the television, choosing the tube over her. He'd told her that watching the evening news was his way of unwinding, but she could only perceive it as a rejection of her.

"I wish you'd talk to me, Michael, tell me about your day."

"Later, Blake, give me a little room right now, huh?"

Blake flounced out of the room in a huff. She knew that people were at Michael all day long, a hundred little problems between the big ones, and that home was supposed to be his sanctuary and all that, but Christ, what about her? She'd been home alone all day, writing and preparing a fabulous dinner. Was he ignoring her already, married such a short time? If he was this inattentive now, what would it be like down the line? Didn't she have to do something now?

Michael padded into the kitchen in his stocking feet and cheered Blake up by grabbing a cheek of her behind and kissing her on the back of the neck. When he lifted the cover on the pot of fish soup and said, "Heavenly," she felt better. But then he stepped in quicksand again, without even realizing it. He asked to eat dinner in front of TV, and Blake exploded.

"Come on, Blakie, what's the big deal?"

"Eating in front of TV is disgusting—it's what people do when they don't want to be together."

"I want to watch the game *and* eat *and* be together with you."

"I cooked a wonderful dinner and set the table—I haven't seen you all day and I want to talk." She said it as an accusation and could see Michael's insides contract—he was being beat up, and he didn't have a clue why. Blake saw that, but her main concern was that he would suggest something so vile: her image of how things were supposed to be was shattered by the thought of eating on trays in front of television.

Blake had spun a fantasy for years about what the texture of her life with a man would be. They'd spend summers in an Italian village watching the black-garbed widow in the bakery become more stooped and gray with each summer, a yardstick for their own maturation. Blake imagined winters stretching out at opposite ends of a pale couch, toes touching, reading and sipping black-currant tea. High ceilings in big rooms, a brown mahogany grand piano, flowers everywhere in odd-shaped vases, Chinese embroidery framed next to modern art. Small dinner parties where everyone ate and drank just a little too much, delighting in each other's company. Falling asleep to a Bach concerto, waking to soft sun and kisses. Television intruded on Blake's fantasies.

Michael came to the dinner table with a closed expression.

"Are you angry?" she asked, hit by remorse. If Michael

was not adoring her, she felt as though he despised her—the pain rose from the very marrow of her bones. "Is that why you won't talk to me?" she pleaded.

"Come on, Blake, don't push. You said you wanted to talk—go ahead."

His annoyance with her felt like torture; the deadly silence after he spoke felt like a kick in her stomach. Blake knew she had been out of line, but when he reacted like this it only propelled her further from her center, from her better self. She hated herself for losing it; she hated him for letting it happen. She sat immobilized, not knowing what to do.

"Why aren't you eating?" Michael asked.

"I can't . . . my stomach hurts," she said. The tension between them felt to Blake as though a grizzly bear were digging his razor rows of teeth into her gut.

After Michael left the table to do work he'd brought home, Blake cleaned up the kitchen. She stuffed a furtive handful of food into her mouth. Her appetite came back with a wallop. She pushed food into her mouth with her fingers, chewing greedily, dribbling and wiping her chin with the back of her hand, gobbling the food with the ravenous intensity of an old woman in some remote village where the emergency rations had just been doled out onto her tin plate.

They went ice-skating one Saturday afternoon. Michael had been working at home all morning. When Blake looked out the window and announced, "It's ice-skating weather," Michael said, "Well, then, put on your ice-skating clothes, woman."

They ran crosstown on Fifty-seventh Street until Blake shouted for mercy and Michael flagged a cab. She snuggled up against him on the slippery black-vinyl seat as the taxi lurched aggressively through the crowded streets. Blake buried her face in the wool scratchiness of Michael's jacket, rubbing her hand on the baby-blanket softness of his cashmere scarf.

"Want to go away on a trip together?"

"Done."

"Really, Michael?"

"Sure, why not—we deserve it."

"Do you promise we can?"

"Want to take down the cabbie's name and number as a witness?"

They tottered as they walked across the plastic floor of the skate-rental room. There was an awkward, slippery moment as they first stepped onto the ice; then they glided easily once the blades were flat on the moonstone surface. They held hands and concentrated on getting their balance, finding a rhythm.

Blake looked across the rink at an elderly couple wearing matching tweeds, skating arm-in-arm, doing leg crossovers and graceful turns. "Look, honey," she said.

The sentimental tone told him that it wasn't just the charming vision of the couple that Blake was pointing out, but also a vision of their own future. He squeezed Blake's hand through his sheepskin gloves.

"When can we take our trip?" Blake asked as they circled with the throng of skaters, frosty air rising off the ice.

"Maybe I can get away next Saturday. We could spend the night in East Hampton."

Blake looked so stricken that Michael thought she'd been hurt, that another skater had kicked her or something. "What's the matter, Blake?" he asked.

"*Saturday?*" she exclaimed contemptuously. "*That's* your idea of a 'trip' away together?"

He was stunned, then angered. "Jesus Christ, Blake, you'd think I said we'd stay home and wax the floors. . . ."

"What do you expect? You say we can go away, but all

you really meant was one puny night in some crummy beach motel."

"Is that what it was for you?" She saw a chilly anger blow through Michael; she had just degraded the memory of their very first trip together, in East Hampton.

"Of course not, this has nothing to do with that. Why can't we stay on the subject?" she said.

"Which is? That if you can't have things your way, you throw a shit fit?"

"No, that I have a shit fit if you promise something and turn right around and renege."

Michael grabbed hold of her arm and pulled her over to the railing. A small girl and her father nearly crashed into Michael, but he was so angry he didn't even see the child fall on the ice or the dirty look her father gave him. "And just when the hell have I ever done that?"

"Saying we could go away, that whole thing about the cab driver as a witness; then you toss me a bone about one lousy night in Long Island when I meant a real trip, a plane, a beach."

Michael stared at her, drove his pupils right through hers like a drill. It made Blake sick to her stomach, Michael glaring at her like that, touching some small corner of herself that shriveled in shame. But she was caught up in her stance and didn't know how to stop, back out.

"Did it ever occur to you that *I* might want a vacation?" Michael said deliberately. "That you aren't the only one who might want a romantic rest on a tropical beach?"

"Then why don't you just do it, Michael, if that's true?"

"It's not that easy, dear. Real life doesn't conform to Blake Marsham snapping her fingers and saying, 'I want.'"

"Don't be a shit, Michael. The point is that you get your kicks from the paper; that's all you've got time for. You'd rather be with the *Herald* than with me, but at least face it."

"You're out of your cotton-picking mind, you know that?" Michael paused and lowered his voice. Several skaters stared at them as though they were an accident on the side of the road, horrible but fascinating. "Do you think about anything other than your precious feelings, Blake?"

She was glad they were out in the open, a public place where he had to curb his impulses. It looked as though he felt like slugging her, hauling off and decking her.

"I'm really sorry I don't have more time for you, Blake, that you feel neglected because I'm working my balls off. But I have to work that hard if the paper's going to be any good. Did it ever occur to you to feel sorry for *me*, because I don't have enough time for myself?"

Remorse hit Blake, a karate chop. "I'm sorry, Michael," she said pleadingly, but that only made him look more disgusted.

"What exactly are you sorry for?" he demanded.

She didn't really know why there was a flag on the play, just that she'd fouled him somehow; she fumbled for an answer. "That I've made you so angry—that you hate me now."

"And now I'm supposed to protest—'Don't be silly, Blake darling'—and everything will be fine again?"

"That's what I mean," Blake said, her lips trembling as she teetered on the brink of tears. "Nothing I say now can fix it."

Michael wanted to hold onto his indignation, to feel strong in his anger, but she was so winning when she was little-girl-blue. He took a handkerchief out of his pocket, and she accepted it with a small, searching smile.

She had stopped breathing a moment before, frightened that she'd gone too far and driven him away this time; now that she had her foot back in the door, she took a choppy breath. "I'm so sorry, Michael," she said plaintively, blowing her nose and keeping a sorrowful expression just a little longer to show how contrite she was.

"Oh, shit, Blake," Michael said dispiritedly, looking up at the golden statue flying beside the Rockefeller rink, "are you trying to bust us up, or what?"

"How can you say that, you know I'd die without you," Blake said, the tears she had controlled a moment before now tumbling out.

He shook his head with all-suffering resignation at the way she went from unforgivable brattiness to irresistible cuteness in the bat of an eyelash. He put his arm around her, but it felt false; she had damaged his trust in a way that kept him from just letting it go, forgive and forget.

Blake felt it, buried her head against his shoulder and moaned, "Oh, Michael, why didn't you stop me?"

"There's no stopping you when you're on a roll, Blake. When your guns are loaded, not even an ABM stands a chance."

Ordinarily Blake would have gotten a shot of pleasure to hear him describe her that way. As they took small, sharp steps towards the exit, Blake wanted to lie down and let the others skate over her, lacerate her, cut the badness out of her. As they were unlacing their skates, Michael gave her a "What am I going to do with you?" look, and she felt forgiven.

For several days afterwards Blake kept a rein on herself. She waited a moment before saying something—a couple of times she even stopped herself from saying it at all. But ultimately all she could do was slow things down. She was a kid out for a joy ride. She knew it was wrong, that she could get into trouble, get hurt or even hurt someone else, but once she hit a hill and picked up speed, there wasn't anything she or anybody else could do to stop her.

Blake found herself going to the supermarket more than she really needed to, buying things that weren't necessary. She felt safe and calm in the store, blissfully removed from the tension with Michael. Looking at all that provender was reassuring, the comfort of abundance. It made Blake feel like the childhood weekends when she descended on the supermarket in the country with her mother and sister. Isabel infected her daughters with a zest for life that made even the commonplace a cause for celebration, made combing a supermarket aisle as much fun as climbing the inner passage of a pyramid. Blake and Cassandra each got a cart. Isabel instructed them to get certain items—paper towels, tomato paste—and after that they could fill their carts to the top with whatever they wanted.

When they rejoined Isabel at the checkout line, Cassie and Blake unloaded Twinkies and ice-cream bars, treats for the dogs and jars of baby corn, chocolate-coated cereal and balls of mozzarella, whatever had grabbed their fancy. Then a new game commenced: adding up the three baskets to see if they had managed to go over a hundred dollars. In those days it really took some doing to spend that much for food for a country house, especially because Isabel ordered meat from a New York butcher.

"OK, girls, let's see if we made it this week!" Isabel would declare, and the girls would begin to load their goodies onto the black-rubber checkout belt.

A trickle of excitement ran down the row of cashiers—everyone had heard about this zany woman who came in once a week with her kids. It would have been impossible to consume everything they brought home, so the overflow piled up in the kitchen pantries and the deep-freeze in the basement. But it had never been a matter of practicality—the game was everything, the giddy feeling that they had it all coming to them in life.

So Blake wheeled up and down the rows at Gristede's, feeling for a while that life was as good and full and nourishing as it once had been. But the gentle coolness of the frozen-food aisles evaporated when she got back home to the smoldering heat of the tense silences with Michael. As he slipped away from her, it reminded Blake of losing that special closeness with her father. When she was fourteen and fifteen and her parents were separated, Blake went everywhere with her father as his date: gallery openings, cocktail parties, movie premieres, and long, boring dinners at Elaine's, in the early days before the glamour seekers invaded and it was just a sort of club where long-winded, self-absorbed writers came to escape from their typewriters.

Blake had loved being Marsh's date, loved to watch people look at them and wonder what their relationship was. She concentrated on never saying "Papa" or "Daddy" when she was out on the town with him, hoping people might think she was his girl friend. He was the most charming man Blake had ever met; charm oozed from him like nectar from a tiger lily. There was no better feeling than being around Marsh when he hooked everyone's attention with an engrossing story, or when he knocked patter back and forth with Blake, publicly flirting.

It had changed when Isabel had the third operation and could no longer carry on with her life as if there were no cancer. Blake had had to choose sides, and her loyalty went where it was most needed: to Isabel's physical pain and her mental anguish over Marsh. In order not to blame her father, in order not to hate him, Blake had withdrawn, but that had meant losing the enveloping closeness. Years later she tried to recapture it with Michael; yet when it didn't stay at its initial peak, Blake was bewildered, felt tricked and fought to get it back.

Things would be fine between them for a while, and then the poisons would start to bubble up again, like toxic wastes that would not stay buried. There was the cocktail party like so many others that Michael and Blake went to; and like many of the others, Blake didn't much want to be there. She mightn't have been so negative except that the gatherings were important professionally for Michael, and she had come to view the *Herald* as a rival for Michael's attention. The same dedication and ambition that had first attracted her to Michael now seemed a slap in her face, made her feel neglected. Knowing that she was being irrational did not make her feel any less put out.

It was a smoky press of chattering bodies. Blake tended to feel lost at these things until she found a familiar face, but even then she felt uneasy: were people currying her favor only as a conduit to her powerful young husband? That, too, put Blake in a pissy mood—Michael was the center of attention; she was just a garnish.

As Blake waited to get to the bar, she watched Michael across the room. He was leaning against a white wall beside a tall, bottle-green fern plant, talking to a ravishing, raven-haired woman. Michael was totally focused on her, as though there were nothing else going on in the room, and Blake recalled what it had been like to have his gorgeous face riveted on her like that. It was at a big, stupid gathering just like this that she had met Michael, she realized—and it felt like a long time since he had devoured her with his eyes. The woman was basking in it. Blake didn't know her name but had seen her picture in *Vogue* or *Women's Wear* or someplace. She was one of those gorgeous women one could have dismissed derisively a few years ago as a purposeless, jet-set dilettante— nowadays those women did respectable, even enviable things, like photographing rare white tigers or interviewing world leaders.

Blake found herself making her way towards them through the throng. A small voice inside her head said,

/   129

"Leave it alone, Blake, don't," but she kept right on walking towards Michael and the beautiful woman. She was drawn to them, moth to a flame, knowing even as she did so that no good could come of it, that she would only make herself look foolish and regret it later. But her compulsion was greater than her foresight: Blake didn't know how to back off any better than her mother had.

"Well, at least one of us is having a good time," Blake said as she reached Michael's side. She shot an icy smile at the woman whose elegantly angular face was framed by jet-black hair. She had just the sort of striking Semitic beauty that Isabel had always held up as the only true beauty. "I'm Blake Marsham," she said, using her words as daggers. "Sorry to bust up such a good time, but the only time I get to talk to my husband is at these silly parties." The woman caught on instantly that there was more going on here than she cared to be a party to. With a sympathetic smile at Michael, she shook Blake's hand and said with excessive graciousness, "Please, don't let me get in the way." With a parting "See you later" at Michael, the woman merged back into the crowd. Michael tried to smile at her; the smile froze on his lips as he turned to Blake. She felt the heat of his anger, but she had an icy wall of self-pitying self-righteousness as protection.

Michael kept staring at her, as though studying a weird piece of hieroglyphic he was trying to decode. "And just what was that all about?" he demanded, keeping his voice very low and steady.

"*I* didn't want her to leave, Michael—she sure was touchy."

"You'd be touchy, too, if someone came over and burned their brand into the man you were talking to."

"So now you're accusing me of playing the part of the jealous, possessive wife?" Blake said indignantly.

"And what part do you think you're playing, Blake, dear?"

"The woman you supposedly love and want to spend time with—but hardly ever do because the precious newspaper needs you more."

"What you need, no man can give you, Blake. At least not this one," he added.

His words sounded ominously true to her, even threatening, but she would not relinquish the offensive. "Yes, I need more than I'm getting—but that may just be more than you feel like giving."

"You want so goddamned much, Blake, like a baby that starts screaming if it doesn't get fed on schedule."

"You grew up in a world where nannies did all that, anyway. You're just plain terrified of emotional demands."

"So it's my WASP upbringing that's the problem?"

"Yeah. Or your refusal to rise above it."

"But what about the way you take a punch, make a bruise, and then just keep pressing on it?"

"God, what a horrible thing to say. If that's what you think of me, what are you sticking around for? Masochism?"

"You can't resist a chance to push it, can you? Don't you know when the hell to shut your mouth, woman?"

When they got back home, Michael opened the two locks and held the door so Blake could walk in ahead of him. They hadn't said a word since leaving the party; his gentlemanly gesture in the midst of his anger towards her touched Blake. He stood with his back against the open door to let her pass—he held his body tall and thin to avoid contact with hers, and it made Blake want to cry. By the time Michael had shut the door and double-locked it behind them, Blake had dissolved into sobs, weeping, leaning her head against the wall and banging her

/   131

forehead several times, rhythmically. "I'm sorry, Michael, I'm so sorry," she moaned, filled with self-loathing. "I don't know what's the matter with me—maybe I just shouldn't go to those parties if I can't be civilized."

Michael patted Blake on the shoulder as he walked into the living room. Her hysterics didn't snag him as they used to, but when she administered self-punishment he could be calmer, more generous. "That's no solution, Blake. We're married, for better or worse. . . ."

"Worse, I know—I've made it that way," Blake interrupted in a burst of despair, but Michael cut her short.

"Let me finish: we're married, and that means we go places together. You've just got to face the realities: at this point in my life my work gets the lion's share of my energies, as it does for anyone trying to be successful."

"But what about us, me? Where does that fit in? By the time you've reached your goal, there'll be nothing between us."

"It's a goal we reach together, Blake—which gives us a shared history. Which we can embellish on down the road. But you're killing us with this desperate intensity, trying to cram it all in right now."

"But I live life that way—as if every day could be my last."

"If you try to impose that on me, on any relationship, it'll be fatal. Nothing can withstand that pressure."

"I'm sorry, Michael, really I am," Blake sobbed, her tears gushing out at the pronouncement of doom.

"I know, Blake, I know you are," Michael said, patting her on the back as she put her arms around his neck. Blake could tell from his tone that Michael recognized that just because she saw the error of her ways did not mean that she was able to do much to change them. She cried and cried in his arms, wondering how it had gone so wrong.

* * *

Blake remembered how magical it had been the night Michael proposed. Hamburgers and St. Emilion at P. J. Clarke's, a late dinner after a long week and a long wait at the bar. Once Blake and Michael were seated at a small, checkered table, she felt a protective bubble blow up around them, shutting out the bustle. Blake was so hungry she took a big bite of hamburger that left ketchup imprints all around her mouth. Michael reached over and wiped her off with his napkin, a paternalistic gesture that Blake resisted enjoying—she didn't want to start imagining how nice it would be to have someone look after you.

"Can't take you anywhere," Michael said. His loving tone and the intense way he looked deep into her eyes unsettled Blake.

"Try taking me to Lasserre, my table manners shape right up," she sparred, a fast line to keep him at bay.

"You want me to take you to Paris?" he asked.

She tried to back him off with Algonquin-table glibness, but he kept coming back, straight from the shoulder.

"No, I want you to take me home and ravish me."

"You're tough to keep up with, you know that?"

"At least I'm not boring," Blake declared. Her smartass comebacks had put him on the defensive, but he continued to look at her in that moonstruck way that made her uneasy, feel out of control.

"It would take a lifetime, and you still wouldn't be boring," Michael said, holding his ground. Blake blushed. He held his wine glass up to her for a toast; she wiped the hamburger grease off her hand and lifted her glass. "To a lifetime together," Michael concluded.

"Oh, Michael, can't we just toast now, the present?" Blake looked really uncomfortable. She was so happy with him, but when he said things about the future it filled her with panic. The future seemed so dicey, so unpredictable—trying to tie it down only reminded her of that. "I know it's neurotic, but talking about it makes me nervous, OK?"

"So we won't talk about it," he said, then added in the same conversational tone, "but you do know that I intend to marry you one day?"

Blake couldn't believe how calmly he said it, how matter-of-factly. He was in control, and there was nothing she could do about it; if only she could slow things down, go back to just flirting and having a good time, not get things complicated by being so serious. She knew her fear of marriage was irrational, but her hands and feet had gone cold; the blood had stopped flowing. "Come on, Michael, we haven't known each other that long—how can you say that?"

"Because it's true. You know it as well as I do."

As frightened as she was, Blake couldn't resist plunging in, even though the water was over her head. She loved being on the brink of peril, she couldn't resist playing along. It was all a game to her: life was a game; getting a man to fall for you hook line and sinker was a game; even the risk that it could turn real was part of the game . . . that there were consequences.

"But it's not like you've really proposed or anything . . ."

Michael's face turned serious; there was a wry twist to his voice, a tone she'd heard him use at the newspaper when a reporter said he'd gotten all there was and another paper had scooped the *Herald*.

"Oh, yeah?"

Michael motioned for the check, and they sat very still, lizards in the desert. It had suddenly become dangerous; the least word or motion could shift the precarious balance. Blake watched him sign the check, barely looking at it, coolly efficient. She liked the way he signed his name with a naturally grandiose flourish, giving the impression that if you were to look at his signature it might just say Edward II. Michael glanced up, as if to make sure she was still there. Blake wondered what it would be like for this to be the only man who ever again picked up her check at dinner, the only man, period. . . .

"Let's take a walk to the river," Michael said, standing up from the table. She followed him through the crowd of chic people pressed together at the bar; she had a premonition that he was going to take her on a walk like the first night, only this time he was going to propose. She couldn't let that happen; she wasn't ready; she couldn't get married. And yet how could she refuse him; he was perfect for her; it was a match made in heaven. The idea of ducking out the side door crossed her mind so that she wouldn't have to deal with it, simply not be there when he got out on the sidewalk. That was how it worked in life: you could be going merrily along and suddenly the other person wouldn't be there; you lost him—or her—through some horrible quirk of fate. That was so much worse than walking alone, protecting yourself from that heartbreak.

Michael walked Blake briskly east past rows of brownstones, propelling her by the elbow as if he were escorting her through an airline terminal. She submitted without protest, without asking for an explanation. She had gotten herself into this. The silence gave her a chance to figure out what she could say when he asked. Just the thought of hearing the question made her freeze. They were only a block away from the river—Blake slowed down, put her arm around Michael's back to slow things down.

"Michael, I didn't really mean . . ."

"You should know better than to throw down a gauntlet with me," he replied, without breaking stride. It was almost an icy smile; he put his arm over hers in back and kept walking her forward. Her mind spun like a wheel of fortune, hoping it would stop on a solution to how to get herself off the hook—at the same time wanting so much to be on it. She wanted this man. Michael's forcefulness was sexy, as was his chiseled blond face and the reins of power he held and the image of how very beautiful they'd be together—two golden children, each holding one end of a rainbow.

They stood at the iron railing looking out at the East River, flowing black, strings of lights on the tugboats churning past. Blake leaned her head against his shoulder; even though he was the antagonist in this drama, he was at the same time her co-star, her leading man. She gazed out at the water and wondered what was holding her back.

Michael put his arm around Blake and held her tight against him. She wondered if they would ever again be as filled with a sense of the promise of the future. Their fantasies had come true when they found each other; it seemed so perfect, such a beautiful combination, an irrefutably good match. They were each just the partner their mothers would have chosen for them. Blake barely knew Michael; certain intensities of passion were missing, but that seemed trivial compared to how right they were for each other. Michael had always been treated like the crown prince but had never really believed it until he met her; Blake made him feel like a king. With him she could be the princess she had been raised to be. Together they would reign, a sparkling example of the best of their generation, a perfect couple.

Michael turned and positioned Blake with her back to the rail, one hand on either side of her. She knew what was coming next, but a feeling of peacefulness was replacing the panic; the soft, spreading light of a street lamp suffused the air around them as if it were a foggy night on the Thames, and all at once Blake felt her mother there, felt Isabel's presence in the ethereal light, as though she had come down to give her blessing. Suddenly Blake understood: she had been waiting for Isabel to tell her it was all right, to give her approval to this man, to sanction them. Isabel's halo shone behind Michael, bathing him in the heavenly light, and Blake knew it was all right, that she didn't have to be frightened any longer.

"Blake . . . will you be my wife?"

For a split second she thought of calling it off, but she wanted him too much, and it had taken on a life of its own. It was meant to be. She nodded, barely perceptibly at first, then emphatically. Michael folded his arms around Blake and kissed her, feeling her resistance crumble as he held his lips on hers and touched her cheek with his hand. He took his mouth away but kept on holding her.

"We're going to knock the world on its ass."

"We're going to make them all so jealous."

"We're going to be impossibly happy."

"Oh, Michael, are we? Promise?"

"Have I ever let you down?"

They walked all the way back to Michael's apartment along the river. He sang Cole Porter love songs to her, winsome words and lilting melodies that reminded her of Cassie singing her to sleep as a child, making her feel everything was going to be all right.

Ten

Isabel created myths about herself by living with spontaneous abandon, careening down intriguing tributaries in a world where other people stayed cautiously to the middle of the road. "That Isabel . . ." they'd say, upon hearing of yet another of her escapades. "How does she do it?" She lived life the way a spirited mare drinks after a hard gallop: plunging her muzzle deep into the stream, snorting with pleasure as she guzzles the rushing water, drinking deeply and giving herself over to the moment. Mama had dauntless enthusiasm and no fear about the world around her —for her, the only danger was not exploring.

Legends about my mother grew out of the smallest incidents, like the exploratory swim in Italy that nearly killed us all. It was the summer she'd taken Cassie and me to the chic fishing village of Porto Ercole, where we watched the old fishing boats outside our window unloading the fish we would eat in the trattoria that night.

One day Cassie and I were practicing headstands in the clear blue water of the cove where we swam while giggling about the German tourists who undressed right out in the open. Those were the days before Americans were considered ugly—the Germans were the ones scorned and ridiculed for being vulgarians. It was an honor to be an American abroad then, when our country was beloved and the powerful dollar permitted expatriates to live luxuriously in the unspoiled playground that was Europe. Cassandra and I got a great deal of attention, with our fluent French and Italian and with our unusual freckles and bright red hair, even though Mama had told us that our kind of coloring just wasn't beautiful. It was one of her definitive proclamations early in our lives that Semitic beauty was the only true beauty. She stated it as indisputable fact, not just the personal opinion of a fair-skinned woman with two little girls straight out of a Gainsborough. Living in Italy, she'd had ample opportunity to point out ivory-skinned, black-haired goddesses; we'd stare wistfully at the beauty we'd never achieve.

"Let's go explore that rock," Mother said, suddenly wading into the water beside us.

She struck out from shore in her powerful breaststroke; Cass and I turned to each other dubiously. Our mother was a marathon swimmer, known to plow out to sea and become a speck on the horizon, to the chagrin of lifeguards everywhere. This rock she was headed for was a good mile out, but we were our mother's daughters, so we followed in our sturdy little crawls. She turned and smiled benevolently back at us, treading water when we needed to float on our backs to catch our breath.

All of a sudden there was a boat bearing down on us from the right . . . there were others behind it. Mother had led us into the center of a harbor channel in the middle of the ocean. We were too far out to make it back to shore, yet still a long stretch from what we now saw was a small island. My exhausted legs froze as I stared at the enormous boat churning water as it headed right for us.

"Come on girls," Mama commanded, unfazed by the impending doom, "let's hurry it up."

Ever dutiful, we huffed and kicked to the rocky little isle, scrambling onto the sharp rocks. Cassandra and I were close to tears, frightened and furious at her, but Mama had us laughing it off before we had a chance to get angry.

Isabel had no patience for timidity about anything, particularly trying new things. Cassandra and I were regular troopers when it came to tasting new foods, willing to take a bit of anything from squid to oxtail. But if anyone traveling with us—friends of ours or hers—turned up their noses at an unfamiliar food, Isabel admonished them with the story of her childhood trip with her parents to Shanghai.

"At the first formal banquet a peculiar platter was put in the middle of the table. It was a mound of pink meat, but it seemed to be moving. Beside it was a stack of small pancakes; each guest had his own saucer of black sauce. I watched the Chinese guests take a pancake between their fingers and pick up one of the pink, wriggling things with it. Then they dipped it in the sauce and popped the rolled pancake into their mouths. I gathered up a pancake and wrapped it around one of the pink pieces; it felt terribly odd, sort of warm and alive. I couldn't resist peeking into the pancake to see what I was about to eat. With a terrible shock I saw it was a baby mouse, newborn before it had any fur. Before I could remember my manners and the rule to do as the Romans do, I piped up in horror, 'But this is alive!' The host turned to me with a patient smile and said, 'My young friend, in your country you eat oysters alive and wouldn't think of eating them any other way.' "

At this point in the story, Mother would smile broadly at whomever she was chastising for reluctance to try kidneys or brains, which suddenly seemed tame by comparison. Speechless and horrified by the thought of the pink, wriggling baby mouse, no one ever really found out if Isabel had put the creature in her mouth.

Mama had such a passion for travel that she fairly gobbled up a country as she sailed through it with my father, sister and me trailing breathlessly behind her like streamers. She dragged Cassie and me into every church and museum in Europe before we were even tall enough to reach the holy water basins without standing on tiptoe. We discovered a way to make church visiting fun: we mimicked Catholic ritual, dipping our fingers in the water, curtseying and making a cross. Half the fun was the effort of keeping a straight face, appearing to be pious angels. I harbored a secret dread that people would be able to tell we weren't the genuine article, that one day a priest would see me make the cross in the wrong direction, tap me on the shoulder with a sinister expression and kick me out the door. I finally told Mama my fear.

"The *Catholics?*" she said with a hoot of laughter. "They want *every*body's soul; they don't care if you don't play the game precisely right."

Cassandra and I tried our best to learn the legends of the saints, identifying them in frescoes by the instruments of their death. We accepted the gory violence as part of the game: Saint Catherine standing with her wheel of torture; John Sebastian dripping blood from every arrow stuck in his body. It pleased Mama enormously when we knew the saints by their symbols, and she made it fun, quizzing us when we got to a room of paintings. Cass and

I played hide and seek behind confessional booths from Saint Peter's to Saint Mark's, looking on all of it as a mysterious adventure, the flickering candles in the cool, musty cathedrals full of secrets. We took it in stride when Mama managed to get us in on a semi-private audience with the Pope—when the moment came for the few dozen people in the chamber to kiss His Holiness' ring, the other guests seemed overcome by the spiritual experience. The thing that impressed Cassie and me was how baby-soft his hand was when we touched our lips to it; afterwards, we debated how he kept it like that. Mother was probably the only person who passed up a chance to kiss the ruby ring.

"I do not want to support the tyranny of the papacy and the centuries of bloodshed the church is responsible for," she told us afterwards. "But I think it's nice for you girls to have the experience, don't you?"

Italy was paradise, the sunny country of my sunny childhood. Pignole nuts are my madeleines: squatting in the park with Cassandra, Maria clucking over us as our wooden scooters lay forgotten on the ground and we scrambled for pignoles in the park dirt, smashing our small fingers as often as the shells, hungry for the tender, earthy nuts. Gathering up pinecones from beneath the wide umbrella pines and smashing the purple-black shells between two rocks, our fingers black-purple dusty as we picked out the sweet white meat, the flavor like mushrooms, like nuts, like the candy of childhood memories.

First grade at the Overseas School of Rome; an entrancing hand-painted ceiling of adorably fat cherubs with dimpled bottoms that smiled down as we lay on our cots after lunch, which was wheeled in by equally fat ladies who ladled out the steamy pasta. Afterwards, we sat on the balcony outside the French doors of the villa converted into a school, our knobby knees poking through the wrought-iron railing as we spat grape seeds into the gardens below; between hedges of oleander and patches of bright flowers were the gardeners with hoes over their shoulders, who kept our universe like a small Versailles.

Living abroad, traveling everywhere, created a conflict between our bountiful life and the poverty we saw all around; Cassandra and I learned early how to block it out, how to look out the car window and see impoverished natives not as individual human beings but as an interesting part of the landscape. We learned how to remark that a peasant girl was pretty, so we didn't have to think about how terrifyingly skinny she was, her stick of an arm stuck straight out begging, matted hair, flies circling her eyes, tatters of a dusty dress and a mournful expression just like in the magazines that say, "You can help this child with the big black eyes, or you can turn the page"; we turned the page, drove past in our air-conditioned, chauffeured car and waved cheerfully at her, the courteous princesses.

I knew there was something terribly wrong in all of it, but I accepted the explanation that, regrettably, that was the way the world was, and seeing it was better than ignoring it entirely. So there we'd be in Istanbul, and a boy with a donkey would rush over when we came out of a trinket shop, imploring us to take a ride. "No, thank you," we'd say politely, smiling as if it were a tea party and someone was passing the crumpets a second time. We weren't in the mood for a donkey ride just then, not thinking that the boy's life depended on it. We even saved sugar cubes for donkeys when the streets of our travels were lined with starving children. Back we went to America and pampered our ponies with carrots and apples, never riding them for more than an hour a day, swabbing them with fly repellent in the summer and covering them in warm blankets when it got cold. No one ever treated that boy as well.

Cassie and I firmly believed we were not spoiled. Our good manners and sense of proportion—not asking for things all the time, appreciating things when we did get them—spared us from such a dreadful accusation. We knew kids who were spoiled, the ones who carelessly left cashmere sweaters in the park or interrupted conversations without saying, "Excuse me, please." We thought we were good sports for not complaining during the sixteen-hour flights to Europe. We helped the stewardesses clear the trays and got the desserts people hadn't eaten; afterwards, we climbed right into our fold-down beds at the front of the plane and closed our eyes so we wouldn't be crabby when we arrived. We didn't think it was spoiled that we could go into stores in New York and say, "Charge it, please," just like Eloise, and they would. We thought our restraint showed we weren't spoiled; when Papa gave us our own American Express cards when we were fourteen and fifteen, we reasoned that with all our traveling it was a necessity, not an indulgence.

Mama's Scotch thriftiness interspersed with luxury on our trips made us think we were far from spoiled. When she took us to see the Roman ruins in Palermo, we stayed at the fanciest hotel in Sicily.

"One meal a day, that's all we can afford," Isabel pronounced as we unpacked in our suite overlooking the seas. "Either lunch or dinner."

Cassandra was upset as we walked past the tanned people all in white on the terrace, stretched out comfortably with cold lobster and salads the color of the Italian flag in front of them.

"Don't worry about it, follow me," I said.

We skipped across the private beach of our hotel in

Taormina and stepped over the rope that kept out the "riffraff." We feasted on plates of grilled shrimp at a beachside stand, colorful Italian families shouting and enjoying themselves all around us. Poor Cassie worried where her next meal was going to come from, but I understood Isabel's madness, her need to create deprivation to keep a balance for herself, to convince herself that we weren't those rich people we always seemed to find ourselves among. The next day, when we went up to Mount Etna, donning gray rubber boots and slickers as protection against the active volcano, we stopped afterwards in the bar at the top of the mountain. There were dozens of bottles of liqueurs and digestives behind the bar, and I asked the bartender about several of them.

"Bring us one of every flavor!" Mama said gaily.

He looked dubious but began pouring out each liqueur, covering our table with small glasses of thick liquids of every color and flavor. Mama vacillated between penuriousness and abandon; riding her waves was the only way to enjoy it. We tasted every liqueur from banana to almond; the ground was moving under us ever so slightly before we even stepped back into the funicular that would glide us down the cable to the bottom.

Mama could make anything fun, even disasters . . . like our cruise of the Greek Islands during a miserable storm. Everyone on board was sick except the three of us, the Marsham Girls, as Mama called us. We stoically lurched up to the empty dining room at the appointed hour, met by extremely pale waiters. The seven-course dinner began with a vegetable—canned peas—served all by itself on a platter. Then the dishes and cutlery were changed, and the second course arrived: what looked like an elaborate pastry creation, a baked-Alaska-type mound of swirling pastel colors. We could barely stop laughing when we discovered it was mashed potatoes, dyed and put through a pastry tube. The boat tossed and turned, just the three of us in the dining room, giggling over the pink and green potatoes and our triumph at being the only voyagers who weren't sick. The stops at the islands were wonderful—grottoes filled with wild butterflies, hilly villages reached only on donkeyback, the palace at Crete where we sat in King Minos' throne—but somehow the most wonderful part was the awful storm, the way Mama made it seem the boat was our private yacht and Neptune had thrown a storm our way as a joke, to amuse himself by testing our mettle.

The best trips were the ones I took alone with Mama, perfect companions because we were so alike, the same exorbitant energy level, devouring whatever life had to offer. Traveling with her, I saw how to initiate lasting friendships in a few moments, to hook into people's lives as though they were fellow travelers on an exciting but somewhat perilous voyage and there was no time to waste, one had to seize every minute. But then, that's how she taught me to view all of life.

The two of us drove through the Loire Valley on the way to Grenoble, where Mama was going to study French. Two wayfarers on a pilgrimage to pleasure, we stopped wherever the green Guide Michelin said there was an important château and took detours every time the red Michelin said there was an important eatery. At the château at Chenonceau I was thrilled by the story of the White Queen, who went into mourning for eighteen years after her husband, the king, died, never again wearing anything but white, the royal color for mourning. I would do the same for Mama, I thought, watching the long-necked swans drift in the moat around the castle as we threw bread crumbs. Our symbiosis was so complete that in memory I cannot see myself as physically separate from her: it is one figure, a little blurry around the edges, as though a knobby-kneed, coltish girl and her long-legged thoroughbred of a mother had fused, become one entity.

For the first weeks in Grenoble we lived in a high-rise student dorm and ate meals in the jolly hubbub of the cafeteria. At thirteen, I was the youngest student ever enrolled in the university and became a mascot to the older students whom I helped with their French, since I was fluent and they came from all over the world. Mama and I must have seemed an odd pair to the rest of them, who were twice my age and half my mother's. After the first couple of weeks, we moved into a two-bedroom apartment near the outdoor market, in anticipation of a promised visit from my father. The prospect of his arrival fueled us both, and we dashed about like newlyweds setting up light housekeeping. We bought bright bath towels, fresh flowers and explored the Friday market for new and wonderful things to cook for him when he arrived. Days went by without word, but we remained undaunted.

We bought a cous-cous steamer and taught ourselves how to use it; Mama and I sat on the floor by candlelight, shoveling the yellow grains into our mouths with our fingers. She told me stories of the palaces in Morocco where she and Papa had gobbled cous-cous the same way, two years before. They had left Cassie and me at the villa of old friends where we were all spending the summer; they had worried that Morocco in the summertime would be too hot for children. I had been shocked when they'd returned with the story of Mama fainting in the bazaar, a woman who, on strictest principle, never succumbed to any travelers' afflictions. It made me think that North Africa in summer had to be the hottest place in the world if it had felled Mama, hotter than hell, hotter than when the planets had first exploded and the earth was formed.

After a week in the Grenoble apartment, Mother and I

pretty well knew that Papa wasn't coming. We didn't dare say it aloud, like miners' wives who live in constant threat of disaster but do not speak of it. We continued to experiment with the cous-cous steamer as if that link to their past, to their hot Moroccan trip, would be a lucky charm to bring him to France. As if once we had the recipe really right, he'd appear on the doorstep, his smiling face covered with the freckles he'd passed on to Cassie and me, and he'd be hungry for dinner. I didn't feel so sad myself, just terribly sorry for Mama's disappointment, her hopes of reconciling with him dashed again.

"What am I doing wrong, Blakie?" she'd implore, sobbing on the edge of the narrow double bed she had intended to share with him.

"You have to back off a little, Mama," I said gently, knowing she didn't know how to do anything "a little," least of all back off.

"I try, honey," she sniffled, "I really do. But nothing seems to work . . . I don't know what to do now, honestly . . ."

Her despair would make her cry harder. She probably didn't even see the damage of drawing me into her marital problems, confusing me at a time in development when there was already so much confusion for a girl/woman. But Isabel was pure impulse, an electrical charge that went off at random; she undoubtedly thought it was logical to ask my advice. I was her friend, and I knew that man.

"It's OK, Mom, you just aren't real good at standing back and letting things happen—and you know how much Papa hates to be *asked* to do things; it makes him feel all pressured." I patted her hand as she cried; my hand felt so small. "It's OK, you can't help it," I went on. "But you and me can still have a good old time, can't we?"

Isabel looked up gratefully and wiped away her tears,

like a kid who's been told she can't go to the circus, but never mind, there's always the ice-cream parlor. I gave her such comfort, barely a teenager whose only experience of loving a male had been her dog Pango, her pony Fortune Cookie and then her horse Lancashire Lad. And, of course, her father, the man causing her mother so much pain.

Eleven

They say that sex is a barometer. The pressure was low and falling between Michael and Blake. In affairs before she'd gotten married, Blake had proven that rule wrong, had continued to have strong sex even when a relationship was a beached whale. Marriage made her more honest: it wasn't a game anymore; it was playing for keeps. It was also that she and Michael had never had the kind of passion that a couple can turn to for salve when all else is floundering. They had made love, but they had never really fucked. When their love was in jeopardy, there was nothing else to hold the sex together.

Michael retreated. He stopped touching Blake when they had sex. He did not caress her, nor did he respond to her touch. His skin did not warm under a warm hand, didn't become more alive beneath the erotic wanderings of a woman's fingers. Blake didn't know what to do; she knew that talking about it would create yet another barrier. But what was sex without hands roaming, grazing with an insatiable appetite over a lover's skin, dipping into the crevices, rolling over the roundnesses, combing through the hairs, never tiring of exploring, pleasuring?

Their lovemaking tapered off, but they continued to share a bed in a sweetly childlike way. "Come spoon," Michael would say when he turned out the light. Blake fit in behind him, cupping her front to fit against his back, hugging so close you couldn't have shone a light between them. Michael felt content when they were playful together, two bear cubs, the asexual tumbling of siblings. It was deceptive, that nightly spooning. The comfort of being wedged together could make Blake forget, for a while, that it was a replacement for sexuality, rather than an extension of it. Her timid attempts at discussing their sexual distance were cut off at the pass; Michael refused to concede that their gentle coziness concealed a deadly problem. Blake felt it was like putting a clean cloth over a bowl of maggoty meat, but she continued to spoon and be spooned because there was nothing else.

Sometimes Michael made a move on her when she was asleep. She would surface from the depths of the first heavy hour of unconsciousness to feel a hand on her legs. Once she nearly screamed, thinking someone was attacking her. It felt like rape, being screwed when asleep. Mostly, it felt like nothing: it was so disassociated from real sex, from the joining of something more than body parts. She let him do it because she knew in some recess of her brain that she had driven him into a corner, that the only time he didn't feel threatened was when she was asleep. She wondered if, before he touched her, Michael gazed down at her the way parents watch a hell raiser of a kid in its crib and exclaim, "But what an angel she looks like now . . ." An inert form cannot complain there's no foreplay; Sleeping Beauty won't qualify the kind of orgasms she has.

"But you *came*," Michael would argue when Blake said she didn't really get turned on without kissing first, touching, rubbing. He found he could get Blake to have an orgasm by faking one himself. She told him early on that she had learned with her first boyfriend to time herself to come when he did; now it happened on its own. Michael got so good at faking it that Blake couldn't tell if his orgasms were real or not—not until he smiled at her afterwards. It made her furious, although Michael said he just liked to watch her come, to enjoy her orgasm, then have his own later. He refused to see that it made her feel betrayed, exposed, angry.

"But you *came*."

"Getting off is not making love, Michael. It's just getting off."

All she wanted was for Michael to look at her meltingly, the way a man does when he's inside and his face says, "Right now you are the center of the universe." She wished he would say her name when they were wrapped together, an incantation; or that he'd say, "I don't want ever to leave," when he was inside her, making that poignant connection between sex, pleasure and the transience of life, the knowledge that it will all end too soon. She kept hoping that when she had him in her mouth he would touch her, instead of putting his hands behind his head as though he were sunbathing, as though he were being serviced.

Blake remembered the day she had asked her mother about sex, the glow on Isabel's face.

"Does the man really put it in?" Blake had said in disgust, her face scrunched up at the very idea. "Isn't it icky?"

Isabel had shaken her head slowly with a smile around the corners of her mouth. "It's lovely," she replied, shutting her eyes for an instant to visualize it. "You'll see."

And Blake *had* seen, when the time came, that there was nothing else that happened to a human that came close to good sex.

Michael stopped kissing, during lovemaking or even as an end in itself. He brushed off the subject when Blake tried to raise it.

"Sometimes I just go off kissing."

"Is it the way I kiss?"

"It has nothing to do with you, Blake, it just happens."

"How can it not have to do with me! Maybe I shouldn't be the initiator—or don't you like tongues? What can I do differently?"

"Nothing," Michael answered impatiently. "Except don't make an issue of it."

She felt like a whore, fucking without kissing. Wasn't that their one rule: they don't kiss customers, they only kiss the man they love?

Before long, Michael found ways to avoid lovemaking altogether. If Blake nibbled at his ear as they read in bed, Michael said, "After the eleven o'clock news."

Blake was usually conked out by eleven, but she would prop her eyes open and continue reading as the day's mayhem flickered across the screen: fires, international disasters, earnest politicians, the human miseries watched day-in and day-out by millions of people comforted that they were safe in their naugahyde dens, far from it all. Blake didn't hear the news, only saw the bright images. Michael had compromised about the television and watched it with an earphone. Blake was disturbed by the sight of him transfixed by the set, a thin wire like a hearing aid joining his ear to the box, but it was better than having to hear it herself. When the news wound down, when the incomprehensible weather map came on, Blake put down her book and tried to cozy up to Michael. But she learned that inevitably there was work Michael just had to do.

A dark, sad corner of Blake wondered what she had ever done to deserve this punishment. She wondered if talking about sex had made him push her away, saying he was too tired or there was something too riveting on TV. She knew she wanted a lot; she knew she could be overwhelming, but she didn't understand being cast off. She stopped trying to reach out: get your hand slapped enough times and you keep it to yourself. Yet she couldn't live in limbo; either she was a sexual animal with a hunger that needed feeding, or the impulse had to be shut off completely. Blake wondered if that was what nuns did, will themselves to become numb between their legs? Blake did that. It became a place where pee came out, nothing else, like when she was a little girl. She stopped putting in her diaphragm at night. Sliding it out, unused, in the morning was too grim a reminder of how things were.

When they argued Blake hated herself, hated the way that her disappointment turned her into a bitching shrew. Sometimes she would stop an argument in midstream and announce that she had to go for a walk. Half in a trance, half with the determination of a foot soldier on a long march, she would take to the street, half hoping Michael would run out and stop her, half hoping never to see him again, hoping most of all that she would walk until she got somewhere.

Blake thought of the things she'd heard about her mother's first marriage, that they were one of those couples who fought a lot but got laid a lot, the two activities being linked. Isabel used to tell stories about the short, smiling man with a slightly satanic goatee whom she could lift off the ground with a hug from her five-foot-nine-inch height. She had towered over him in more ways than that; their short, ill-fated liaison had been a series of shouting matches that wound up as passionate truces between the covers. Blake wished that she and Michael could make silk purses from the debris of their fights, rather than a pile of festering pigs' ears. Perhaps they could have had something grand together if they had known how to fight and fuck.

It was hard for Blake to believe that this was really her life, that things were so ugly. It had been so sweet in the beginning, a courtship so rosy that it foretold a lifetime together seen through rose-tinted glasses. Those early moments with Michael were like scenes from a movie, so pretty that they stayed in her mind like famous paintings. But as bad as things became, it still didn't deface the loveliness that had been.

The day after they met, Michael had picked Blake up in his lovingly cared-for old Rover, gray with red leather seats. He was taking her to his tennis club, and they drove over the bridge, murky water churning below them as a tugboat chugged past.

"Our river doesn't look quite so appealing in daylight," she said. "Kind of like women past a certain age."

"I love this river, pollution and all," Michael said. "I wouldn't live anywhere else."

Blake liked his loyalty, felt like a bitch for what she'd said.

They pulled into the parking lot of the River Racquet Club, set in a grimly industrial, partly abandoned area on the other side of the river. It didn't prepare Blake for the shocking beauty when she went through the doors; on the other side of the wall of glass there were terra cotta-colored clay courts, a patch of green grass on the far side and then the river. The sun was high in a blue sky with cottony clouds; the bridge they'd just driven over arced boldly across the shining water, where a few boats glided past. Blake went straight out the glass doors, past the courts to a wooden deck with chairs on the riverbank. On the other side of the river, skyscrapers reflected the sun like sheets of mica. She had never seen the city from this bank, never seen New York so beautiful. It was an exquisitely innocent beauty, the beauty of a girl who doesn't yet know how gorgeous she is. The river and the Chrysler building and the bright sun and the boats and the sound of tennis balls filled Blake with a surge of joy, gratitude to be alive.

Michael came up behind her.

"You sure hit a home run with this one," Blake said.

"How about hitting some tennis?"

Blake couldn't take her eyes off the crystalline vision of the river.

Michael put his hand on her shoulder. "It'll still be here when we finish, I promise."

Blake smiled and followed him back to the court. She looked down at the blond hair on his tanned, muscular legs and was struck by the Greek-statue-perfect proportions of his body. She let her eyes travel past his crisp white shorts to his white knit shirt. She noticed it was fraying around the collar and thought how she could mend it the way Maria had taught her—and how bloody absurd it was for all that domestic bullshit to click on the minute she liked a man.

They hit the ball well together, long, solid ground strokes to the baseline, finding a rhythm that was almost hypnotic. Blake hit the ball hard—graceful, tough strokes that gave her a rush of pleasure. She felt sexy hitting the ball that way: aggressively, powerfully, like a man.

Afterwards, they leaned against the wooden deck railing, resting their drinks and watching the river. Two small children ran and played on the grass, their exuberant laughter filling the air. Their mother was hitting on an adjacent court and stopped for a minute to watch them. Michael and Blake both saw it, saw the woman's loving expression, saw the joyous delight of the little ones.

"Nobody seems to want kids these days."

"Couples who want them are looked at like freaks," Blake replied.

"*Couples*—ones that stay together—are considered weird!"

They watched the murky water slap against the wood pilings beneath them. They thought about couples, the sorry state of modern relationships, about being different, beating the odds.

"Children are a gift," Michael said. "A second childhood, except this time it's how *you* want it to be."

"No religion, though," Blake said. "I'd never let a child of mine be brainwashed."

"Absolutely," Michael agreed. "Atheism, free will."

Discussing it moved them to another level, across a threshold. Once they'd raised the subject, there was no turning back, like an Italian country boy who is automatically engaged to a girl if he sets foot inside her parent's house. Now Michael and Blake's children were linked in their minds. She pictured their offspring scampering around naked, bright-eyed, godless.

"I wish you could have met my mother," Blake said as they drove back into the city.

"I feel as though I have."

"Katharine Hepburn in *Philadelphia Story*, that was my mother to a tee," Blake said, smiling a cheerfully sad smile. She thought of the way Michael had looked at her, as though he had seen Isabel and fallen a little in love with her, too. "The last time I went riding with my mother was the second time we lived in Rome," Blake reminisced. "We rode in the Borghese Gardens, miles of bridle paths in the middle of the city. We rode the horses of an amazing sixty-year-old contessa who rode with us, sidesaddle, in a dark-green, long skirt. It made me eager to reach sixty and be just like her, a prancing horse with an arched neck dancing underneath her. 'Never say a word about money to the contessa,' Mother would caution me. 'Italians are more sensitive about being down on their uppers than the English.' The contessa's family had once owned the Borghese Gardens, and there she was, reduced to renting out her horses."

Blake paused as she remembered how her mother's hair dissolved into wispy Victorian curls around her face after a good canter and the stately, lace-up hunt boots she wore that had been made for her when she had hunted as a young woman in Canada. Blake wondered what sort of castles Isabel's family had owned in Edinburgh before crossing the ocean. "Edinbra!" Isabel used to pronounce it triumphantly, accenting the last syllable. "The Stewart clan!" Blake finished her story: "So after we rode, we shook hands with the contessa and thanked her graciously for the pleasure, and she asked if we wouldn't take tea with her, and we declined because of other engagements but thanked her profusely all over again. Then, once we got home, Mama sent her a check in the mail, protecting her aristocratic illusions."

"Nice," Michael said. He put his hand at the back of her neck. Blake could feel her pulse, deep and strong, against him.

They were sitting cross-legged in front of the fireplace back at Michael's apartment. Blake's hair was stringy wet, and she was only wearing one of Michael's Brooks Brothers shirts. He had on a terry robe and a towel around the back of his neck, tucked in the front like an ascot. They had taken a long, hot shower together. The pizza they'd called for had arrived sooner than they'd expected. There was still a trail of dark, wet footprints across the wood floor from the bedroom to the front door. They ate the pizza and listened to Mozart quintets.

"Listen to that," Michael said, and they both stopped chewing, listened to a melody and shook their heads in wonderment.

"Oh, I love this part," Blake said, and they did the same.

Michael tried to take a swig out of his empty beer bottle, and Blake stood up. "I'll get you another." When she came back, Michael had such an odd expression on his face that she hesitated before sitting back down.

"Come here," he said, reaching out to take the bottle of Beck's with one hand and her with the other. Blake sat down close to him. "I want you to do something for me," he announced. Blake looked at him, waiting to hear. "OK?" he prompted.

She wondered what sort of test he was going to put her to—that they not see each other for a while, that it was going too fast? "Sure, of course," she said.

Michael took a leather jeweler's box out of his bathrobe pocket. Blake's heart skipped; her stomach clamped down. She was filled with a sense of doom—she dreaded the ring that was in there. She didn't know what to say, how to explain, but the idea of marriage—of admitting her vulnerability when there were no guarantees, of letting herself depend on his love as she had on Isabel's—well, it was too scary. It was just so damn chancy. She looked at him tentatively, pained by her misgivings because he was so fabulous, so perfect for her, really. It had happened so quickly, she'd barely had time to come up for air. She didn't know what to say, because whatever words came out they would both remember for the rest of their lives—so she said nothing. She opened the box, forcing herself not to shut her eyes. Her smile was as much relief as was delight in the glimmering emerald earrings.

"What I want you to do for me is pierce your ears, OK?"

"Just for you," Blake said, putting her arms around his neck. "Oh, they're so beautiful, Michael, I . . ." She took them out and held one up to the firelight. "I have to look in the mirror," she said, starting to get up.

Michael caught her by the wrist and looked at her so intensely she had to look down for a minute. "Next time it's going to be what you thought," he said. When he was sure his words had sunk in, Michael took Blake in his arms and buried her in a kiss lit up by flickers of firelight.

When she looked back on how sweet it had been in the beginning, Blake was even more horrified by how bad it had become, at how paradise could turn into an inferno in front of her very eyes.

Twelve

When I was Papa's little girl, life was a fairy tale; vibrant, delightful. We were in total synchrony, like a silver anniversary couple we could telegraph thoughts with a glance, see something and both burst out laughing. I found my prince early in life. Everything since then pales by comparison, as if the early years were deep red on a color chart which fades lighter and lighter as the years go by. No matter how good it may get now, there is always that pure dark red up there to measure the present against. No man really has a fair chance when I had such a charmed childhood.

Magic could happen at any time. One summer our family took a cottage outside the town of Honfleur with its boat-studded harbor. It was almost absurdly picturesque: every Impressionist painter represented in the Jeu de Paume gallery did a rendering of Honfleur. Our month under the thatched-roof cottage covered in hotly pink roses was so pleasant it drifted by like a dream, a wash of days under wide, colorful umbrellas on the Deauville beach, sand and water shimmering for miles under the soft Normandy sun. Then one day Cassandra had a tummy ache. Mama and Maria, our Italian nanny, stayed to soothe her; Papa and I took off for a bite of lunch *à deux*.

Heading on the road towards Deauville, planning on a hot sausage sandwich and some ice cream, Papa impulsively turned down a steep, narrow road into a small seaside village. We drove slowly, admiring the quaint old buildings and cobblestone street, until we came to a white stone archway with the word "Restaurant" above it. Papa and I looked at each other, then back at the entryway, a rabbit hole for two Alices.

"How bad can it be?" he said rhetorically. "We're in France, right?"

Walking under the arch, we reached a white gravel courtyard with flower-hung balconies on all four sides and a cluster of white-linened tables in the center under a trellis of pale green vines. Somewhere birds sang.

A smartly attired maître d' welcomed us, bowing slightly as though we were the guests of honor they'd been waiting for at this mad tea party. The place was much fancier than the flimsy beach clothes we had on, but no one seemed to notice. With a secret smile at each other, we followed the captain to a table in the middle of this gleaming jewel of a place. They brought my father's Heineken and my Coke in separate silver ice buckets that gleamed in the midday sun; the waiter wrapped each bottle in a white cloth with the same attentiveness one would give champagne and poured our glasses half full. Whenever we took a sip, someone was there to replenish the glass.

Papa and I hadn't said a word since he'd ordered the drinks, afraid to break the spell. We sat grinning like kids at a birthday party. Rows and rows of shiny silverware fell away on either side of our hand-painted service plates, and I imagined we'd be there until nightfall if we had to eat enough courses to justify all that cutlery. We unfolded the starched white napkins and bobbed our heads in thanks to the solicitous maître d' when he presented us with huge, hand-written menus, holding them so reverently they could have been the Dead Sea scrolls. Papa lifted his beer glass towards me, a toast which I mirrored reflexively so that we both swallowed our cold, bubbly drinks at the same moment.

My father's lobster bisque was served in a bowl that sat on two plates, and when he finished the thick, clay-red serving they offered him seconds, bringing a fresh spoon and bowl. My country pâté was bordered by a little garden of greens and shiny cubes of gelatin that jiggled gaily in the sun. I ate them one by one, spearing each one on a tine of my fork to make it last longer.

"Cass hates the gelatin," I said, congratulating my own sophistication. What I was really acknowledging was the touch of guilt about having this magical treat while my little sister sat at home with a stomach ache.

"No kidding?" Papa said sarcastically. Cassie's dislike of "that gushy junk" was a well-known fact which she reiterated at every charcuterie stop. "You mean I shouldn't fill my pockets with jelly to bring back to her?"

I gave him an "Oh, Papa . . ." look, loving to be teased by him, loving the undercurrent of flirtation.

The whole meal went on like a feast at the Aga Khan's —endless tureens and new plates and crisply starched waiters—so that by the time the individual apple tarts arrived, swimming in custard sauce, I could barely pick up my fork. I was paralyzed by its beauty, the steaming apples against the pale yellow, yet unsure whether I could fit in another bite. I glanced up at Papa, who was giving his dessert the same weary look. We started to laugh as we caught sight of each other, giddy with our good fortune, with the perfume of the hanging flowers all around, the opulence of the meal and the joy of being off together.

When Papa's espresso came, he pushed the cup towards me automatically, and I unwrapped a sugar cube. I dipped the edge in his coffee, the blackness seeping into the white square. I sucked on it like sucking nectar out of a tiger lily. I dipped the cube again, and this time it came apart in my mouth, the sweetness dissolving around the spicy bitterness of the espresso. Then Papa took a cigar out of his breast pocket. I took out a match from the box on the table, waiting for him to get the cigar ready. He clipped a hole in the end with the silver folding cigar clip on his key ring, then he leaned forward for me to put the fire under it. I struck the match and let the sulfur burn off as he had taught me. I held the flame far beneath the end of the cigar so that only the heat reached the tobacco, not the flame itself. Papa slowly turned the cigar between his lips until it was evenly lit all the way around. I blew out the match as it reached my fingers and watched solemnly as he took the cigar out of his mouth, then blew lightly on the end to make it glow, to be sure it was well lit so it would burn smoothly. He nodded his head and took an appreciative puff. I put the matches down proudly. When we finally got up from the table in the crystal-white courtyard, we held hands and vowed to keep this our secret, never to come here again with anyone else, ever.

We got back into the hot car, steamy vinyl replacing the aroma of hot pastry in our noses.

"Want to see where you first learned to ride?" Papa suggested.

We drove past miles of beach with gay rows of umbrellas spinning in the wind like multicolored flying saucers; jaunty waiters intent on their trays navigated with drinks between the canvas sling chairs. I could see people in the water pulling themselves up onto the off-shore floats, covered with damp sisal mat. It smelled like a hayloft when you lay down on it, puffing from the long swim out there, and left marks on your cheek if you stayed very long. Papa took one wrong turn, but otherwise the force of his memory got us right to the stable with its small sawdust circle, bordered by low blocks like a circus ring.

"There's Monsieur Roberge!" I said in wonderment, as much because I'd remembered his name as because he was still there. Waxed, pencil-thin mustache, ascot tucked in at the neck, riding britches with a wide crescent flared out at the thigh and brown lace-up boots against which he slapped a riding crop.

Papa and I got out of the car and went over to the three-horse barn. There was a small girl cantering around the ring on a bareback pony. I had been only five when I had ridden here, but I could tell that she was fighting the impulse to grab hold of the handle on the bareback pad. The patient horse went round and round as she held on for dear life with pudgy little legs clamped around the pony's fat sides, while Monsieur Roberge's whip-crackling voice barked out a command I remembered too well, *"Deux mains en air!"* The child timidly stuck her sunburned little arms up above her head like the victim of a stickup as the pony cantered on.

"That's the part where poor Cassie always fell off," I whispered sympathetically to my father as we watched.

We all used to cringe when Cassandra hit the ground and turned her tearstained face plaintively towards the three other members of her family on the sidelines. We tried to smile encouragingly, knowing that what she really wanted was rescuing; when it wasn't forthcoming, she bravely picked herself up out of the sawdust where she'd fallen, thump! under the belly of the pony who picked his way carefully over her before coming to a well-trained halt. Most of the students bit the dust from time to time. Cassie's problem was that her older sister never did. When Cass took too long brushing off the sawdust, buying time on terra firma, M. Roberge would command, *"Allons-y, mademoiselle!"* With a last pleading look in our direction, she remounted the pony, standing on one of the blocks that formed the circle, pulling herself up in a vaulting motion onto the horse's back like a little circus performer.

Mama would turn to Papa and say, trying to convince herself, "It's best for her."

"That's the way they learn," he would reply dispiritedly. Then they would look over at me for confirmation, their elder daughter, the one who stuck like glue, a natural little jockey.

I graduated to the saddle before Cassandra. M. Roberge would say, *"Le cheval noir pour mademoiselle"* to the stable hand, whom I would follow proudly over to the larger circle where a small black horse awaited those who had passed muster bareback; here one performed the same acrobatic feats in a saddle, but without using reins. Each time my knobby knees would be rubbed raw, but I was so pleased with this badge of accomplishment that I wouldn't let Maria fuss over it, even when the blood seeped right through my pants. Cassie, meanwhile, continued in the bareback ring, an expression of utter terror coming over her when she got the command to stand on the horse's back at a canter. Sometimes she'd manage without falling, making her ascent the way we were taught: first she got her feet on the pony's back in a hunched-over, leapfrog position; then she slowly rose as she got her balance. It was a toss-up whether she was more terrified of that or the order to *"Girez-le-monde, s'il-vous plait.*" She had to swing both legs onto one side of the horse, clinging tightly to the handle on the pad, then shift so she was cantering facing backwards, then swing both legs to the opposite side of the horse until she came full circle again, with one leg on either side facing front. I never knew why she didn't just quit.

"Do you think that's still Sambo?" I asked my father of the pony going around with the girl on its back.

The brown markings on her white sides looked different from Sambo's, but there was the same sad look in her eyes, resigned to a lifetime of carrying children around in circles. When I asked the stable boy, he said it was Sambo's daughter, that Sambo had gotten too old. It made *me* feel old that my first horse's daughter had already taken her place. Papa and I stood side by side, watching the girl as she tremulously stood up on the pony's back, the circle so small that she and the horse leaned in towards the center like the tower of Pisa. My memory of myself merged with the girl, and for a moment my father and I turned back the clock, history turning inside out on itself.

Papa used to come in every night to tell us a bedtime story, but he didn't read from a book like other fathers. Our father made up stories just for us, spinning out a yarn bit by bit each night and incorporating into it things that really happened to us. He made a monster seem harmless by naming it after our diminutive, soft-spoken Chinese piano teacher; he built in double jokes, like naming a flying dachshund Alberto after our gardener because Cassandra had once said his fingers looked like sausages. Papa told the stories sitting on one of our beds, and I never took my eyes off his face, riveted on his expressions and the different voices he used, acting out the story. I wondered at the magical mystery of where it all came from, how Papa could pour out a saga for weeks, remembering the characters, inventing new ones, creating dreadful dangers, thrilling escapes and puzzling clues, pulling us along like a pied piper. It was the best way in the world to fall asleep, knowing that under the same roof was a wizard—who could tell stories, fix anything, make good things even better. The sun rose and set on him.

As a girl I made a secret vow that I'd die for him. I had visions of an enemy army coming up the driveway in a tank and demanding hostages. The threat of invasion came from bomb-shelter practice at school, where we had to huddle together under our desks with our coats pulled over our heads in a sort of demented game of "sardines." In my fantasy the captain would not accept me when I offered to be taken instead of my father, but with red-flushed cheeks I'd insist, "It doesn't matter if I'm younger; he's more worthy." My imagined scenario didn't frighten me; it made me feel good.

There was nothing Papa could not do. I went to him if I got a splinter, was stumped by homework or had a bad fight with Cassandra. Sometimes I'd shout up at the window of his third-floor office so he'd watch me canter figure eights with Lannie down on the front lawn. Sometimes it was for more important things. He was the one I told when I first got my period; I got home from school aching with cramps, having survived a whole day of anxiety about whether the toilet paper I'd stuffed in my underpants was going to fall out in the lunchroom. He came downstairs to have a snack with Cassie and me after school; he could tell something was up and asked. He kissed me on the cheek and said, "Well what do you know! That's great, you're becoming a woman, Blakie."

Cassie scowled, envious of yet another in a string of things I'd gotten and done before her. "I don't see why you're *smiling*, Blake," she said, as if calling my bluff, "if it really *hurts* so much . . ."

Papa gave her a kiss, too, and said, "Don't worry, Beensy, all in good time."

One of the loveliest treats was peeking into Papa's study for no good reason, even though the rule was not to disturb him unless necessary. I'd sneak up behind his big oak desk and beam with pleasure when his face lit up. He chewed gum when he was working; I'd hop onto his lap and open my mouth like a baby bird in the nest. "Oh, *Blakie* . . ." he'd say, feigning annoyance. I made hungry-little-bird cheeping noises until he put the Doublemint gum he'd been chewing into my upturned mouth and sent me scampering back downstairs. Most of the sweetness was gone, but it was warm and soft and seemed the most delicious prize in the world.

As though I were his firstborn son, I was a valiant tomboy, covered in sticky black resin from climbing the tallest pine tree, knees scraped from playing flies-up, my arms aching from practicing lay-up shots into the basketball hoop above the garage. Papa did everything with Cassie and me; we hit tennis balls, played a modified version of ice hockey when the ponds froze over up in the country and we built a rabbit hutch following the instructions of a U.S. government pamphlet. Papa even cooked us pancakes on Sunday mornings and created one of our favorite treats, hard-boiled eggs, fried. One Easter we had baskets of leftover eggs, which he put through the egg slicer and cooked crispy brown in butter.

Going fishing with Papa was a major expedition as we sallied forth into Long Island Sound, surrounded by coolers of beer, root beer and multi-ingredient sandwiches. Mother was a big believer in generous sandwiches, and when we picnicked in Europe, Cassandra and I were often shocked by the meager sandwiches of English or Italian friends—a speck of filling, mostly bread. Chintzy sandwiches were one of our criteria to judge people by as we dribbled mayonnaise down our chins from sandwiches of cold roast veal, peppers and cheese.

Cass and I knew how to bait our own hooks—an accomplishment of particular pride, since most girls were too squeamish. After lacing the centipede worms onto our hooks, we sent the lines down to the bottom with weights. Papa cut the engine way back and we trolled, holding the rods to the side of the boat, the putt-putt-putt of the engine creating background music for our chatter.

We wore hats to protect our fair skin from the sun, great straw boaters we'd chosen that morning from the luggage room. There were mountains of suitcases and trunks plastered with tags of long-ago journeys; on the shelves above was Mother's eclectic accumulation of hats, collected over the years while sightseeing in sun-parched villages or lounging on blue-water beaches. Sometimes the hats went flying into the water when we got a bite and jerked up and reeled too hastily. Papa dipped the net under the fish as we pulled it out of the water, shiny and flapping, and onto the deck with our sandwich remains. Blowfish were a startling thrill; touching the sandpapery skin as it blew up with air, expanding until it looked as if it would explode. Then we circled the boat to where the hat had landed, and Papa nabbed it with a long-handled hook. After a long day in the sun and sea air, it was as comforting as mother's milk to get home and sit at the candle-lit dinner table while Reggie served the sweet, firm fish we had caught ourselves.

Going to the theater with Papa was the quintessence of being his little girls, out on the town with him and Mama. They took us to see every play and musical that would even remotely interest children, and afterwards we went to Sardi's. There were always people Papa knew . . . it felt as though the air around us were full of silver sparkles on evenings like that; when handsome people embraced my father and mother and exclaimed over Cassandra and me in our matching dresses, puffed up with petticoats. Papa adored the theater, and our enthusiasm was partly vicarious. As a poor boy he had snuck into theaters at intermission—he knew the second half of a hundred plays. But by the time he was taking us to Broadway, we always got producer's seats, fourth row center. Everything was peachy when we were all together; it seemed as though my seats in life were fourth row center.

It's hard to say at what point Papa's travels kept him away longer and longer, because the times when he was home were so jubilant. Like the huge meal a bear eats before hibernating, our times with Papa sustained us long after he left again. He never failed to materialize on a birthday to put on one of his elaborate puppet shows, dozens of exotic puppets which he brought alive in a full-size puppet theater. And he took movies of every birthday, chronicling the children's costumes and clowns' tricks, the games and prizes and the grand finale of Cassie or me cutting our cake, wedding-size creations with miniature merry-go-rounds twirling above the gooey white icing or artistic renderings of Fortune Cookie and Pennies from Heaven. Perhaps Mama made such a big deal out of our birthdays not just because she did everything big, but because it was also a celebration for her that Papa had returned. Years later, when the movies were all that was left of a certain time in our lives, they gave the illusion that he was there, had not been gone so much. He'd been there, hadn't he, behind the camera, capturing it all for posterity?

As Cassie and I got older and Papa was around less, we learned to seize time with him and make the most of it. There was the end of one summer when Cassandra and I wound up in Malta, a dreary spit of land the English had once controlled and then wisely relinquished. It was hot, boring and claustrophobic, and Cass and I wanted to get back to the States to see our father. We had joined up with Mama in Malta, where she was tracking down some terribly important ruin with an art-historian friend. Cass had been assisting on an Etruscan dig near Rome, and I'd been on a trip with the Touring Club de France around Greece. I'd already been there twice with my mother and sister, but it was a whole new kettle of fish to eat and sleep my way through a country second-class instead of deluxe. I discovered how sheltered I was, despite all my travels, when I was utterly shocked by the whispered stories told me by Greek students who said the CIA had subsidized the cruel Greek junta. Until then I'd thought the worst thing America had ever done was export Coca-Cola.

Cassandra and I were fidgety young teenagers that summer and begged off going on Mama's island expeditions. That left the grand old British Officer's Club as our sole amusement, a remnant of their once-glorious domination of the island. The attendants still wore colonial white with braided gold epaulets, but they were as rickety as the retired colonels they served. Tall mugs of Pimm's cup slid precariously across their trays as they shuffled arthritically through the imposing salon; the ice was melted by the time they reached their destination. Wood fans turned somnambulistically, uselessly. By the time a waiter reached his destined customer, a wide-mustached brigadier who had "done India" and wore the medals to prove it, he had often fallen asleep, his bulldog face twitching with dream-memories of the grand days when Britannia ruled the seas. The only hope for Cassie and me was to go see Papa.

After four days of walking to the Malta telegraph office and getting no reply from our father, we booked a plane anyway. I told Mama that we'd find him, or there was sure to be at least one person we knew stuck in New York at the end of August. We had one of our rare arguments— she called me a spoiled, ungrateful teenager when I said that getting mugged on a hot subway was better than being stuck on the ass-end of the earth—but the tiff was at least in part about Papa. By now she had learned to live with the fact that we would see him and she would not, but she didn't like it any better.

In the New York airport, giddy from jet lag and our successful escape, we got a handful of dimes and started dialing. We managed to track Papa down through his lawyer. Papa sounded genuinely delighted and not very surprised at our solo trip home that had required two plane changes; we'd been making grand and grown-up jaunts alone for years.

"Can I go get Pandora before we come to East Hampton?" I pleaded. All summer long I'd fantasized my reunion with Pango's sweet puppy, imagined it as a romantic, slow-motion run towards each other with Pandy jumping up into my arms. I adored her ebullient affection.

"Let's wait; come out here first, Blakie."

"I can't wait, Papa. I've just got to have a hug from that little rascal," I insisted, even after he pointed out the impracticality of getting to a kennel in Connecticut.

"Darling, I wanted to be with you when I told you this," my father said, pushed into a corner. "But Pandy's gone, Blake, there was an accident. . . ."

I dropped the receiver; the blood plummeted to my feet and I went down with it, my bottom hitting the cold, hard floor, my back braced against the wall. A terrible acid taste sprang into my mouth, and everything went still—all I could hear in the tumult of the airport was the thumping of my heart.

Cassie picked up the receiver and nodded, listening carefully to whatever Papa was telling her. She looked down at me with the desperate empathy that only siblings can feel, experiencing the same pain and injustice when the other one is hurt or punished. She put out her hand and touched my head; through the tears I saw crushed cigarette butts on the floor around me, baggage-claim stubs and bits of crumpled paper, the remnants of people's long journeys home. It is always such a long way home.

My sister handed the phone back to me, and I controlled my sobs enough to hear my father's soothing voice. "I wish I could be there right now to hold you, darling, the way I wanted to. I'm so sorry you had to hear like this, but you were so eager. . . ."

"But I loved her so much, Daddy," I said, then broke into miserable sobs again. I hadn't even told him yet about the lump Mama had found in her breast, that her friend had been so worried about.

"I know, Blakie, I know," my father said, his voice pained. "It hurts like hell to lose Pandora, but you were lucky to have loved her, for her to have loved you back. No matter what, you'll always have that. . . ." He waited awhile; when my crying went on and on, he made his voice even softer and said, "Now, you two get your freckled bottoms out here so Papa can make it all better, OK?"

Somehow, those five days at the beach were idyllic, a reaffirmation of life. Papa, Cassandra and I rode the surf by day and went with undaunted optimism to the drive-in at night. And every night it was so thick with fog that they sent everyone home with free tickets for the following night. Somehow, the pain of losing Pandy made those unexpected days with Papa all the more glorious. We floated in that suspended piece of time together, stuffing ourselves full of the last corn of summer and brick-red lobsters.

One night after eating, Cassandra and I went out on the night-damp sand and danced together in the moonlight to the faint, scratchy strains of an old record that Papa had found and put on a record player, perched on a windowsill. I could feel him watching our wonderfully foolish turns on the awkward sand, and it gave me a feeling of being a flashback in a lovely, old-fashioned movie— a misty scene recalling the way things were.

Dancing can do that, twirl you back to simpler, sweeter bygone days. The first night I met Michael, we danced together. He stole my heart.

Michael's apartment overlooked the East River, which was visible from nearly every room. When he lit the candles scattered at strategic points throughout the living room, the city's night-lights reflected off the black surface of the river far below; it was impossibly beautiful. Michael put on Willie Nelson's *Stardust* album—romantic, old-fashioned songs from before our time that managed to make me feel nostalgic all the same. We stood talking beside the fireplace, two tall candles in pewter sticks quavering near our faces. What a pretty picture we must make, I thought, how perfect we were together.

"All of Me" started to play. Michael took two steps and held me in his arms. We began to dance, slow and easy. It was just one of those things; it happens, that's all, but even as I was wrapped up in it, I knew I'd look back on this moment years down the road, a keepsake to take out and hold in my palm. Michael danced like a man from his father's generation, real dancing. It reminded me of Miss Harris' ballroom-dancing classes in fifth grade.

Inside Miss Harris' prim town house a group of chil-

dren gathered every Wednesday afternoon. The invitation
to attend the series involved an interview and two recom-
mendations—my mother told Cassandra and me that she
thought it was "all a lot of social hooey, but it's your free
time, and you can use it in jackass pursuits if you want."
I loved standing at the top of the stairs, music tinkling
up from down below, where dozens of dainty cushioned
chairs surrounded the shiny parquet dance floor. A be-
spectacled old maid was the pianist, a dried-up old prune
who would have joined a nunnery if she hadn't found her
calling preparing little lambs to enter Society.

Miss Harris greeted each child at the bottom of the
stairs with a tight-lipped smile. "Good afternoon, Miss
Harris," each little girl said, curtseying in her Mary Janes
and lacy-white ankle socks. "Good afternoon, Miss Harris,"
the boys said as they bowed, their hair slicked back with
water. Then we were each formally introduced to the
guest for the afternoon, whatever snow-haired, pearl-
strangled biddy Miss Harris had corralled into contribut-
ing to the social indoctrination of the next generation.
The half-blind, half-deaf old codger gingerly shook the
children's immaculately white-gloved hands, the sweaty
grime of a hard day's play at school concealed. "I would
like the pleasure of introducing Miss Muckety-Muck,"
Miss Harris intoned, and we had to curtsey and bow all
over again.

The boys and girls warmed up to each other after the
first few stiff fox-trots, breaking their self-imposed segre-
gation of the sexes. We were really enjoying ourselves by
the time Miss Harris announced, "Ladies' choice: a cha-
cha, please." I tried valiantly to follow when dancing—
tried hard well into adulthood, where Miss Harris' crinkly
voice pursued me with the admonishment, "It is the *gen-
tleman* who leads, Miss Marsham. Young ladies do not
lead." I tried everything: I tried to forget about my feet,

tried not to listen to the music, not to second-guess the boy's next move. I tried not to be a leader, to be a young lady, but I couldn't. I simply had not been raised to follow.

Michael and I stopped dancing as naturally as we began. I wished it could have gone on forever. Michael kissed me tenderly on the forehead, a longish kiss. We hadn't said a word to one another since we'd started dancing, which made the kiss even more important, a receptacle for all our thoughts. I turned my face up to Michael's, expecting to start a serious kiss, but he took my jaw gently in his hand.

"I'm going to take you home now," he said softly, with a hint of apology.

"OK . . ." I said, drawing the word out so that he could explain if he wanted to.

"We've got all the time in the world," he said, still gazing into my eyes.

I knew he meant this was special, worth waiting for; there was no sense letting him know that my philosophy was that nothing delicious should be delayed in life. I wanted him more than I could remember wanting anything; I could imagine the taste of his skin in my mouth, the feel of him deep inside me. If it meant waiting, so be it. It seemed as though it would always be like when we were dancing: effortless, dreamlike, as though we knew the next move by osmosis, as if we'd been dancing partners for years.

Thirteen

Blake's craziness first surfaced at night, in bed. Suddenly the darkness would engulf her, swallow her into a black hole; the bed seemed to disintegrate beneath her, and Blake would freeze, afraid to move, afraid of free-falling into the bottomless blackness. It happened on nights when she and Michael had had a fight—which was to say when she had pushed, had wanted a response, and he had withdrawn further and further into his shell, which whipped her into a frustrated frenzy. He tried to escape, to go into another room until it had blown over, but she pursued, trying to push buttons in him until finally she gave up, slunk away in ashamed anger; only to slink back, tail between her legs, apologizing. But the problem was still there, immovable, unresolved, and the fight would permeate her like a drug that stays in the bloodstream. The darkness in bed got deeper and deeper until she knew that she had to get up, get away from Michael, from the malevolent forces binding her to him.

She had to summon all her courage to pull herself out of the sinking blackness, summon all her strength to creep across the bedroom floor. She was terrified of waking Michael, a dormant Jack in the Beanstalk; she had to creep by him, escape with the golden goose, her sanity. Halfway out the door, her tiptoeing awakened him.

"Where are you going?" He had smelled the blood of an Englishman.

"I want to sleep on the sofa." She was trembling from the horrible black pit beneath that bed; she knew she had to get away to survive.

"Come back to bed and cut it out," Michael snapped, annoyed with what he thought was her manipulative attention getting. His tone of voice frightened her in its sternness, the fear of a child confronted by authority.

"Please, I want to sleep in there; just let me do it."

"I don't want you sleeping on the couch; it's absurd."

But she was already in the living room, wrapped cocoon-like in a mohair lap blanket. She lay in tense, alert silence, not breathing, an animal in the forest waiting for danger. She heard Michael throw back the bedclothes and the dull sound of his bare feet heading towards the living room. She was panic-stricken, terrified of what he would do to her, although he'd never indicated the least sign of violence.

"Please don't," Blake mumbled through her frightened tears. "Stay away, leave me alone."

He sat down on the edge of the sofa, and Blake pulled her legs aside as if he were fire. She was shivering all over; she twitched when Michael put his hand on her.

"No, don't! I'm scared," she pleaded.

Michael stroked her trembling body, distressed. "What are you afraid of?"

"You . . . I want to die, it's killing me."

"I'd never hurt you, Blake."

"I can't bear it anymore; I hate myself in this marriage; I hate how I am to you. . . ." She started to sob.

"It'll be all right, Blakie, we'll work it out. Come back to bed."

"No, please let me be alone." She felt shriveled and trapped, thinking of how she'd spoken to him earlier, ugly, bitter snarling. "There's no way to fix it," she said, trembling. She hated herself for pushing him away, hated him for frustrating her into self-loathing, into the shame of sounding like a fishwife.

"I don't want you to be unhappy, Blake."

"I know you don't, Michael."

"You take the bed; I'll sleep in here."

Blake protested hysterically, begging him just to leave her, sobbing, not knowing whether she felt sorrier for how low she was sinking or for the tortured confusion on Michael's face. She didn't even try to explain how terrifying that bed was, the air over it thick with evil, the black hole beneath it that wanted to pull her down. Out of exhaustion she followed him back to bed and lay there stiffly beside Michael, who fell asleep thinking he had patched things up by bringing her back in. Blake lay rigid, keeping vigil against the horrifying madness that had engulfed her, wondering when it would return. She slipped out of bed and onto the floor, comforted by the solidity, hard as the monks' cells she had seen as a child, with indentations in the stone floors from penitent years of sleeping there, emulating Saint Peter or Paul; it had seemed so severe, but maybe only a hoax. Blake had always been so happy; life had been so delicious; who could have guessed she was capable of such misery? Blake could not understand where this torture had come from, or why. It reminded her of when they had gelded her pony.

They had told her parents it was dangerous to have a stallion, so the vet came over one afternoon. The doctor's nonchalance made her think it was a simple procedure, although he said it would be best if she waited indoors. Fortune Cookie was lying on his side, his front legs bound together and his hind legs tied to a tree; he seemed calm after the tranquilizer. She patted him a friendly farewell, expecting that he'd be out cold under the anesthetic when she saw him next.

When she came back outside, they told her he was in the barn. It took a few moments for her eyes to adjust to the darkness from the sunlight, and then she saw him, standing in a corner, still as a statue. She walked slowly towards him, sensing something was very wrong. As she got closer, she saw the blood pouring from where they had cut him, running down the inside of his back legs, soaking the straw a bright red. He stood stock-still. His eyes didn't even seem to register that she was there; he just stared straight ahead.

"Oh, sweet boy, I'm sorry, I'm so sorry," Blake whispered, holding her cheek against the soft side of his muzzle. His nostrils were flaring from the pain, but otherwise he remained motionless.

Blake ran out to where her father stood talking to the vet. Out of breath, she blurted questions with her hot tears of anger. The doctor replied that they didn't use painkillers to avoid complications; they didn't use stitches because the wound healed by itself; he said not to worry. Her father put his arm around her shoulder, but Blake yanked her head away; her braid caught on his belt, and some hairs ripped out on the buckle. *She* wasn't the one who needed comforting.

Fortune Cookie refused the carrots and apples she brought him. It made her feel worse, but she admired him for it. He still would not budge. He flinched when she sponged near the cut with fly repellent, but it was only a reflex; he didn't even swish his tail at the flies buzzing all around him. Blake cleaned out the straw from beneath him, half expecting a kick in the head. Then she got a brush of water and tried to scrub the wall where the blood had spattered. It would not come clean; that angry bloodstain will not let anyone forget, Blake thought.

She stayed by his side all that afternoon and evening. Maria brought her supper out to the barn, but Blake sent it back, refused to eat if he wouldn't. Finally—finally—he lay down. She sat beside him, running her hand lightly on his fat brown flank the way her mother sometimes stroked her head when she was reading aloud. The afternoon faded into a hot, dark summer night; the flies left, the fireflies came to life out in the field. What had this poor dear animal ever done to deserve this? Blake wondered. How could she have permitted this horror, this betrayal? She had imagined it was going to be a little nick, a vasectomy; she'd had no idea they would subject him to such butchery. What must he think of her, of the world?

"Life isn't fair," she whispered in his ear, "and I'm sorry for that, Cookie." But until her marriage, Blake did not truly believe that, did not understand such torture.

What Blake could not understand was that she could not change Michael, could not force him to be a man who responded the way she wanted him to. Yet she believed her mother's puritan work ethic: she would succeed if she kept her nose to the grindstone. All Blake managed to do was rub her nose raw. Nonetheless, she kept at it, determined to conquer, watching disdainfully as other couples split up.

"Everybody in our generation is so impatient," she said to Cassie. "They won't tolerate adversity, don't know to work things through. It's a TV generation: get some static, change channels." Blake was determined to be different, clinging desperately to her conviction that hard work would pay off. And little by little she began to come apart.

When she began crying during a fight, she could not stop; deep, racking sobs like a shrouded mother mourning for her children dead in a famine, crying so deeply that it felt as though her bowels would rise up and pour out of her eyes. Sometimes she cried so long and hard she wondered if she would dissolve. After she and Michael staggered away from each other after one of their clashes, Blake retreated into her closet, her essence draining out of her with every sob. She leaned against her clothes, touched the soft wool and silk, mumbling through her tears, "It's OK." The little words whispered to an inconsolable child whose puppy has died. "It's all right," she said, even though she knew it wasn't.

Michael's anger from the fight would subside, and he'd come looking for her. "Knock that off and come out of there," he said, wondering what in hell she'd think of next. Huddled in the closet, of all things.

"I *can't*," Blake wailed pathetically. "I'm scared, I can't move." She was terrified of sinking into such humiliating powerlessness. The four walls around her clothes gave her a sense of security; the idea of standing up and going back out there was beyond her. She could see the disdain on Michael's face, which only made it worse. "I'm sorry, honey, I know I'm being a lulu, but I can't move . . . I'm just all fucked up."

Michael went in and pulled her up, let her adjust to standing, then tried to lead her out by the hand. Blake was a horse trapped in a burning barn, too paralyzed by fear to put one foot in front of the other and exit to safety. The problem was that no place felt safe. Michael eased her out gently; for a while things would be all right.

Her crying really made Michael angry. He didn't understand it and felt it was a tool to get at him. So Blake learned to save it until nighttime, crying herself to sleep without him knowing. She strangled her sobs and let the tears pour out, while keeping her body perfectly still. But in the middle of a fight she had to do something to stop the release of tears: she became catatonic. She stared straight ahead, motionless, and within minutes would feel blissfully paralyzed, unable to move or hear clearly, removed from the reality that was so painful. Her mind left her body and stood outside it, outside the argument where it didn't hurt so badly.

When Michael saw her glazing over he told Blake to cut it out, but it was too late—once she had crossed over into her self-hypnotized state, she was physically incapable of responding. At first the catatonia was a relief, but then it got scary; she didn't know how to get back. Michael yelled at her, thinking she was in control of what was happening. Then his anger turned to fear when he realized how far gone she was. Inside her head Blake repeated over and over, "Please hug me, please hold me," praying that he'd hear even though she couldn't speak. Michael slapped her face; the sting pleased Blake, reassured her that he cared. As she began to come back into focus, she wondered if she were losing her mind—had already lost it?—and wondered how far it was from here to dying. She had lost her instinct for self-preservation. She needed so badly to be loved—for Michael to love her the way she wanted, when she wanted—that she was willing to destroy herself to get it.

Blake wondered if this was what it had been like for Isabel. She felt sure that not all bad marriages got this bad. She didn't know how much more Michael would put up with, but she didn't know how to stop herself. She was afraid that she might drive him away for good. And she was torn between her fear of that and her wish for it.

She was in the sauna at the health club one day, staring at a woman's silicone breasts that perched like hard hills, the nipples pointed down at the owner's belly button instead of looking out into the world. Blake hugged her knees to her chest and was startled when the woman next to her touched her on the shoulder and whispered, "Are you OK?" Blake suddenly realized she had been rocking back and forth, unaware of a low moaning sound in the back of her throat. She forced a smile.

"Yeah, thanks," she whispered back; she felt like adding, "Except that I'm dying—my marriage is destroying me, but otherwise I'm fine, thanks." The bruises inside her were so large, the pain branched all over her body. It was too dark in the sauna for Blake to recognize the woman in the locker room, but she was thankful that she had responded, that someone heard her.

And then one night Blake went over the brink. She had been especially vicious to Michael, accusing him of being unable to get close to anyone, of not having the guts to be intimate. Blake had been crying the whole time, feeling hopeless and trapped, in misery about what their life had become, shocked by how dreadful she could be. The potential for their vileness to each other seemed infinite, crimes beyond punishment, infractions against the human soul that were suffered doubly by the person committing them. Life was too, too horrible. Michael slammed out of the room, and Blake didn't think she'd ever stop crying this time, silent sobs that shook her entire being, cups of tears from a bottomless well. If only I can stop crying, she thought, I won't melt, I won't disappear altogether. I must stop crying or I'll die.

Blake opened a drawer and took out a pair of antique

silver embroidery scissors that had been a present from her mother, one of her no-occasion, just-because-I-love-you presents. Blake felt calmer just touching the sharp steel blades that ended in a knife point. If I hurt myself, she reasoned, give myself real physical pain, I'll be able to stop crying. Her mind stepped aside and said, "Look, this girl is going to cut herself." The prospect of the blood entranced her, compelled her as though she were a vampire, intrigued her as though she were watching a movie about a person possessed. She scratched the scissors across the back of her wrist, and her mind stepped aside and snickered, "She's chickenshit, copping out and not going for the vein, the underside." But that only made Blake dig the blade deeper into the freckled skin on top and say back, "Bullshit to you—I don't want to *die*, fool, I just want pain, to hurt myself. I want blood." She dragged the scissors point along her skin and made a red track through the blond hairs, the freckles disappearing as the blood seeped out. She felt nothing, anesthetized, just an eerie calm as she watched the trail of blood follow the scissors point. She dug another line alongside it, two parallel red streaks that became one as the blood oozed together. Then she drew a line across those two, a tick-tacktoe pattern. "She's smiling, how fucked up," her mind said, but Blake didn't care. She felt peaceful, so much better. She wasn't crying anymore, it worked, what bliss.

She heard Michael coming back into the room, and she jammed the scissors into the drawer. "She belongs in a loony bin," her mind said. "This is *Never Promised You a Rose Garden* time."

"What are you doing?" Michael asked, suspicious of her faraway, guilt-ridden expression.

"Nothing," she answered dully, robotlike.

"What have you got there?" He narrowed his eyes at her hand which she was holding behind her back.

"Nothing."

Michael strode over and grabbed her arm. His face went ashen. "What in the hell have you done?" He looked so angry Blake thought he'd kill her. Perspiration beaded on his forehead.

"Go ahead, kill me," she said. He couldn't really hurt her; she felt dead already.

"Never do this again," Michael commanded, breathing hard, then louder, "Never! Do you hear me, Blake?"

She smiled a goofy smile, the smile of a mental patient who has sat on her mashed potatoes and is enjoying it.

"I mean it, this isn't funny," he went on, not daring to look at her wrist again but afraid to let it go. "Do anything else you want—hit me, throw something—but never this."

"It was me I was trying to hurt, not you," Blake corrected him.

"*Promise* me you won't do it again," he demanded, kneeling down by her chair to make direct-line eye contact. He continued to hold her arm as if it were a baby rabbit he'd found dead by the roadside. She stared at him dumbly, wondering who he was, what he wanted. "Promise?"

"I promise," she whispered after a long pause. But she kept her fingers crossed behind her back.

It took her forever to leave the marriage. She didn't get the message, kept banging her head against a wall, begging, mutilating herself, knocking on the front door when Michael had gone out the back. It was Chinese water torture for her—there was nobody home, but she kept being fooled by the shadows moving behind the drapes. Yet she was afraid to leave, had gotten used to being supported, to being half a couple, to having a safe harbor. It was the idea of marriage that she wanted to preserve, the concept of a lifetime mate to share life's delights and problems with.

It was that idea she was afraid to give up, replacing it with aloneness . . . even though that marriage was the loneliest place she had ever been.

Cassie talked to Blake, reminded her that even though their mother had been a strong, adventuresome woman, she had been imbued with her generation's indoctrination: that life without a man at the center of it is a fearsome and powerless place. She had passed that notion along to her daughters in silent messages, a communicable disease that took root insidiously. And every day inside marriage took Blake further away from the time when she had been on her own, satisfyingly self-sufficient. Her memory of it grew dim, as if it were a remote island on which she'd once survived but would now be too harsh and threatening for her without a man.

"I know it's dumb, but I'm afraid, Cassie."

"Of what?"

"Pain, loneliness, failure."

"How much worse can it get?" her sister asked gently. "You already live without sex, without communication. You already live in lonely pain. And you are capable of a magnificent life."

"I know I have to leave. I just want to find a time when we're both ready, when it'll be smooth, painless."

"No such thing, sis. You can't avoid pain in life—it's part of it, part of change."

"But I don't *like* it!" Blake said, self-mocking. "Mommy said it wouldn't be like this, not for me, at least."

Cassandra smiled at her, a smile full of faith in her, hope, caring.

"Well, it ain't the first time you found out old Mom was wrong, huh?" They smiled at each other, then Blake frowned.

"But how will I decide when to leave?"

"One day soon you'll wake up, and you'll just know."

And one day Blake woke up and knew she could do it. She packed a bag and told Michael. It was the fall, and she wanted to go up to New England. Walking to Avis, Blake felt alive, strong, fresh. The city was at its best: terrifyingly tawdry and elegantly exotic, a parade of incredible characters. Blake drove up the Merritt Parkway so that she could see the first trees, let the leaves do their glorious last dance for her; maples so red they seemed on fire, yellows and oranges bright as Halloween candy corn. She wanted to go up to the country and watch the earth die where it did it so gallantly.

Fourteen

That house was Camelot. Perhaps Cassandra and I would never have been princesses if we hadn't grown up in a castle: it confirmed our feeling of specialness. It was our family's idyllic retreat, cut loose from reality like a hot-air balloon miles above the earth and ordinary people's lives. We drove up from the city every weekend; our private paradise began the minute we hit the loose gravel of the long, birch-lined driveway with the majestic, white-stone turreted castle at the end, carpets of green grass as far as you could see. We packed the car at the Beresford, a lovely big apartment that was basically a place to live during the week while we were in school, every day aimed towards our Friday departure. The car was jammed with special foods like croissants, veal roasts and cheese, mundane necessities like bed pads and yellow slickers from Bloomingdale's, the dogs and a school friend or two.

My father and mother went looking for a house when

she was pregnant-out-to-here; with two little redheads running around and a third on the way, their New York town house was bulging at the seams. They didn't exactly need a mansion, mind you, but they fell in love with the house, a copy of a Norman château originally commissioned by the Rockefellers. It was a white elephant that hadn't been lived in for years and would cost a fortune to restore and maintain. There was also a rumor about a ghost which had kept the house from selling. Two hard-boiled atheists like Malcolm and Isabel thought it was silly, the tale of a ghost that could be appeased only by a death in the family. Once we'd moved in, they did hear a faint noise up in the eaves like the sound of bouncing tennis balls, but they thought nothing of it. It wasn't until the third Marsham child, a carrot-topped boy, died several days after he was born that they realized the sound had stopped. Cassandra and I understood very little about those events. We didn't know that Mama nearly died giving birth, that our fairy-tale life was almost shattered at the very beginning. Somehow, the house held us all together, swallowed up what must have been hideous pain for my parents and gave us a paradise in which to grow and play.

Our friends, even those who came from wealthy homes, were inevitably knocked out by the huge house. "Don't you ever get lost in here?" a friend of Cassie's once asked, wide-eyed, as we showed her through the labyrinthine hallways that led to various wings of the house, vast spacious rooms next to odd little ones. Later that day Cassandra and I found her friend in bewildered tears at the top of the back stairs. She had come upstairs on the wide, burgundy-carpeted, winding front staircase, traversed various rooms and halls, only to arrive at the narrow back stairs she'd never seen before. "Don't worry," Cass lied diplomatically, "I get lost sometimes, too."

"When they built these places, the back stairs were for

servants," I explained. "But they're really much better for bum-bumping." I sat down and slid down step by step, bumping on my behind. Cassandra followed my example, and her friend forgot her tears and joined in, our shrieks and giggles echoing everywhere.

The cares of the city, of the week, fell off our shoulders like heavy capes as we breathed in the rich country air. While our parents sat on the patio having before-dinner drinks and reading, Cassie and I rode our sorely missed ponies. My first steed in life was Fortune Cookie, a sly devil of a Welsh pony who would nuzzle you one minute and two minutes later dart out of your grasp and across the field. Cassandra's pony was a quixotic, copper-colored mare named Pennies from Heaven whose specialty was cantering like a perfect lady until you were off guard—then she'd stop short and thoughtfully lower her neck as a ramp for the rider to slide right down. The horses loved Friday evenings because we'd hop on bareback and let them graze on the lawn; Cassie and I challenged each other to daredevil tricks which activated our parents' protective sensors. How could a man read a week's worth of mail and magazines when he heard one daughter shout to the other, "Bet you can't jump over the wrought-iron bench!"

Papa would stand up, hands on his hips, then he'd put two fingers in his mouth and give an earsplitting whistle that would bring both dogs running, as well as Cassie and I who'd trot over with angelic faces. "If you two want to mutilate yourselves, please don't do it in front of your mother and me. It will ruin our appetite for dinner."

I would roll my eyes at my sister, then I'd lie flat back on Fortune Cookie with my head right above his tail; Cassandra forced herself to follow my example despite her unease, a foot soldier willing to do anything her big sister commanded. "Let's get out of this joint," I'd say, exchanging a smile with my father as I kicked Cookie, who tottered off with my head jiggling on his rump, Penny reluctantly following.

Friday-night dinners were slightly giddy, as though we four shared a secret, having escaped into our castle. Reggie, the butler who lived in the house all the time, carried in the first course with the dedicated composure he brought to his work, his face softening into a hint of a smile when he served Cassie and me, his little princesses. When we had all finished, Mama would ring the crystal bell beside her water glass, and Reggie would appear instantly, clearing the dishes into the butler's pantry and replacing them with warmed plates for the main course. We became more jovial as the meal progressed, a sense of well-being spreading through us at being there. Cassandra and I always helped Reggie clear the table before dessert, a part of Mama's attempt to keep us from being spoiled that had the added benefit of giving us a chance to persuade Maria to give us ice cream for dessert. Our Italian nanny never learned English so she was self-conscious about eating dinner with the family, even though we all spoke Italian after our time living in Italy. Cassandra's and my favorite treat was chocolate and vanilla ice cream, which we would mush together in our bowls to achieve a strawberryish flavor all our own. It made it even more fun that Mama and Papa would pretend to be aghast at our bad manners in playing with our food; the best moment was when we asked them to shut their eyes because we just *had* to lick our bowls. As our pink tongues licked like kittens at the ice cream coating the bowls, our eyes darted between our parents' faces. It was another kind of dessert to see the smiles beneath their closed eyes, the all-accepting love they showered on us.

At night Maria would tuck us in with a kiss on both cheeks and a cheerful, "*Sogni d'oro*," golden dreams. Maria had sailed back to America with us when I was six, nearly missing the boat because she'd gotten on the local rather than the express train to Le Havre. Mama was too thrifty to reserve a first-class cabin for this Italian woman we'd only met a week before the end of our year-long sojourn in Rome, so Maria had to come up to our cabin every morning to braid our hair. Mama got angrier by the day as Maria arrived later and later to get us ready; finally, my mother demanded to know why Maria was sleeping so late. "Oh, no, Signora," she said in Italian, her face lit up like a Christmas tree with her own silliness, "I start out in plenty of time, but I cannot find my way up here. I climb stairs and stairs and stairs, but they take me right back down where I started. They are *furbi*, these ship builders, to keep the people from sneaking into first class, no? But eventually I do find the passageway. Thousands of stairs, but I made it!" Maria would cackle with wholehearted joy, the rest of us joining in on her delight with life's small absurdities. Her favorite ploy was eating a meal in the second-class dining room on the deck below, then being able to eat all over again in the first-class dining room as our nanny, never quite recovering from the endless courses with a constant flow of red and white wine.

Our braids had to be done every day, a laborious chore since I could almost sit on my straight hair and Cassie's was thick and curly; Mama liked a ribbon twisted into the bottom half of the braids, so it took Maria quite a while. She would sing snatches of songs, bursting into thrilling little melodies like a canary for no apparent reason, making us feel that life was joyful, worth singing about. At home our closet door fluttered a rainbow when it was opened; inside the door was a rack with neatly ironed rows, two by two, of every imaginable color, ribbons to match whatever we might wear. For dressing up there were single wide, satiny ribbons that wound around a high ponytail, thick and curly once released from the braids. Along with the ribbons, Maria braided into us a sense of unending good cheer, the joy in today and faith in tomorrow that is so splendidly Italian.

"*Ciao, Maria, buon giorno!*" I would call out in the morning, dashing towards the kitchen door. When I woke up, a voracious hunger welled up in me the instant the terrible waste of sleep was over. I could once more dive into the delicious offerings of daylight.

"What will you eat?" Maria would call after me, using one of her Italian nicknames like "the little red ball of fire."

"Leftover spaghetti warmed up!" I'd say, turning to lick my lips as I placed my order. As if she hadn't heard it a hundred times before, she would feign horrified amazement at my choice of how to start the day. I'd give her an exaggerated wink—knowing full well that she often cooked pasta just so there would be some for my weekend breakfast—and I'd be out the back door, running full speed across the dew-sparkled lawn.

By the time I'd caught Fortune Cookie in whatever field Jim, the caretaker, had put him, brushed the dust off Cookie's back and the hay from his mane, Maria's lyrical Italian would be calling me to the table. I closed Cookie in the barn and ran to the front patio where we ate, instead of the circular breakfast room, when it was warm enough. I kissed Papa good morning on both cheeks, wading through the sea of newspapers surrounding him. He and Maria would give each other a look, shaking their heads at the bowl of red-tinted strands she brought me. I attacked the spaghetti, torn between wanting desperately to be back with my horse and wanting the pasta to last forever. I let my father read the paper in peace, but he would catch my eye with a secret smile, a smile that said I was half-crazy and he was half-crazy about me. Mama was asleep in their bedroom with its balcony right over the far end of the patio, and Cassandra was a late sleeper, too. Papa and I shared our mostly silent breakfast, saying more to each other with glances and a few words than people who might jabber all morning.

I rode my pony until we were both shiny with sweat, sending him over the jumps that Jim had built for us in our leveled-off riding field: a small stone wall, a brush jump with a ditch in front of it, a bright red panel, just like the Hunt Club where we kept the ponies in the winter. By now Cassandra would have joined me, mostly walking around not quite awake on Pennies and getting off to set up jumps that Fortune Cookie knocked down. I'd let her give me a course to jump, as though she were a judge, by way of thanking her.

When we finished, I put Cookie's saddle inside the rack Jim had built near the gate to the field, from where he'd later take it back to the tack room. I sprayed the pony to cool him off, hosing down Cassandra and her pony in the bargain if she wasn't quick enough to escape my spray; then we let the horses loose in the field and watched them roll, their short legs kicking up in the air, the aroma of wild grasses filling the air as their fat backs crushed them. "Race you!" I yelled to Cassie; we ran from the field towards the pool, stripping as we went, a trail of bright bits of clothing dotting the dark green lawn.

Around lunchtime Reggie drove us to the beach, where we deposited pails, shovels, plastic molds for castles, snorkels and flippers in a heap beside Maria, who settled under the striped umbrella to do Italian crossword puzzles. Cassandra and I combed the beach for sea glass and shells, sunken treasure in the tangled mass of seaweed and drift-wood that snaked parallel to the water along the curve of the beach. Then we ran lickety-split across the burning-hot sand, reaching the swinging screen door to the hamburger stand just when we thought our feet would sizzle to a crisp. The barbeque smell hit as we got in line, juggling the terrible decision between a cheeseburger or a hot dog bursting at the seams, discussing whether it was just too piggy to have a milkshake *and* french fries. How incredibly good life was.

At the end of a summer's day in the country, Reggie put out a wide glass pitcher of sangria, slices of orange and peach floating in each guest's glass. While they played croquet, Cassandra and I would sneak up and fish out the leftover fruit from the pitcher, smacking our lips over the piquant, wine-soaked slices. The sharp clank of the croquet balls smacking together, the warm, green smell of the lawn, the gay straw hats and rippling laughter of women made it a scene from the English novels Mama sometimes read to us. If Cassandra and I started playing badminton across the lawn, it would lure our mother and anyone for whom croquet was a bit too tame. Mother had been a badminton champ in her day and did stunning maneuvers with a feather-light ornery birdie. Everyone else did their best just to keep it afloat, but she knew tricks that made it spin right past a waiting racquet or fly over the net and nose-dive for the grass. Her expertise would delight and frustrate us, who eventually fell to the ground in giggles. Mama would lie down with us, laughing on the cooling grass that began to take on the smell of night as the sun faded away.

When we were little, Cassandra and I took our before-dinner bath together, sitting at opposite ends of the tub and making up stories and games about the mountains of bubbles between us. The old-fashioned bathtub was big enough for us to wiggle our toes pinkly at each other through the white clouds of soap, letting our bodies float to the surface. Beside the tub was a glass-topped table where Maria put tall, cool drinks for us—mock sangria of fruit juices or iced tea with a sprig of fresh mint. We lay, two rosy mermaids, reaching out of the hot, soapy water over the smooth, cool porcelain edge to take a sip. When we stepped out, Maria wrapped us like cigars in pink towels, our names embroidered in curving white script. We were very good about folding them properly afterwards, the outside edges folded in so that our names faced out in the center of the soft pink terrycloth.

Dressed like twin cherubs in dotted Swiss dresses hand-smocked above the sashed waist, Cassandra and I joined the adults downstairs. We were allowed to help Reggie pass the hors d'oeuvres, weaving in and out of the multitude of legs, sometimes having to tug on them to call attention to our silver tray of smoked salmon on rounds of cucumber or stalks of celery filled with sour cream and red caviar. The air was alive with loud arguments and equally vociferous laughter, a dynamic mixture of people who often had nothing in common but their friendship with Isabel. Mama circulated, wearing a black satin hostess apron over one of her exotic housedresses; she created just the right spark between people to stir things up, and you could feel the release of energy as people discovered things about themselves in the mirror of new encounters.

The best part of the evening was early on when Isabel gave a rundown of the yet-to-arrive guests. It was a habit which encouraged early arrivals: people were eager to hear the scoop on others while sparing themselves her uninhibited behind-the-scenes dissection. She told stories of people's fortunes: "He's a multi-multi . . . but it's from his family's sugar-cane empire. Ridden with guilt about all those brown-skinned workers he's oppressed to make white sugar. So he spends buckets of money improving the Chinese porcelain collection at the Met and civil-rights things." Or stories of misfortune: "Poor Nathan, he's so handsome and smart—and such a born loser it's incredible. They've been bankrupt twice, and poor Naomi had to sell all her beautiful French clothes to that resale place in the city. She has such style, though; she can put together three dime-store handkerchiefs and look as good as a Balenciaga." There were sagas of friends' skeletons in the closet: "He spent time in a Roman jail—rats as big as cats, mind you—which was surprising, considering that it's a Latin country where they understand crimes of passion. He *did* stab a man, but it was over his wife. Some people say he overreacted, that the fellow simply looked at her the wrong way at an embassy party, but I say, grow up . . . you don't stab a man if there isn't some real hanky-panky going on."

Cassandra and I were mesmerized by the stories, which improved with the embellishment of each retelling. I sat on the seal-gray, art-nouveau couch, leaning back against the glamorously curved assymmetrical arc. Mama would invite me to join the conversation. "Isn't that true, Blake?" she'd say, after telling of a friend's personality or past. With precocious bravado I'd prompt, "Yes, Mama, but you didn't really tell about his wife. . . ." Isabel would smile a sunburst at me, torn for an instant between scooping me into her arms for a public hug or completing the story.

"One probably shouldn't tell," she'd begin, lowering her voice so that everyone had to lean in, "but I think Denise is actually quite proud of it. The woman has had everything lifted, absolutely every single thing you can. She's a monument to plastic surgery: eyes, neck, stomach; then her bazooms had a lift, even her behind—they raised it up two inches. And the incredible thing is you can't tell, you'd never know." And just when you thought you'd gotten all the tidbits, the sound of fresh tires on the gravel would prompt Mama to say, "Ah! That's probably the Ashleys. Now, originally Bob was Valerie's best friend's husband . . . and when he left her for Valerie, she killed herself, jumped right out of their apartment at the Dakota. He sold it, natch, but even so, you'd think it would weigh on them, but Bob and Valerie are as happy as can be."

Sometimes Mother got carried away with her love for entertaining and invited people who happened to telephone or whom she'd just met and wanted to draw into her net. It was a wondrous collection of people, so many silvery, exotic fish brought together. There were times when she overinvited, and it looked as though there'd be just barely enough food instead of the usual excess. Before every one sat down to dinner, Mama would whisper, "F.H.B." to Cassie or me, and we'd whisper it to Papa, who would nod with a rueful smile. "Family hold-back" meant the four of us would take very little on our plates. If a guest commented, Cassie and I knew to say that we'd ruined our appetites with Creamsicles before dinner.

Mother was also resourceful with culinary mishaps. Once she was given two crates of impressively large oranges; in her thrifty fashion she decided to have them as dessert for a very large dinner party. She had Reggie and Maria working for hours with her, scooping out the pulp and chopping it together with ingredients and refilling the orange shells, transforming them into a spectacular dessert. It wasn't until forty of them were arranged on a silver platter that Mama thought to taste the filling. The way she wrinkled her nose made Cass and me refuse even to try it; Reggie did so reluctantly, and his lips puckered. "A bit bitter, don't you think, ma'am?" he suggested diplomatically. Anybody else would have tossed them out, but Isabel met the challenge head on. "I wouldn't dream of letting your beautiful work go to waste, Reggie. Just carry them in like the crown jewels when the time comes."

My mother waited for a particular guest to arrive, an easily impressed mile-a-minute talker who was known for the speed with which she spread rumors and gossip. Mama kept me nearby when she approached Silvia, so that I could share in the escapade. "Darling," Mama said in a conspiratorial whisper, "we have such a treat for dessert tonight. Don't tell a soul, but an old admirer sent me a whole crate of rare Basque oranges!"

By the time Reggie carried in the artistically arranged orange bombs, everyone in the room knew their origin. "Basque oranges, just flown in," Isabel announced with a smile. Cassandra and I held our breath as we waited for the moment of truth when people tasted them: they proclaimed them marvelous and unique. Some even had seconds. We need not have doubted our mother's cleverness; she knew how to play people the way she sometimes strummed the antique harp in the corner of the living room, inlaid with ebony and mother-of-pearl.

Fifteen

~~~

T he preliminary divorce papers arrived in the mail and Blake looked at them with emotionless curiosity, like reading a lease on a house. One item puzzled her, so she called the lawyer.

"What does this part mean, about there being 'no dead issue'?"

"No deceased babies," she replied.

That got to Blake: their dreamed-of babies died with the end of them. There had been times in the beginning, lying in bed together talking about their future baby, that had made it so real she could practically smell the baby powder. The courts wanted to know if there had been 'dead issue', if Michael Lowell and Blake Marsham had had offspring that died? Damn straight, Blake thought to herself, there was dead issue, all right: my dreams, my hopes. She cried herself to sleep that night.

Blake's nightmares disappeared as soon as she and

Michael split up. It was a startling revelation to her. During the marriage she had dreams so frightening she'd awaken in a sweat, sobbing tearlessly; as she came awake, real tears sprang into her eyes. They were nightmares of such chilling realism that she was afraid to go back to sleep, afraid to get into their grasp and be overcome again. Michael held her tight and soothed her back to sleep; Blake thought his ability to comfort her was a sign of how much she needed him. His tenderness convinced her of his loving understanding as he took away the razor edge of the nightmare. She had wondered how she had ever managed to live without him—yet as soon as she did, the nightmares vanished. Either they had been the result of the daily horror of the marriage or were yet another method devised by her resourceful subconscious to get the attention she so desperately craved from him.

The first days back on her own were exhilarating: cool sheets beside her instead of a snoring body; no one to pick up the check automatically in a restaurant; no one else's social plans to take into consideration. Blake was on a filly's wobbly new legs, filled with an exquisite joy at having gotten herself back, as though she'd rediscovered an old friend. Marriage had shaped her life, eliminated options . . . avenues that she had thought were barricaded forever were now magically reopened. It was awesome; she could do anything she wanted—the whole world was waiting. She was in a state of grace; she had gotten a second chance.

She had told her father she was leaving Michael, and instead of the soothing sympathy she'd hoped for, her father stunned her with his directness. It was better, she knew, to be reminded just how wrong her mother had been. There were some things that could *not* be made to work in life—and neither Isabel, nor Blake, could manage *every*thing.

"You've given it your best shot; it didn't work out," Marsh said when Blake told him that she and Michael were splitting up. "So cut your losses. I know from experience—from *not* having done it—that what you have to do now is cut your losses."

It made Blake sad that Marsh had not done it for himself; she felt that in some small way her decisiveness could even the score for her father.

Blake felt a surge of angry disappointment at her father. At first she had been glad that he was so non-judgmental about her divorce, but then she wondered if it was just that he didn't care. Several weeks passed before it struck her as pretty odd that her father had not tried to find out how she was, whether she needed anything.

"You know, Papa hasn't called at all since my separation," Blake told her sister.

"So what else is new?" Cassie replied.

They exchanged a sarcastic smile. Their bitterness was encapsulated: they let it out by dribs and drabs, only when they were alone together, and even then, cautiously. It was like the green sac of gizzard that Maria used to pull out of a freshly killed chicken, the little bag nestled against the liver. Maria had explained that you had to be careful not to puncture the sac or the bitter green liquid would pour all over, ruining the rose-red meat. Blake and Cassie were careful about their righteous anger, releasing it only with the other one there as sentinel. They did not want to spoil what little they did have with their father; he was, when all was said and done, the only father they had.

"Let me ask you something, Blakie," Cassie went on. "Why did you get married?" Blake took a step backwards, retreating from her sister's question, but Cassandra added, "And why did you marry Michael, which may be a whole other answer?"

"Cassie! Why do you think?" Blake said, mild indignation in her reproach. "Because I loved him."

"You mean because he loved you?"

"Yes, of course, that, too."

"But why did you get married, Blake?" Cassie's probing tone was laced with such loving concern that Blake didn't feel too threatened, just thrown off guard. "And after six weeks . . ."

"Why didn't you say something then?" Blake said, getting out of answering by questioning.

"What?" Cassie laughed. "And risk getting flattened? At the calmest of times, being with you is like socializing with a mild tornado. That was more like a twister, cutting a path."

"I guess I was a little swept away by Michael," Blake concurred, smiling at her sister's analogy.

"Or the *idea* of Michael . . ."

"Meaning what?" Blake said, a defensive edge returning.

"Meaning he was a very glamorous package that appeared on your doorstep at a vulnerable moment in both your lives."

"Cassie, we loved each other," Blake said, as though explaining something to a dunce. "We were deeply in love. Now, it might have been stupid to do that Romeo and Juliet whirlwind courtship, but I . . ." Blake stopped and shook her head in self-reproach. "Real stupid, actually . . ." She looked as though she might cry. Cassie put her arm around Blake. "Too bad you have to do such jerky things and have so much pain to learn anything," Blake said and started to laugh through the few tears that had formed. "I just hope life is 'pass/fail,' because otherwise I've got a shitty grade so far!"

"Don't be so tough on yourself, Blakie. Everybody makes mistakes, makes fools of themselves . . . at least you learned something."

"But I can never erase the ugly things I did and said in

that marriage—it's part of my personal history now. I feel as if I got soiled, as if it made me dirty and I can never be totally clean again."

"I guess that makes you human, like the rest of us," Cassie said gently.

For a split second Blake began to protest, then stopped herself. She and Cassandra burst out laughing and put their arms around each other in a big hug.

Before she'd gotten married, an essential part of Blake's identity had been the wildness of her love life, the variegated retinue of suitors. There was always the wonderful choice between going to St. John's with the Stockbroker or to Los Angeles with the Doctor. Once married, she missed those extravagantly dramatic liaisons, the fun of deciding which fantasies to live out. She had always avoided saying "my husband" because it made him sound like a possession, but also because it was an admission that she had forsaken all those sexy dramas. Yet she said "my ex-husband" with relish; it was an announcement she was back in the game, suited up.

The idea of dating, the newness, scared her a little. How to kiss a stranger? Hell, how to kiss at all; she could barely remember what it felt like after living with Michael. But she plunged right in, figuring that cold water is easiest if you jump, both feet.

When the phone rang, Blake would panic if it was a man—she didn't know which one it was, but they all said, "Hi, there, it's me," in a low, seductive voice. Each figured he was the only "me" in her life, and they all sounded the same with that lowered, sexy tone. Her nerves jangled every time, and she prayed for a shred of identifying information—anything would do. "I've been in court all week," or, "It was foggy in the Hamptons this weekend."

The other problem was that she needed a complex mental file to keep track of particulars: which guy liked what drink; his sister's, ex-wife's and dog's names; which outfits she'd already worn with him and where they'd gone to dinner. She was mortified when she slipped up. "How is Susan?" she'd ask.

"Who's Susan?" the man would reply. How could Blake explain that she was the daughter of the guy she'd been out with the previous Thursday? Or what could she do after saying, "There aren't any good movies around except the new Robert Redford picture, have you seen it?"

The fellow would look at her cockeyed and say, "Yes, with you."

Blake's flurry of lovers after Michael was the hedonistic gorging of someone who had been on a strict diet; one slice of walnut torte wouldn't suffice. Some of her friends were shocked that she wanted to be back on the town immediately; she felt they would rather a discreet period of time during which she wore some sort of widow's black. But Blake wanted to celebrate, not mourn. To dance on the grave seemed the best possible solution.

"Oh, shit," Blake said as she looked in her date book. "My period's late," she added, sitting across from Cassie in the Palm Court. Their mother used to take them there for tea cakes and violin music every so often—they were keeping up the tradition.

"What's your date book got to do with it?"

"Just checking to see when in my cycle I was with a man," Blake said, counting days on her fingers.

"You mean you write down when you sleep with a guy?" Cassie tried not to sound judgmental, but her effort at neutrality made her sound even more shocked.

"It's a date book; I write down when I see anyone."

"I guess you're what they call promiscuous," Cassandra said, trying to joke to cover her disquiet. "Do you just sleep with them and never see them again?"

"Sometimes."

"But afterwards, doesn't that make you feel . . ." Cassie's voice gave out before she could find a word that wouldn't sound terrible.

"It doesn't hurt later if you go to bed with a guy you don't love," Blake said calmly.

"But doesn't it hurt to fuck without feelings?"

"Mostly it feels best not to feel anything for a while," Blake said, knowing that her sister wouldn't understand, having been in a solid relationship for a long time. Then with a big smile Blake added, "And it feels lovely to fuck again!"

"So it's going to be the good old days all over again?" Cassie said. "Like Il Vagabondo?"

"Oh, God," Blake laughed. "That was priceless."

"I thought Michael was going to faint."

"Him? What about me?"

Blake and Michael had gone out to dinner with Cassie, her boyfriend Rick and two other couples to a funny Italian restaurant that had a long, sunken bocce court beside a row of tables. One of the women, inspired by a formidable consumption of Bardolino, had proposed that they all write down how many lovers they'd had. A few in the group protested the game but gave in when the majority searched in pockets and purses for writing implements. They cleared off the white paper placemats that protected the tablecloth in front of each person.

There had been some self-conscious joking as people began writing down names, but Blake had jumped right in and had a good-sized list going in no time. She was absorbed in jotting down names and smiled to herself, either in memory of a good time she'd had with whatever man she added to the column, or laughing because in some cases she knew just what the guy looked like and what he'd been like in bed but couldn't remember his last name. She began a second column and wondered how she'd had the time and energy.

Suddenly Blake had a feeling that she was being watched. Michael was on one side of her and Cassie on the other, and she could feel their eyes. She shot a warning glance at Michael—as though he were a kid in school trying to cheat by looking at her paper—and then she returned to her list, scribbling down several names that came to her all at once. Blake had the feeling again of being stared at. She looked up sharply, intending to shame Michael into minding his own business, only to find that all seven pairs of eyes at the table were scrutinizing the long columns of names on her placemat. It was dead quiet except for the clack of bocce balls as they smacked together. Blake's hand slid protectively over her placemat. She noticed the modest lists in front of the others and looked up at the amazed expressions with which they were examining her. The pause seemed to last forever. Then Blake put on a dignified smile and slowly, deliberately, tore up the tomato-stained placemat with the evidence of her checkered past. Her sister broke the awkward silence by declaring in a cheery voice, "And she gave it all up for Michael! Let's drink to true love!"

When the divorce papers arrived, Blake stared at them and felt nothing. She waited, her own third eye ready, the cyclops syndrome of the Writer Watching Her Life, expecting a momentous response. There wasn't one. She waited—the nothingness was a shock. Was it a defense mechanism? No, she decided, she just didn't feel anything. To feel nothing—*that* made her sad. Nothing between her and Michael mattered anymore. Doors shut fast, don't they? she thought.

Scattered realizations: Michael Lowell was now an entry in her address book, a person whose zip code and telephone number were different from hers, might even slip her mind. Incredible, Blake thought, when I believed those numbers would be forever linked to me.

Would she always avoid the small things that annoyed Michael: the sound of a metal spoon scraping the bottom of a pot, or of her fingernails scratching on a silk blouse? Was she destined to think of him forevermore when she heard those sounds, to stop herself out of habit? Would she always worry about using lip gloss because Michael pulled away and wiped his lips in annoyance if she wore lipstick? Are these the ties that bind, she wondered; is *this* the backwash of that stormy sea?

Michael resigned himself to their parting of the ways. He slid back into his prior life as if he'd never left, as if there had never been anything that engaged him except the paper. It was over, and he simply cut it out of his life. But he was worried that Blake would talk about their marriage to people, violate his privacy.

"Don't worry, they all think I was the villain, anyway, bitching at sweet old you," Blake assured him.

"I just don't want a lot of people knowing the specifics of what went on between us." Michael looked nervous and sad. Blake wanted to put her arms around him, but he spoke again. "I just don't want you to tell anyone that I wouldn't fuck you." Blake stared at him, dumbfounded, speechless. "OK?" he urged. "That's all I'm asking, that you don't go telling people *that*."

"That you wouldn't *fuck* me?" Blake shouted. "Is that what it boils down to: that your reputation as a stick man might be tarnished?" Her rage boiled up, and she thought the top of her head would blow off. "What about the fact that you wouldn't *talk* to me, you son of a bitch? What about *that?!*" She felt as close to being able to kill as she ever hoped to get.

"I don't see why you're starting a fight now," Michael

said, perplexed by her explosion. "Now that it's over, and we're finished . . ."

They stared at each other blankly, as though they were staring at a stranger. Neither of them knew who the other was. Michael did not understand the deep river of angry sadness flowing through Blake, did not see where he fit into it. Blake did not see how the very force of her personality had incapacitated him.

"Never mind," she said wearily, "I promise not to tell anyone that you wouldn't fuck me."

Sixteen

When I was little and Papa was away from home, I'd go up to his office and sit in the creaky, brown-leather chair and play with the things on his desk: a silver apple Mama had given him that said, "The apple of my eye"; a mother-of-pearl-handled letter opener; a clay figure Cassie had made for him at school; and a wooden box for paper clips that I'd carved for him in shop class. My favorite thing in his study was the photograph of him dressed up in bullfighting clothes at the entry tunnel to a bullring. The costume itself was tacked on the wall above the photo, a pale green satin suit embroidered in gold with a matching two-cornered hat. They'd given it to him, he always said, for having had "the *cojones* to go through with a challenge that had been made in a state of severe drunkenness."

Papa had spent a lot of time in Spain with a famous painter. Through him Papa had come to know Antonio Ordoñez, the Spanish idol matador who was dying to learn

American baseball. Antonio told me, some years later when I met him, that my father had agreed to teach him baseball, and he would teach El Pecas, the Freckled One, how to fight a bull. Ordoñez told the story with a wide Spanish smile that melted a little girl's heart. So after baseball lessons—which included accidentally hitting a makeshift ball right through the window of the Gritti Palace on one of their trips—Ordoñez had dared my father to join his procession into the ring when he fought a special *mano-a-mano* with Dominguín. Each matador was to fight three bulls; if either man was hurt, his seconds took over.

"If Ordoñez had gone down," Papa loved to add at the end of the story, "I was next at bat: El Pecas would have had to haul his freckled ass into that ring. Can you imagine?"

One summer I went to the bullfights with my father. Our family was spending the summer at the villa in Málaga of old friends whose avocation in life was to entertain people from all over the globe. Cassandra and I were given a small suite in the children's wing with Maria. The fifteen servants who worked in the house slept in that part of the house, too. The Harley children went to boarding school in England and only came to the villa on holidays, so they were used to a regimented life of restrictions. But Cassie and I were aghast at being segregated from the adult world. Even more insulting was the handle on the heavy wooden door that led to the part of the villa where the grown-ups held court: the handle had been placed so high on the door that a child could not reach and turn it. The Harley kids were wide-eyed when I put Cass up on my shoulders to get the door open.

We loved going into the huge kitchen early in the morning, when the house servants and the twenty outside workers convened for breakfast at a long wooden table with huge platters of sliced onions, garlic, tomatoes and oil, sopped up with their rough, crusty bread. We loved their garlicky hugs and kisses, listening to them chatter and break into song, hearing the backstairs gossip about the guests and the inside news of their own lives. Since we already spoke French and Italian, it took only a week or two for Cassie and me to get by in Spanish. As much as we enjoyed that part of life at the villa, we had no intention of being restricted to the children's dining room. We ate breakfast with our parents and the other adults on the trellised terrace, fresh-churned butter and home-made jam on flowered porcelain breakfast dishes.

It was an opulent summer, a house full of worldwide people, like the Iranian who left behind so many big blue tins of Malossol that we got sick of caviar after a while. I loved to watch my father's amused expression as I refused the toast and onions and nibbled the shiny gray eggs from the end of a small silver spoon. Dinner was rarely served until eleven, and although the Harley kids couldn't wait that long to eat—I was convinced their parents kept scrupulously late Spanish hours just to exclude them—I filled up on caviar and shrimp and hung in there. My father suggested that the pre-dinner hours would be a good time to do something special with the Harley children and the few other kids who had come with their parents. I wrote a play. It was called *The Cocktail Party*: in the first act people were seen at their most socially grand and phony; the second act showed the same scene as it would have been if people had been honest. We children performed it on the balcony that jutted out over the main staircase—renowned figures from the international scene sat on the cool marble steps and craned their heads up at us, listening attentively to our childish cynicism and applauding roundly.

The best part of the summer was the bullfights, the *corrida*, going every week to our box where Papa initiated me into the great art of bullfighting: what to watch for; how to appreciate the power and grace; and how to avoid misunderstanding the blood in the sand. After hiding my eyes the first time, it came clear to me. I began to shout, "*Olé!*" spontaneously with the overflowing, one-voiced crowd, applauding a pass with the cape that was as beautiful as anything Nureyev ever did. The matador's body bent backwards in a powerful arc, his head back over his shoulder, watching the cape as it trailed in a circle, making an echo of his body's curve in the sand, the as-yet-unbloodied sand. He tempted the bull to pass so close to his body that one fast flick of the menacing horns—which formed curves all their own, the entire pas de deux a curving Calder mobile—and the blood in the sand would have been the man's, not the bull's.

We hissed with the rest of them for dirty playing, when the picador leaned really hard on the bull, black-red blood oozing thickly on the black hide, pushing the bull off balance and tiring him out, cowardly up there on his padded horse. And when a good bull—a strong, proud bull —fought back at the picador, threw his head sideways and gutted the horse, we'd give a small cheer even as we gasped for the steed: poor rickety horse, halfway to the glue factory. Its flanks covered with padding, it was yet vulnerable under its belly where a bull's deadly horn could rip in so that the horse trotted out of the ring, knees buckling, with a piece of its insides dangling below . . . only to return trembling for the next bull, its guts stuffed back in with sawdust until it could be fixed properly or sent off to the glue factory, after all, the end of its terrifying days in the bullring, blindfolded, with the scent of the terrible bull filling its nostrils.

Papa taught me how to tell if a bull was good from the moment he entered the ring, the red marker flag flapping from his shoulder to denote which ranch had bred him

/ 215

for this thrilling, horrifying sport. The first charge into the ring could tell you how angry he was just to be there: when the assistants taunted him, would he charge the wood barriers where they took cover, throwing up the slats of wood with a toss of his horns as though they were so many popsicle sticks? The matador watched as we did, standing by the fence in his glorious satin colors, the black cap he had bowed with when he came in now clutched by some lucky lady in the boxes to whom he'd thrown it, dedicating this bull to her, this bull he now studied to see how it moved when his assistants made a fast, frightened pass to get the bull going, running behind the barrier at the slightest danger. Because if the matador knew what kind of adversary he had in this bull, it meant the difference between fighting and killing it elegantly, or making a botch of it, not finding the rhythm to wrap the bull around his body behind the wide passing cape that matched his costume, not finding the way to bring out the best in the bull; or, worst of all, winding up gored again, his stomach and thighs a battlefield. How incredible the scars on Ordoñez's stomach when once he lifted his shirt to show Cassie and me after a fight, in a jovial mood because he'd been awarded two ears, a tail and a hoof, the highest honors from the judges, and had been pelted with flowers, shoes, hats and pillows for a full fifteen minutes as he strode round and round the ring like a king, one arm crooked with his cape over it, the other hand acknowledging the cheers of the people who adored him, who felt prouder to be Spanish because of him, who revered him because he brought danger and death that close to them, right there in front of their faces, and taught them it could be vanquished, that man *could* triumph.

Even a child, even an American girl of eleven, could feel that, could feel the deep chill as the bullfighter faced the bull, having finished his final passing with the red cape, having turned that wild, mad beast into a dancing partner, a conspirator in his own death. The panting, bleeding bull stood inches away, black-red rivers of blood down his shoulders, head down, watching the man in the skintight pants and dainty black slippers up on his toes in those ballet shoes, the long killing sword hidden beneath the red cape, poised in front of the long, curved horns, frozen still to keep the bull hypnotized in front of him. Then came the moment of truth, that enchanted instant when the matador raised a half-inch higher on his toes and came over the bull's horns with his one steel horn, going right over the bull's head and ramming the sword deep into him, right up to the brass hilt, so that instead of the bull throwing his head and killing the man, the bull fell to his knees in homage to his conqueror and died at the matador's feet. To a really fine bull, one who gave the man a beautiful fight, who was strong and brave without being foolish, who ran and turned and charged to his death gallantly, to a bull like that we would throw flowers and even cry. I would rest my forehead against Papa's shoulder, warm in the sun, and cry, not because of the blood, or the brutality, or the unfairness of many-against-one, but because of the great spirit of that bull, because such a spirit existed on earth, and we had been witness, our breath taken away. If I ever felt anything like the existence of a God, of something bigger than me, it was sitting there next to my godlike father, shouting "*Olé!*" in one massive human cry, watching death in the afternoon and understanding it.

Seventeen

Michael was made editor of the paper, and Blake decided to call him, maybe to invite him out for a celebration dinner. Enough time had gone by. "Michael Lowell's office," an officious secretary said in a tone that challenged any callers to convince her of their right to speak to him. When Blake said her name the secretary repeated it, "Blake Marsham?" without much conviction, the way the headmistress of a desirable school might say the name of a child unlikely to be admitted. "May I ask what this is in regard to?"

"I'm his wife," Blake said, enjoying the shock value of understatement. "I think he'll remember."

When Michael took the call he said, "Blake!" with such false cheeriness that she imagined he was trying to conceal his dread that her call portended problems, some messy vestige of that tourniquet called a marriage bond.

"Listen, I've changed my mind, I *do* want alimony," Blake said.

She waited a beat, then added reassuringly, "But not a lot, and just for a little while." She claimed not to be a vindictive person, and yet she got indescribable pleasure from the five seconds of silence on Michael's end while the impact of what she'd said registered on his gray matter—she could almost see her words like a stone thrown, splat!, against the squishy, intestinelike folds of his brain as it collated what she'd said, the cranial computer telling him it was her smart-ass way of making a joke; some joke.

"OK, Marsham, what's up?"

"I'll settle for dinner instead."

"*You* and *me?*"

"If you'd prefer, we can send our seconds and just read about it in the morning paper."

"You know what? I think you like being divorced; it's a new role for you to play," Michael said without rancor. "It's a war medal you can flaunt."

The observation sounded right to Blake; that had been one of his attractions, how well he could psyche her out. "Hey, I called to make peace."

"Why?" Michael asked.

She could tell he wasn't being contentious, he was just asking. "Maybe I want to see you, how's that? To congratulate you on your promotion. You're a pretty cute fella—I even married you for it once."

"I wouldn't be surprised if your plan now was to seduce me," he said.

Blake had thought about it, of course, had wondered what it would feel like now. Part of her just wanted to see if she still pressed those buttons in Michael . . . or maybe if she ever really had. Yet she figured that getting him into bed could be quite difficult—a horse to water, based on the past. Michael's manner on the phone had maintained a certain cautious distance, a demilitarized zone; Blake decided it wasn't worth getting blown up in a mine field just to see if she could get him.

She was therefore utterly astonished when Michael walked through the door Friday night and kissed her fully, aggressively, on the lips, then pulled her closer and forced his tongue into her startled mouth.

Dinner was a spinning top, as dizzying as being a virgin, only this time knowing ahead of time what it would feel like. The food was exquisite, one dazzling presentation after another, but Blake could not connect that it was really happening to her; she was aware of it as though she were watching the meal in a French film. The only thing that seemed real to her was the way she and Michael held hands across the table, their fingers laced beside the base of their wine glasses, woven together as if they had a will of their own, assuming they belonged together. When they were married, Michael often seemed only half there in restaurants and didn't like to hold hands; his fingers would not respond when Blake tried to hold them. Now he was looking right at her and they were talking like old friends, not the disconnected way they used to dine together, Michael looking over her shoulder and Blake pouting because he wasn't paying attention to her. Here he was, the way she had first known him, the way she had wanted him. Had it all been a bad dream, she wondered; was this the real Michael, the man she'd first thought he was? Maybe all the bad stuff had been a hallucination, a *trompe l'oeil*, a devilish trick of perception, and this feeling she had again of falling in love with him was the truth.

The waiter brought wine sherbet between courses, and Blake realized that the best memories, what came back to her now, were not the big times with Michael, the fancy dinners or early courtship romanticism or the trips they'd taken. She was struck by the tiniest moments, sharp pinpricks that filled her with love and yearning for him, quaint little memories that stuck in her throat as though he were a meal she hadn't digested, as though they'd never had a chance to finish the banquet they had laid out.

There was the moment after a long breakfast at the Plaza. They had taken a room there one night on a whim, walking home from a dinner party, and the next morning they sat by the window in the Edwardian Room, overlooking the horse-and-buggies going into the park. Blake ordered enough to feed a football player in training, and Michael's eyes widened as it all disappeared, remarking that he wondered if there was *anything* for which her appetite was not Herculean. The moment had happened when they stood up from the table; Blake patted her stomach as if it were a good little pooch, and then Michael helped her on with her jacket. It was the way he reached beneath her hair in back and pulled it out from inside the jacket, letting it fall loosely around her shoulders, that had made her feel like crying for joy. It didn't look like much to anyone else, just a natural, thoughtful gesture, but to Blake it felt like heaven, a caretaking gentleness that bespoke love to her more than a thousand erotic caresses.

There was the moment when she'd paraded into the ocean in East Hampton, the cold surf hitting her frothily against the shiny oil on her thighs, plunging into the water despite Michael's booming voice on the beach telling her not to. She had fractured her elbow riding—hardly any pain and not even a cast—but thrashing around in the surf would not have been anyone else's idea of the best possible road to recovery. Blake knew it was foolhardy, but she'd wanted to do it all the same, all the more because an edge of recklessness gave the world a brighter shine, made her feel more alive; when she ducked into the churning cold water she laughed right out loud, it made her feel so wild and free. She swam around until her arm hurt, then headed for shore, looking back over her shoulder at the waves following her, timing her strokes so she wouldn't get caught in the churn. And there had been that divine instant when she looked to the beach and saw Michael sitting there on the sand, his elbows resting on his bent knees, piles of seaweed around him. He was watching her, standing guard. She had taken a few more strokes, body-surfed one wave and then been able to stand up. When she looked again Michael was gone, had gone back inside, assured that she wasn't going to drown or perhaps unwilling to let her know how much she mattered.

Vigor. As she and Michael made love, Blake thought of that word, of how John Kennedy had used it in his inaugural speech and pronounced it vigah, in that especially vigorous way he had, and now she and Michael were going at it with such vigor, such dedicated intensity to make up for all their sad, fuckless nights. Then they made love a second time. The wine buzzed in Blake's ears; Michael could feel it pumping in his blood right to the tip of him, and he made love to Blake as though it were the only thing in the world. When they made love a third time, Blake was astonished. She wondered what it was all about, why this man who had avoided her like the plague was now fucking her brains out, what she had done wrong, what had been done to her. Whatever it was—pent-up anger, proving himself, unspoken regrets—it was divine.

But it made Blake feel she owed him one. She knew now that it was that demanding, engulfing energy of hers—Isabel's painful, wonderful legacy—that could drive people away, that had suffocated Michael, but it was also what made people adore her, what Michael had loved and wanted when he married her, then rejected and blamed her for once he got it. It was her very essence, though, not some purposefully damaging behavior, and deep down she would never find a way to forgive him his betrayal.

They were lying together, exhausted from lovemaking.

"If I'd known you were going to be so energetic," she said, watching him smile contentedly, "I would've been more careful."

Michael's body tensed, then relaxed. "What?" he said, hoping he'd misunderstood.

"I didn't know we were going to," she said and shrugged.

"Knock it off," Michael said sternly. He raised up on one elbow and stared down at her, trying to see if she were kidding. She was surprised by how intense he looked; she only meant to give him a little shot. "Tell me the truth," he insisted. Blake smiled enigmatically, getting off on how serious he was. "Yes or no?"

"I am not wearing my catcher's mitt," Blake answered obediently, knowing she couldn't remain quiet without pissing him off.

"Very funny," he said, letting his breath out and lying back against the pillows. He knew her well, but Blake was a step ahead, knew she could make him think she was lying by telling the truth a bit clumsily. When he lay back down she said nothing, shrugged her shoulders as if to say, "OK, don't believe me."

"Blake," he said sharply. "This isn't funny." Now he wasn't sure.

"But it sure felt good," Blake said dreamily, trying to snuggle up against his chest, Southern belle tactics. That did it; he grabbed her arm tight. "Ow! That hurts!"

"Just tell me you've got it in and I'll let go."

Blake squirmed out of his grip and jumped out of bed. She came back from the bathroom with the blue plastic container. She opened the lid and a light shower of powder puffed out; the pale rubber dome perched there in all its glory. "See? I really didn't think we were going to." Michael had no way of knowing that Blake had two diaphragms. She shut the case with a click and got back into bed. She tried to cuddle with him, but he pulled away.

"Shit. That's the stupidest thing I've ever heard."

"I always wanted one of your blue-eyed babies," Blake said with a sweet smile.

She had dreamed about sturdy, mischievous children who would give new perspective to their lives. She had imagined Michael's and her child soapy in the tub with her, Michael sitting beside them on the floor, telling stories. TREE/MOUNTAIN/TREE she'd had inscribed on an old silver box of Isabel's as a wedding present to Michael. When he'd proposed to her he had said, "I will be the tree following you up the mountain, and when you get a little tired from climbing, you can lean on me. The tree will be following you. And you will be the tree for me." Blake had cried when he'd said that and dreamed about children who would climb the mountain with them. Except that right from the start, they hadn't given each other a fair chance to be the tree.

"Life is so strange," she mused. "It's the middle of the month." She put her hand on her belly with a serene maternal expression, rubbing her hand as though this baby were already beginning to grow inside her. She was carried away by her own game, almost beginning to believe it was true, that with all that fucking one of those little sperms probably had made it, bless his plucky little heart.

Michael was distraught. "Goddammit," he said, shaking his head, scowling, his mind running ahead to all the consequences, to what could be or might have been, to the lack of absolutes even when you thought you knew something absolutely. They both lay silently, caught in their fantasies. How powerful it was for both of them, that baby they'd never had, that they had married each other to make and watch grow, that had died when they died as a couple; the baby seemed to lie there in the bed between them, sweetly pink on the flowered field of sheets, waiting to have its toes counted and its belly tickled and kissed all over. Babies are so good, Blake thought, imagining what a hot, wet little mouth would feel like on her breast, sucking not just for pleasure like a man but because it needed her, because it had a hunger only she could feed. Babies were so good, the best thing in the world.

"I'm going to keep it if it's there," she declared. "But you don't have to worry, Michael. It's my decision; it doesn't have anything to do with you."

"What do you mean?" he bellowed. "Has nothing to do with me?"

"I mean," Blake said in her most sensible voice, "I'll have it alone. You don't have to be involved."

"The hell. It's my baby, too," he said firmly. "But you *can't* have it, Blake." He paused. They were both thinking, not clearly, just a jumble. "It's over," he concluded sadly. "I don't want you having it; you can't, Blake, it's impossible. We're getting divorced."

It was sobering to hear him say it out loud, the finality. It was the first time it really sank in for both of them. Blake patted his back comfortingly; Michael didn't pull away, just let her pat him like a baby.

It was sheer madness, she knew it, but when Michael left she thought about taking the diaphragm out, about lying down afterwards with her hips raised so it could all flow up into her womb, so those sperm could really have a chance. How frightened and angry and confused he had been, she had made him; the games people play, the tricks they play on themselves, the simple crimes of passion.

Eighteen

"Six-centimeter cyst on the right ovary," Cassandra said. "Exactly like you, right?"

"Oh, shit."

"That's the way the cookie crumbles."

"When are they going to do it?"

"As soon as you can get here," she said.

The day before Cassie's operation Blake took her to Maxwell's Plum for a big lunch. They conferred on what to order as usual and split everything precisely in half, even the garnishes. Ever since childhood they had driven people crazy in restaurants: bouncing questions at the waiter about how things were prepared; asking other people what *they* were having; deciding on an appetizer but then changing it when they chose main courses that were too similar. They felt it was an aesthetic duty to pick out the most stunning offerings of the kitchen, covering as much territory as possible while harmonizing the dishes. Isabel had given them a feeling of urgency about the world—this might be their last chance.

Isabel was too much of a muchness for Marsh. Blake had an abiding image of them: Isabel was leaning over his shoulder at the breakfast table and said, "Kiss me, Marshie," a diminution of his nickname which he hated. He pushed her arm away and averted his face as though he were smothering. Michael once pushed Blake away like that, and she nearly hit him; the rage—her mother's unspoken rage—flew up in her so hot and fast.

She reminded her father of Isabel; the memories pressed buttons. All Blake had to do was display an extreme of emotion and her father looked as though he'd like to escape, facing her with the gritted teeth of a person in the dentist's chair. Did he see the irony? He had spent all those years trying to leave a woman, to get free of the ties that were slowly cutting off his circulation. As she was dying, he finally got a divorce. But there was no escape: he was tied by blood to Isabel's mirror image, her replica haunting him.

"You live with a reckless disregard for danger," he once said; Blake took it as a compliment. "Sort of like a free-fall parachutist."

"Life isn't supposed to be taken in careful teaspoonfuls like medicine."

"I don't know how the words 'impulsive' and 'compulsive' ever got into the dictionary before you were born." Marsh said it as though she were a wild beast he had helped raise but was still wary of.

"Michael used to say it was like living with someone shot out of a cannon—that I was spring-loaded. I'd leap out of bed in the morning and would have read the paper, cooked that night's dinner and be settled at the typewriter before he'd even stumbled into the shower."

"Poor bastard."

"What about 'poor me'?"

"You're doing fine, Toots," her father said. "Poor old Michael has to recover from being flattened by your tornado."

"No fair, Papa." The wounds were too fresh for her to have much resilience for teasing.

"Who promised you 'fair'?" he said.

"*You* did!" Blake nearly shouted. "Mama did!" They stopped and stared at each other, accidentally having stumbled on a truth.

It was a long wait during Cassandra's operation, four hours during which Lily kept Blake company. She considered it miraculous that they continued to live and breathe normally while one floor below, her sister was out cold, sliced open, scraped, stitched. When she thought of her laid out, Blake had twinges of pain in her groin: it was her flesh they were cutting, too, when they cut her sister, her flesh and blood.

There were reverberations of other hospital waiting rooms, for her mother, but also for her father's baby boy. It had been the same hospital where they were now cutting Cassie. On a crisp, wintry night just before Christmas —the same time of year Isabel had died a couple of years before—Marsh's wife had gone into labor. She'd had contractions that afternoon, so when Blake called their apartment and got no answer, she took a cab right to Doctors' Hospital. How nice, she thought, I can keep him company during that interminable wait, get the cigars ready, even reminisce about my birth if I can get him talking. But the maternity-floor nurse was a dried-up old prune who wouldn't let her go to the fathers' waiting room or even take a message. She was cold and nasty; Blake figured she resented every new baby born, a reminder of her own barrenness.

So Blake was forced to pace in a waiting room one floor

above her father without him even knowing. The frustration was awful, knowing how hard the hours had to be for him, stirring up memories of his first baby boy, dead after three redheaded days on earth; the agony that must have been, the ghastly fear that he would be punished again. If only she could get down there and tell him it was going to be OK, that this baby would be fine, like Cassie and her.

It was odd to Blake to conceive that she had once been his adored little baby. Things had changed so dramatically when she grew up. It was as though he'd turned off a switch. She felt a distant, fond familiarity from him, as though she were someone with whom he used to share a summer-house rental. There were times when it caught in her throat, when she was driving and suddenly realized she could be killed at any moment by some drunk—and that it probably never occurred to her father. She wondered whether as he drove the Long Island Expressway or the autoroute out of Paris if he worried about Blake on a back road somewhere. She wanted so desperately for him to worry, to care.

She wanted to get down to his waiting room and say, "Just please don't stop loving this baby when it gets big"— she'd say that to him, just that—"Don't go South on that kid when it gets big enough to think on its own, to question your throne, like you did with us; oh, please, because even now we still think you are King." She paced alone and watched a light snow come down outside the dirty windows, which made the whole world out there seem chill and lonely, people cut off from one another, segregated in waiting rooms, airports, labor rooms, even taken away from their mothers at birth. It took so much effort to fight it, to batter down the doors, the walls between people that have to be hacked away at constantly, like wild brambles that overtake an uninhabited house.

Finally Blake gave up and got back on the creaky hospital elevator. It stopped one floor down, and they asked her to get out so that a severe-faced nurse pushing a cloth-covered box on wheels could get in. As she passed the white box she saw a sheet of paper on top, imprinted with a baby's footprints. It looked as though they were transporting a dead baby all covered up and didn't want her in the elevator with it. She had wondered if it were her father's baby. And now in the same hospital, her sister was under the knife. Would they keep Cassandra intact, reconstruct her ovaries, too, so that one day they could have little munchkins of their own who would run together across green lawns as they had?

Lily took Blake to a coffee shop around the corner from the hospital once Cassandra was safely in the recovery room. A lady wearing a thick sable came in and asked the cashier for a packet of Parliaments. Blake thought how New York makes you want to be rich, to have anything you want when you want it. The lady walked out, a tiny Yorkie on a leash behind her, a yellow bow holding its hair out of its eyes. Blake wondered if she were happy, if her life made sense to her or was just a blur of days.

Lily and Blake decided to share a hot-fudge sundae with coffee ice cream. It was their special treat, something they allowed themselves at Serendipity's about twice a year, but today was an exception. Blake watched the lady in the fur get into a limousine; the small, beribboned dog popped in ahead of her. "I used to love going out with rich men to fancy places; long, shiny black cars to whisk you around. But now—if I even think about it at all—the fantasy's not about a man with a limo anymore."

"What changed?" Lily asked.

"Marriage beat some sense into me. I found out that the knight on the horse isn't the guy who rescues you. You do it yourself."

"Is that so terrible?"

"What's terrible are all the white lies Mama and Papa told me about how life was going to be. My marriage threw them all back in my face."

"If it was so painful, why were you so determined to stay married?"

"Because I couldn't give up the fairy tale."

"Or give up the part of you that is Isabel—that wanted to be loyal to her, to the way she managed her situation with Marsh."

"You mean holding onto Michael was a way of holding onto Mama, to the lies she taught me?" The excitement of discovery, pieces of the puzzle falling into place.

"You are a very stubborn lady when it comes to holding onto how you wish the world could be."

"I know that my memory of the ivory tower is partly a dream. But it feels so good, Lily."

"Just as long as it doesn't keep you from living well right now, from living the rest of your life."

"I *want* to go on, I really do—but no matter how far I travel, I think I'll always be a little homesick for my childhood."

"I think the little girl who wanted a daddy to protect her is ready to become an independent woman," Lily said affectionately.

"I guess I've gone from wanting to have my father to wanting to be him. . . ."

Blake took Cassandra up to the East Hampton house to recuperate. Their father, his wife and their young son were away skiing in Europe. They drove up the long driveway where the baby birch of their childhood had grown to fat, gray-and-white-trunked trees. Both of them were hit by a deluge of memories: things as they had been, as they wished they'd been. Blake stepped out onto the gravel and went around the car to help Cassandra out. The pebbles under her feet reminded her that about a year after Isabel had died, the widow of an old family friend had called. She had found a box of her husband's keepsakes; inside, there were three small stones. At first she had assumed they were from one of his favorite places, probably Le Mans, which had been his favorite race. He had been a well-known writer about cars and racing, until one day, quite out of the blue, he had blown his brains out.

He had visited Isabel often in New York in the last year of her life. Once Blake walked into the living room, and they were on the couch in a way that made her think they'd been kissing. She couldn't be sure; it made her too uncomfortable to think about it. Her mother had been dead a year when she read in the *Times* that Bill had killed himself. She burst right out crying; the tears she hadn't been able to shed for Isabel sprang instantly to her eyes for Bill. Several months later his widow had called about the box of pebbles and the note she'd found that said, "Came back to Isabel's house—strangers here—walked the driveway to find a trace of her."

Blake hadn't known what to say to the woman, couldn't imagine what she made of it, so she just said, "How nice. I guess that was when the house was rented for a little while after my mother died." It made her realize what a deep hole Isabel had left in many lives, how much they all would have given to have her back. It also made her think they probably *had* been kissing. Whether they'd ever done more than that hardly mattered. They must have been in love—how good that she had that at the end—because you don't keep common stones as mementoes for anything less.

Michael had found a picture of Blake and her mother in a box of photographs. She was three years old, wrapped in a towel on Isabel's lap on a beach on the Riviera. "Now I understand why you want a girl so much," Michael had said. Earlier, they had discussed children in a general sort of way—the highly charged, specific generalizations that people make when they're afraid to say things head on—and she had insisted she only wanted a girl. When Michael came across the picture, he held it reverently. Isabel and Blake were gazing at each other with huge grins, a child's joyful face craned over her shoulder to meet her mother's adoring gaze. Isabel's arms were wrapped totally around Blake, her little legs were stuck straight out. The toes were curled over, the way kids' toes can curl from the pleasure of eating ice cream. The love between them was that strong, an enveloping, sensual treat.

"You want to be loved the way your mother loved you," Michael said.

"And I want to love someone that way," Blake added, understanding for the first time why she wanted a girl-child so much.

"This is a picture of sheer ecstasy," he said. "Most people never experience a love like this, not from their mother or anyone."

It was not a blessing to have been loved that way. It spoiled Blake for any other loving—everything else was tepid by comparison. As long as her mother was around, life was a honeysuckle rose. She had only to enter a room, and Isabel would interrupt whatever she was doing and announce, "Blake!" in a glee-filled voice. One almost expected a band to strike up. Love emanated from her mother the way steam rises off a horse on a cold morning. Blake was the Christ child incarnate. Every glance, every word and touch said, "You are divine. You can be—can have—everything, anything."

Cassandra and Blake went into the empty house and felt something: a wisp of their mother. This would always be her castle. The few times they had visited their father and his wife—disoriented by the changes in furniture and rugs

—he would say, "You girls should go through that stuff in the cedar closet, get rid of it." The "stuff" he referred to was what was left of Isabel's belongings, most of which he had disposed of in the weeks following her death. They had been only teenagers at the time, too young to know the nostalgia they would later feel. Marsh had decided for them that they'd never want any of it, so all Isabel's clothes and racks of shoes and shelves of big Hermes alligator purses went to the Salvation Army.

Cassandra and Blake had developed a ritual when their father instructed them to deal with "the stuff." They unearthed the few remaining boxes of Isabel's things, took them out, touched them, let stories flow from them and replaced them in their boxes. The small stockpile was a comfort: if they were to whittle away at it, that would diminish her power, her presence. They mentioned things of hers they remembered, discarded so unceremoniously, wistfully saying that they'd like them now, that they were back in style. Meaning that they missed her, that was all. They were two stones striking against each other to find sparks of their past.

Blake liked the idea of putting Cassie in her childhood bedroom to recuperate, to get well where she had recovered from mumps and chicken pops, as she had called them, but the room had been transformed into a little boy's paradise: a riot of primary colors, a drum set, a puppet stage, electric trains; all the trappings of a late-in-life only child. So Blake put her in the master bedroom, in the wide bed they used to crawl into after bad dreams, the bed where those giant, omnipotent, omniscient people had slept, the ones who made anything, everything, possible. A life like the most fabulous dessert trolley in the world.

*　*　*

How could anyone ever understand our shared child-hood, that enchanted forest known only to us? How could anyone else in the world understand what it was like to run across bridges in Venice with your almost-twin sister in matching shorts and sandals, race into Saint Mark's Square and say to the corn vendor, *"Due, per favore,"* then tear open the little sacks of corn, sprinkle it in each other's hair and stand in front of the whimsically majestic cathedral—four bronze horses above threatening to leap right off the edge and gallop through the long, arcaded square—where we posed stiffly with arms stuck straight out, palms up, full of corn, so that pigeons swooped down from the porticos to feed off us, the warm flutter of their beating wings swirling around our ears, the prickly-tickle of the birds' feet as they boldly landed on our heads, peck-ing corn from the straight parts down the center of our hair, other pigeons roosting on our arms, until a crowd of people gathered at a whispering distance, snapping pic-tures of this pair of pigtailed statues who stole the spot-light for a moment from Saint Mark's in all its glory. . . .

Could anyone but Cassandra understand what it was like the next day when I broke out in wide welts, terrible hives from those birds? The Italian doctor had to come early in the morning to our rooms at the Gritti Palace, wearing a beige linen, three-piece suit in the middle of July, bringing with him the pleasant aroma of coffee on his breath and the scary smell of disinfectant when he opened his black bag (unlike American doctors who didn't dress like real people and had no smell at all). He pulled out a hypodermic, then scrubbed my bottom with chilly alcohol as I lay, stomach-down, on the heavy linen sheets, holding Mama's hand and waving one finger at Cassie, who stood at a respectful, wide-eyed distance. I barely felt the little slap on my bottom when he jabbed the shot in,

the gleaming needle left sticking in my round pink but-
tock while he flicked the glass cylinder of medicine with
his finger before attaching it to the needle, turning the
glass tube round and round onto the metal post, while I
watched Cassandra's horror-stricken face and thought she
was going to cry, staring at that needle sticking there so
long, even though I told her it didn't really hurt. Cassandra stayed close to me all through breakfast, her bottom
sore in sibling sympathy as I sat on a fat, hotel-bed pillow
out on the balcony overlooking the Grand Canal, waving
at the silly tourists in gondolas like resident royalty out
to greet their subjects. I was allowed only plain rice the
night before and for breakfast weak tea and toast, so Cassandra snuck me a bite of her cream-filled sweet roll,
dunked in the creamy, bittersweet hot chocolate. It tasted
better than anything I could ever remember eating.

The days ran together as Cass mended, the luxurious
monotony of hours and hours to read, the tearful exhaustion from a short walk to the patio; the days compressed
into a solid block by the boredom and pain and pills, im-
patience with the body, waiting for it to heal so that ordinary life could be resumed—when it did, we would lose
sight again of our delicate mortality. I read a poem to my
sister:

> *Is life a wound*
> *which dreams of being healed?*
>
> *Is love a wound which deepens*
> *as it dreams?*

We lay on the smooth expanse of what had been our
parents' bed, with the gilded wooden angel still hanging
overhead, kitschy and benevolent under the velvet valance,
just as it had hung there for as long as we could remember.

that we could meet for the first time,
open our scars & stitches to each other,
weave our legs around
each other's patchwork dreams
& try to salve each other's wounds
with love—

if it was love.

I read poetry aloud the way my mother had, lying on the bed and reading to me from Kahlil Gibran when I was a little girl who had just had her tonsils removed. It was peaceful, airy, protected; my mother had covered me with a mink lap robe meant for winter evening reading, and there was the dulcet perfume of a bowl of potpourri by the bedside. The poems Isabel had read took a different view of love than the modern woman poet I chose to read:

(I am not sure at all
if love is salve
or just
a deeper kind of wound.
I do not think it matters.)

I read as we lay beneath the round golden cheeks of that suspended angel that had flown there almost forever.

If it was lust or hunger
& not love,
if it was all that they accused us of
(that we accused ourselves)—
I do not think it matters.

I read out loud, and the angel flew above us as it had over our mother and father, sanctifying their silent, sad nights—cold even in the heat of summer—when they kept strictly to their own sides of the tightly stretched field of sheet, a stone wall of unspoken wishes, spoken barbs, be-

tween them; the angel had also sanctified the nights I came
into their bed shivering, from a big black nightmare that
wrapped around me like an octopus, even though Maria
said every night when she tucked us in, *"Sogni d'oro,"*
golden dreams.

It had sanctified bright mornings when Cassandra and I
clambered into that big bed and snuggled with them, turning us into a happy family.

> *& if it wasn't love,*
> *if you called me now*
> *across the old echo chamber of the ocean*
> *& said:*
> *"Look, I never loved you,"*
> *I would feel*
> *a little like a fool perhaps,*
> *& yet it wouldn't matter.*

I read to Cassandra as we lay with the angel singing over
us, as it had that day when we were ten and eleven and
asked our mother what breast-feeding was like. She let us
have a try, then screeched in pain from our toothy enthusiasm, falling into a giggling, apologetic threesome hug.

> *My business is to always feel*
> *a little like a fool*
> *& speak of it.*

Cassandra stretched out with me, and the light came in
soft and ferny-green through the long tendrils of the ancient willow outside the bedroom window. One day men
had come to cut off the tree's most graceful, curving
branch, and our mother had run out—made a last-minute
plea for a cure, for a reprieve from the saw—and then had
cried right in front of the tree surgeon, Mama's softness a
shock to us. We lay on that firm, wide bed, our fingers
intertwined, cool yet warm, blood-flesh strong together;

Cass's hand felt like my daughter's hand, my mother's hand, my father's hand when he used to let me hold it, before the time when he pulled away, didn't like it if I even hooked arms with him walking down Fifth Avenue, taking his hand out of the pocket of his camel's hair coat to break the link, vanishing, like a circus pitching its tent in a small Italian town, filling the night air with the caramel perfume of cotton candy, bedazzling the townspeople with acrobats and bareback horses, but when a child returns the following day there's nothing there: a trampled field, paper wrappers, a lost scarf . . . as if the circus had never been at all.

> & I am sure
> that when we love
> we are better than ourselves
> & when we hate,
> worse.
>
> & even if we call it madness later
> & scrawl four-letter words
> across those outhouse walls
> we call our skulls—
> we stand revealed
> by those sudden moments
> when we come together.

Silence fell over us like a blessing, the churning noise of a chorus of crickets at night seeped in, the thick sound fluttering down on us like a gossamer blanket, the same crickets that had lulled us to sleep as children. We lay on our Mama's wide, warm bed, holding each other, and that angel smiled down, sanctifying us.